T

A WOLF SIX THRILLER

ALEX SHAW

B
Boldwood

First published in Great Britain in 2026 by Boldwood Books Ltd.

Cover Design by Nick Castle

Cover Images: iStock

A CIP catalogue record for this book is available from the British Library.

Paperback ISBN 978-1-83678-414-2

Large Print ISBN 978-1-83678-415-9

Hardback ISBN 978-1-83678-413-5

Trade Paperback ISBN 978-1-80656-231-2

Ebook ISBN 978-1-83678-416-6

Kindle ISBN 978-1-83678-417-3

Audio CD ISBN 978-1-83678-408-1

MP3 CD ISBN 978-1-83678-409-8

Digital audio download ISBN 978-1-83678-412-8

This book is printed on certified sustainable paper. Boldwood Books is dedicated to putting sustainability at the heart of our business. For more information please visit https://www.boldwoodbooks.com/about-us/sustainability/

Boldwood Books Ltd, 23 Bowerdean Street, London, SW6 3TN

www.boldwoodbooks.com

PROLOGUE

SIX YEARS AGO

Joaquín Sorolla, Valencia, Spain

The rain in Spain may have generally stayed on the plain, but today it had fallen on Valencia. It hammered on the windows of the Alta Velocidad Española train like stormy fists as it departed Joaquín Sorolla station. A myriad of brightly coloured, dripping, umbrellas battled for space on the streets outside. Valencia was yet another city that Akulov's nomadic existence prevented him from knowing better. Guessing and second guessing the opposition, those who hunted him, who sought to kill him, made for a life of continual movement. Like a shark, Akulov mused, he may only rest in death.

A couple, maybe his age, probably younger but definitely much happier, ignored the rain and ignored the world. They walked hand in hand, without an umbrella between them. Hair plastered to their faces, clothes clinging to their bodies, their eyes were locked on each other. Loneliness gnawed at Akulov. He was on a crowded train but was a man forever alone. This was not the life he had been forced to choose; this was the life he had been created for. Forged out of Ukraine's strongest steel and tempered by experience, Akulov was no longer a man. He was Wolf Six, a weapon. A weapon for hire.

The train gathered pace, rushing into the relentless rain. Akulov was sat in an aisle seat, the last one in his carriage before the doors to the next. His fellow first class passengers appeared to be mostly businesspeople. Dressed in formal attire, or a little neater than the average traveller, they were scrolling on their smartphones or working on laptops or using e-readers. He retrieved his paperback from his courier bag. It was a Spanish edition of *Dubliners*, a collection of short stories by James Joyce. Akulov knew the work in its original English and was now reading it in translation to improve his already highly competent Spanish. He opened the book and pretended to follow the words, although his eyes now assessed those who were seated within his carriage. A man in a leather jacket, with cropped, neat hair, occupied a seat facing him, at the opposite end of the carriage. He had his phone in his hand but was not looking at the screen, he was staring past Akulov at the entrance to the next carriage as though waiting or watching for someone. Akulov averted his eyes before the man noticed he was being evaluated, and started to read the next story, 'A Painful Case'.

Akulov enjoyed reading about places he had never been to but really should have, and Dublin was a place he must visit especially as, on many occasions, he travelled under an Irish passport. Movement caught his eye. The doors at the end of the carriage, behind the man in the leather jacket, opened and a suitcase edged through, followed by the woman who pushed it. Her eyes darted around as she searched for an empty seat. There were none at that end, but several at Akulov's, including two directly opposite him and one at his side on which his courier bag rested. She approached him, and he sighed, not wanting to share his space with anyone.

Akulov overrode his compulsion to help as the woman struggled to place her case in the luggage rack. He averted his gaze and watched her reflection in the window as the passenger in the seat across the aisle, a man in his sixties, gallantly assisted her.

"*Mil gracias*," she said, before sitting heavily, in the seat directly opposite him.

Akulov felt her eyes on him. He didn't return her gaze. He finished his page and turned it over for the next. The woman's phone rang. She answered it, was silent for several seconds and then launched into a loud tirade of abuse in Spanish. The man across the aisle flinched whilst Akulov tried to keep a poker face, he spoke the language well enough to understand many of the insults she was using, and several of them were anatomically impossible. He studied her now via her reflection in the window as her volume rose, until eventually she ended the call.

Her eyes met his in the window. "Are you going to stare at me like that all the way to Madrid? Are you some kind of pervert?"

Akulov turned his head, and before he understood why he said, "Yes."

"Ha!" She folded her arms.

Akulov had no intention of getting into conversation with anyone, let alone someone who was drawing attention to herself. He didn't want to be remembered. His gaze moved over her shoulder and down the carriage aisle.

"What is it with you men?" she asked, he didn't reply. "Why can't any of you be normal?"

He was searching for empty seats. He needed to move.

"My name is Carmen." She was addressing him; she wanted to talk. She peered at him, expectantly. "And?"

"And what?"

"Do you have a name?"

There were no more seats in the carriage away from the woman that Akulov could see, he was marooned. He sighed. "I'd rather not talk. I'm trying to read. Please enjoy your journey."

She nodded. "And I'm trying to place that accent. You are a foreigner, not Spanish. Not fat enough to be American."

Akulov felt his mask weaken but he remained silent.

"I'm going to Madrid, and you?"

"Yes."

"You really don't want to talk?"

"No." He surreptitiously studied her again via the window. He undoubtedly found her attractive, and there seemed to be an unusual energy about her, but there was no point thinking any more of this or of her, it was a chemical reaction that he had been trained to ignore. He needed no one and that was how it had to be.

She switched her gaze to the man who had helped her. He was smiling broadly. "What are you looking at?" He mumbled something, turned away and raised his phone as a defensive screen.

A regular traveller could close his eyes, go to sleep, but as an irregular, Akulov had no such luxury. At any moment they – the opposition – could come for him. And unless he smashed through the reinforced glass window, he had only two escape routes, up or down the crowded carriage. He was essentially a prisoner, trapped in a steel tube for two hours, gliding inexorably towards Madrid.

Carmen asked, "Is your book good?"

"I don't know, I haven't read it yet."

"The parts you have read. Did you enjoy them?"

"They were fine."

"Wine can be fine, a book cannot. Literature is either fantastic, invigorating or it is simply awful."

"It is interesting."

She glanced at the cover. "James Joyce is interesting?"

"Yes."

The carriage fell silent. Carmen ignored him. The express train would make no stops, Akulov pondered if he should or should not move away to another carriage.

The woman's phone chimed. She opened the message and gasped. And then eyes becoming moist, her face contorted with anger. And then the phone rang. An incoming call. She wasted no time. "You are dead, do you hear me? If I see you again you are dead!" Her chest jerked erratically as she seemed to fight for breath as she ended the call.

Akulov looked at her, a moment of weakness, a moment of humanity, the question obvious on his face.

She held out the iPhone. "The bastard strangled my dog!"

Akulov viewed the screen. What it showed was not pleasant. "Why?"

"Why?" Carmen snatched the phone back. "Because he's a psychopath, my ex-boyfriend is insane."

Beneath his outward veneer Akulov too became angry. Those who preyed on the innocent were contemptuous, and although he was by no means an animal lover, there was nothing more innocent than a pet. "Where is he?"

"Valencia."

"Good."

"Good? What do you mean, good?" Akulov could see Carmen was trying to regain her composure, her breaths becoming more regular. She retrieved a travel pack of tissues from the pocket of her denim jacket and wiped her eyes. "What can I do?"

"Kill him."

"That's not funny at all!"

"It's the best solution."

"The idiotic thing is, I've never been a pet person, yet he bought me that dog." She closed her eyes. "The little thing used to slobber all over me."

"Everything and everyone dies. If you accept that, grief becomes a passing emotion. A memory."

Her eyes widened and she stared at him for an overlong moment before she asked, "Who are you?"

"No one."

She now switched languages to English, and without a trace of an accent said, "You're English, aren't you?"

"Yes," he lied, "I am."

"An emotionally stilted Englishman, hiding behind his book and a trimmed, pseudo-hipster beard."

Akulov felt his chin with his hand, he'd have to lose the facial hair. "How many more languages do I get to be insulted in?"

"How many more do you speak?"

Akulov said nothing.

"Do you have a name yet?"

"No."

"I should call the police. About the dog."

"I see."

"You are meant to say 'sorry'." She glared at him, he remained silent. "You really are shit at comforting people, aren't you?"

"There is nothing I can do. The dog is dead, you are not. That should be comfort enough." He'd given too much away by speaking at all. Now she knew he spoke English and Spanish, and this made him unusual enough to be remembered. This was the most real interaction he'd had with another human for months, alarmingly he realised that he'd started to like it. It needed to stop. Yet something compelled him to talk to this woman. Akulov chastised himself.

They lapsed into silence, which was broken every now and then by her angry huffs. He tried to avoid eye contact, which was now easier as she wasn't trying to engage him and turned his attention to his book and the blur of countryside rushing by outside in turns. Yet Akulov yearned for company, for verbal and physical contact. It would pass. It always did. His classified Spetsnaz unit, the Werewolves, had settled for bottles of vodka and prostitutes, he'd mostly just taken the booze. But he never drank until he was safe. And he wasn't safe. Not yet.

Akulov checked his watch. They had another hour to go. He was uncomfortable, he felt exposed, but at least it had now stopped raining outside.

The doors at the opposite end of the carriage opened and two men stepped through them. Instantly Akulov felt his threat radar ping. Both men were tanned, looked to be in their mid-thirties, seemed physically fit, had no-nonsense haircuts and dark sunglasses were part obscuring their features. They wore leather jackets, just like the man they were now passing. The first of the newcomers was holding a plastic shopping bag in front of his body with his left hand, whilst his right was inside as though supporting something hidden. The second man had no bag, but his own right hand was in his jacket pocket, and he gave the slightest of nods to the seated man in the leather jacket as they passed.

Carmen must have sensed something was wrong because she asked, "What is it?"

Akulov spoke slowly and quietly in English, "I need you to keep still, remain quiet and stay low in your seat."

A third man now entered the carriage; his hand was also conspicuously hidden in his pocket. The seated man rose to his feet, and thrust his right hand into his jacket, as though retrieving something from under his left arm... and Akulov imagined he knew what that was. He stood directly in front of the doors and glanced back out of the carriage. The first two men were now more than halfway up the carriage, striding towards the door behind Akulov. The first man's shopping bag caught against a piece of luggage protruding from between the seats, and was tugged away to reveal a weapon Akulov knew well, a Heckler & Koch MP5K.

Akulov felt as though time was slowing around him, as his training and instincts fully switched on. It was medically called tachypsychia, and was a neurological condition where his own perception of time became distorted during stressful situations. What it did was give him milliseconds more to react than those around him. He saw Carmen dig her right hand into her jacket and pull something from a hidden pouch. At the same time he noticed the older man across the aisle throw up his arms and his mouth open in panic.

The anguished yell of the elderly Spaniard was met with an almost instantaneous suppressed double tap from a 9mm Beretta fired by the second man. Carmen's right hand was now clasping a sub-compact Glock 26, and her eyes were on Akulov's. For the briefest of moments, and certainly for less than a second, Akulov wondered if she was with the men, and they were a kill team there for him. However, she sprang up and out of her seat, twisting as she rose and bringing the Glock to bear on the group of men. She fired her own pair of rounds. Roaring from the unsuppressed barrel they instantaneously struck the nearest gunman, the one with the HK, a perfect double tap, the first 9mm round striking the man's chest and the other splitting his skull.

Akulov wasted no time. As the man fell, he threw himself into the aisle to grab his machine gun. A moment later he heard rounds fly from behind him as Carmen fired again. The carriage now became a cacophony of panic as yells and screams filled the confined space. On his haunches, and HK up, Akulov sought out the remaining gunmen. Carmen's rounds had found their target. Only two were left, the first man he had seen seated at the very rear of the carriage, and the last one to arrive, who had grabbed a panicked passenger as a human shield and was backing away. Before Akulov had chance to react, a single round slammed into the shoulder of the gunman who had taken the hostage, making him shudder and his pistol arm fall away. And then a second round made his face explode. As the body fell Akulov could now see the last remaining gunman, weapon raised and pointed in his direction. Rounds zipped past Akulov's head, smashing the window to his right. As the howling wind was sucked into the carriage, Akulov returned fire, a controlled burst which stitched a line of holes from abdomen to chest and slammed the final gunman backwards against the doors.

Akulov rose to his feet but almost fell again. There was a grinding noise and the carriage started to shudder and decelerate. Someone had activated the emergency brake system.

"Drop it."

Akulov slowly turned, letting his left hand fall away from the HK sub-machine gun as he did so. Left palm up he locked eyes with Carmen and slowly started to place the weapon by his feet, noticing that his courier bag was also lying in the aisle.

Brakes moaning, the train jerked to a halt and Akulov grabbed his bag.

Glock trained on his centre mass, Carmen asked, "Who are you?"

Akulov had his own questions but as he backed away, replied, "Just a tourist."

Carmen moved towards him. "I'll ask you once more."

The carriage doors to their immediate left hissed open and a stern voiced shouted, in Spanish, “Armed Police!”

As Carmen’s hands raised, and her eyes darted to the door, Akulov bounded backwards, turned and vaulted out of the carriage via the shattered window. He sailed into the void and landed hard, his feet slamming onto the gravel next to the rails before tumbling forward and away from the train.

He found himself at the bottom of a steep, stony verge sparsely covered by grass and bushes. Akulov assessed his options. To his right ahead of the end of the train was a tunnel through a hill, and to the left was a bridge. His only way out was to climb directly up the bank, and he noted there were several paths which did just that. He moved left, quickly picking his way through the grass and gravel, knowing that at any moment either Carmen or the local authorities could come chasing after him. He started to climb, his bag slung across his shoulder, his feet slipping on the bare soil of the eroded path. Leaning forward he scrambled with his hands to aid his purchase. He heard voices from behind, but dared not look back as he concentrated on powering upwards.

Commands in Spanish were barked at him. “Stop! Armed Police! STOP!”

A round was fired, its unsuppressed retort rolling off the banks of the cutting. A second shot now. This one landed a metre ahead of him and to his right. Akulov had no intention of stopping, whatever had happened back on the train was something he didn’t want to and couldn’t get involved with. He had killed an armed man, in front of a train full of witnesses and of course could not let the Spanish authorities hold him for questioning. He reached the top of the slope. His feet finding traction on thicker grass, he started to jog away from the noise and outraged shouts from the police below, before they could chase him down.

1

JENNER, CALIFORNIA

Present Day

Tomas Torres mopped his brow with a handkerchief and slapped his son-in-law on his back. He'd worn himself out chasing after his grandchildren across his daughter's lawn. He straightened his back and let a wide smile split his face as the twins continued darting around their mother's legs. Past the fence at the edge of the clifftop garden, gulls soared and a distant ship smudged the horizon. This part of California couldn't be more different to his hometown of Bahía Blanca in Argentina, a port city whose shores were constantly busy with cranes and container ships. Torres was more than happy his daughter had married her American boyfriend and settled in his home state. Torres saw himself as a man of the world, he was equally as happy in Argentina or the United States, yet he preferred Europe. He took joy in exploring one of the many fascinating old towns dotting the Spanish interior where the landscape had remained unchanged for centuries and the pace of life was relaxed. This summer he would take the family with him. Torres was sixty-one, and whilst he knew this was by no means an old age, he understood that he had begun to age, started to slow. This annoyed him. Torres took a great lungful of sea air. He had to push himself, he knew, he had to remain active, if not for himself then for the two little girls who needed their grandpa, and potentially their as yet unborn brother.

The scuddering clouds overhead heralded, he knew, an incoming storm. Shadows fell across the lawn as, watching his granddaughters, he felt his own shadow of grief land upon him once more. It had now been over ten years since that day when the love of his life had been ripped away from him. He still had flashbacks of the split second before the impact. He'd been stood on the pavement waving her goodbye, when he suddenly saw the incomprehensible image of the other car barrelling around the bend to T-bone his wife's ancient runaround, then immediate aftermath and the uncomprehending face of his wife as she tried in vain to speak whilst he brushed her hair away from her bloodied face. The driver of the stolen vehicle which had hit her had never been identified, never been prosecuted by the local Argentinian police, and the fire of revenge still burned inside Torres because he knew who was behind it. He vowed to make them pay, one way or another. This is what had kept him alive and preserved his sanity until the twins had been born almost a year later, to the exact date their grandmother had died. Renata had missed her grandchildren by a year, the dream she had shared with him since they'd met when he was a battered soldier in his late teens, fresh from the Malvinas conflict, and she a nurse. All he had wanted to do was grow old with Renata, and all she had wanted to do was see her children, grandchildren and, she had joked, her great-grandchildren take their first steps and laugh their first laugh. A flash of lightning sparked on the horizon, followed by a distant rumble. The twins ran to their mother, and flung their arms around her legs. Torres remembered when their mother too had feared thunder. He called out, "Time to go inside!"

Maria turned towards him, each hand holding a different twin, a beaming smile on her face. Christian, her husband, picked up the dolls the girls had inadvertently left on the grass, and together they walked inside.

"Here comes the rain," Christian said as he drew next to Torres, "but of course it'll be nothing compared to Bahía Blanca."

"No, it won't," Torres replied, thinking of the recent floods in his Argentinian hometown.

"How are your cousins?"

"They are fine, they were lucky. You know their places are away from the shoreline on the higher ground, but others were not. I wish I could have done more to help."

"You can't help everyone, Tomas. You did make them partners in your shipping business."

"True."

The group trudged up the lawn towards the decking then back into the house. The twins rushed up to their room whilst Maria headed to the kitchen. Torres took a seat in the living room and switched on the television whilst Christian headed to his office to attend to an urgent email from a supplier. Torres selected the Argentinian state channel which, through the wonders of modern technology, he was able to watch even in California. The news programme had already started. As had been the case for the last few days, the two major national news stories had been the provincial elections and the Bahía Blanca floods. Yet now, however, the two stories had started to converge as one of the candidates for the governorship of the Province of Buenos Aires had arrived at Bahía Blanca and was giving a press conference about the destruction caused by the flooding and what he would do, if elected, to rebuild the town and help prevent any such future catastrophes from happening due to unforeseen natural disasters.

Politicians lied, and begged until they were elected, then continued to lie. After that, they started to steal and boast. At least all those who had sought his support when he still ran his shipping business did. In his opinion they were no worse than the racketeers he'd had to work with over the years, who had also wanted to tax him. Torres had long since taken a disinterest in politics and he had no idea who was currently campaigning for office. In his opinion, all sides and all political parties were as bad as one another, and worst of all, they looked and sounded the same.

The suited, moustached man on TV, in his late-thirties, whilst seemingly speaking with passion, was no different. Torres continued to watch as Hector Orosco fielded questions and affirmed that even before he took office, starting from tomorrow, he would pledge his own money and that of the foundation his father had started to help Bahía Blanca. The camera zoomed out slightly to reveal a tall, robust looking, white-haired man standing at the side of the stage. Orosco gestured towards the man and introduced his father, the man who had already done so much for the Argentinian people, General Franco Orosco.

An abrupt blanket of cold enveloped Torres, and he felt a sudden constriction in his chest, as though he had been punched by a giant invisible fist. He opened his mouth wide and tried to breathe, failing on his first attempt and then taking in a greedy, heaving lungful. Eyes wide, he could still not quite believe who he was seeing on the TV screen. It was the first time he had laid eyes on the face of the man in almost a decade, the same man who, all those years ago in seemingly what had been another life, had been the officer who had brutalised him during the Malvinas conflict. Torres started to shiver as mentally he was transported back in time to that freezing hillside in nineteen eighty-two. The faces of his fellow conscripts flashed before his eyes, including his two school friends who had been placed in his same group. The two friendly, happy-go-lucky, wide-eyed boys who, like him, had been scooped up to do their patriotic duty and retake the Malvinas from the British occupiers. His two school friends who had died on that same hillside, not at the hands of the British but due to the direct actions of the white-haired man he was watching on the television. Rage had now replaced fear and Torres started to shake as he watched his old tormentor walk across the stage, right hand held up in a friendly greeting to the assembled press.

"Is that the Argentinian news?" Christian entered the room and sat on the sofa, "Reminds me of the aftermath of Hurricane Katrina."

Torres raised his right arm and pointed at the screen. "I know that man."

"The one with the white hair? An old friend of yours?"

"An old enemy." Torres had never spoken about the evils that had happened during the conflict with his daughter or Christian. For him it had been something that, whilst unresolved, had been buried yet never forgotten since he had become a grandfather, but he couldn't let that monster stand there and pretend to be a hero, the saviour of their shared hometown.

Christian said, in his usual light tone, "You want me to make some calls and have 'some of the boys' pay him a visit?"

"That would not be a bad idea."

"What did he do?" Christian's tone was light, as though not realising the truth behind his father-in-law's words.

"That man murdered my two best friends."

"I... I'm sorry. I had no idea."

"Nor does anyone else," Torres replied.

At the time, Torres had of course fantasised about killing the man responsible for the murder of his friends. Then, when his wife had been taken from him, this had grown into an all but soul eroding obsession, which he had hidden from his daughter, to hire a hitman to take out Franco Orosco. Torres had spoken to people he knew who had taken illegal business shortcuts, their businesses as murky as the waters his cargo ships sailed on. He had been given a couple of names, and then the twins were born. Life suddenly mattered to him more than death then. But now, seeing that man standing tall and, in the spotlight, once again, well that was something he could no longer accept.

* * *

Atlantis The Palm, Dubai, United Arab Emirates

It was relaxing to be away from both Europe and the Americas for a while. Although Ruslan Akulov, the Ukrainian assassin known by his military call sign "Wolf Six", could never wholly relax. Yet of all the places in the world to sit, enjoy breakfast, and people watch, Akulov accepted that Dubai was, if not the safest, one of the safest places in the world to do so.

He sipped his reassuringly rich Atlantis coffee as he observed those around him. He had of course stayed at the hotel before, but then he had been observing a target, someone whom he'd had to chase out of the UAE to liquidate. Dubai was not a place to enact any type of wet contract, the county's internal surveillance gathering and monitoring capabilities were just too efficient. Which was why he was perfectly happy to sit, eat his buffet breakfast and look out across the restaurant terrace. Even so, he had checked in using an Irish passport and disguised his appearance with a pair of light-orange tinted oversized sunglasses of the type favoured by Hollywood film stars. He was not the only person wearing such eyewear, which seemed to have been designed for indoors rather than any real exterior sun blocking usage. He had a pair of black oversized Oakley's he reserved for that purpose.

Akulov's table was, as per his preference, away from the food stations, in the lower part of the restaurant and in the corner, against the rear wall overlooking the doors to the ground-floor terrace. This meant no one could creep up on him unannounced. It also meant it was somewhat quieter. Even though he knew his environment was as safe as it could be, ignoring all his own stringent security protocols would be unwise.

A trio of long, wide, white marble steps to his right led back towards the main restaurant seating area, and gingerly navigating these was a boy who, in Akulov's estimation, could not be any more than eight or nine years old. He had a smattering of chocolate sauce around his lips and was holding a plate piled high with pancakes. What struck Akulov the most, however, was the expression of pure joy on his round face. A step behind him was a woman. Like Akulov, her features were part obscured by a pair of "indoor sunglasses". She wore a tight-fitting dress which repeatedly featured the "Gucci" logo. She had a glass of champagne in one hand and a ginger shot in the other, Akulov knew this because he has passed her at the champagne station. He hadn't indulged. He'd have a little cognac later, at the pool bar, as he doubted the Atlantis stocked any Ukrainian vodka. A portly man with close-cropped dark hair, and a scowl, appeared two paces behind her, his left hand too held a champagne flute whilst his right grasped a plate piled high with cheese and cold cuts of meat. He was also wearing a tight-fitting Gucci outfit, but unlike the woman, his was not flattering. Akulov followed the trio, behind his orange lenses, to their seat at the far end of the room, directly by the peacock blue, wooden framed French doors leading to the beach path. Both males immediately started to eat, whilst the mother sipped her champagne and ignored them. Akulov knew from experience that the clientele of the ultra-luxury statement hotel was a mixture of foreign tourists, Emiratis and UAE residents taking staycations. And the other guests dotted around him were further evidence of this. Although, now more than ever, Russians seemed to make up the largest percentage of tourists. As a Ukrainian, this annoyed him. He finished his coffee.

It was a little after eight-thirty a.m. and the restaurant had started to grow busy. Akulov was in no rush to move. A member of the waiting staff brought him another coffee and cleaned away his plate. He realised that this may well be the first time in a long while that he had no ulterior motive for being where he was. He was waiting for no one, he was tracking no one and he was certainly not planning on killing anyone. But then everything changed.

The woman had platinum blonde hair which rather than ageing her, had the reverse effect. As she gracefully took the steps down, Akulov noticed the male diners start to stare at her.

Valentina Tishina had an aura about her which he could still not fathom. It was more than her physical attractiveness, it was a confidence, an inner strength which radiated outwards and was impossible to ignore. She was dressed immaculately in a long, flowing designer dress – which drew not too subtle looks from the Russian woman in the Gucci – and had an oversized branded handbag in one hand, and the de rigueur glass of champagne in the other. Without saying a word, she joined Akulov's table, taking a seat at a right angle to him, so she too could see the entire room.

"I won't ask you how you found me," Akulov said to his broker.

"Good, because I won't tell you," Tishina replied, speaking in English with a clear-cut, crisp, home counties accent. "I knew you were in the UAE."

"Is this business related, or do I have a stalker?"

A smile appeared on her lips. "Dubai must agree with you, you do sound relaxed."

Akulov took a sip of coffee, and swallowed it before he asked, "What's the job?"

"Straight to the point I see, even here. No time for pleasantries."

"I am sorry."

"You should be. We've not seen each other since the last time we shared breakfast together, and on that occasion, if you remember, we ordered room service."

Akulov never knew what he was supposed to say, or how he was meant to navigate their occasionally non-professional relationship. So, he asked, "How are you?"

"Thank you so much for asking. I am very well. How are you, Nick?"

"I am fine." Akulov frowned. The passport he had used to enter the country and check in to the hotel was in the name of Nicholas Furmidge, and he didn't know how she had found this out. "Are you staying here?"

"I'm at the Royal next door, with a friend."

"Nice."

"It is. Don't be jealous. There are fewer families there." She paused and raised her glass at the Russian woman wearing the Gucci, who nodded before looking away. "So, to business. I do in fact have a new contract for you. I've sent the file to the usual place. The client is paying a premium because this is time sensitive."

"You know the money does not matter to me."

"It matters to me."

Akulov finished his coffee. "When?"

"You can fly out tomorrow."

"I can?"

"What else would you be doing, hanging around the beach and pretending to be happy?"

"Where?"

"You'll see."

"And if I don't accept?"

"You will, once you've read the file. There is a five-day window starting tomorrow."

"That doesn't give me much time at all."

"Time is overrated, and the client has been meticulous in the intelligence he has supplied me with." Tishina finished her champagne then slowly stood. "Take care of yourself."

Akulov watched her walk away, as did the other guests taking their breakfast on the terrace.

2

BUENOS AIRES

The dark-green walled building was situated close to the Recoleta cemetery. Its function, however, was far from sombre. It was a café popular in former times with racing drivers and writers. Nowadays it also played host to tourists, Instagram influencers and would-be writers. It was a place where its patrons preferred to sit outside on its ample terrace which spilled out onto the street and the edges of the square. One of these patrons, according to intelligence supplied by his client, was Akulov's target – Franco Orosco. The client had requested Orosco be liquidated at his favourite café. Perched on the roof of the twelve-storey residential block across the street, Akulov had a bird's-eye view of the scene below. The café was on the corner of the street where it met a park and then wound to the right. Wooden chairs and table sets were arranged nearer the rear of the building, part obscured under awnings. Further away from the café were the cheap seats littering the cobbled area. These were made of green plastic and seemed to Akulov like an afterthought. The entire space was hemmed in with low glass and steel walls. Rather surprisingly, given the country's former relationship with the

United Kingdom, just in front of this on the pavement stood two old-style, red British telephone boxes. Akulov watched as pedestrians wandered past the café and towards the park area beyond. It wouldn't have been his choice for a strike point, but it was where his client had paid for the assassination to take place. In an ideal world Akulov would have much rather taken the man in a far more controlled environment, one that he himself had chosen after undertaking a full and unhurried threat assessment, but once more that was a luxury he had not been allowed. Yet who could he complain to, his broker? Tishina's face fleetingly flittered through his mind's eye; he knew that what he felt for her he shouldn't and what had transpired personally between them in the past must not be repeated. Akulov moved away momentarily from his position to drink from a tepid bottle of water. Whilst it was not the height of summer, the September sun was still warm enough to make him hot beneath his thin blouson style jacket. He moved back into position and continued to await his prey. His weapon of choice for this operation was a HK416 A5 11" as the range to target from his position was not far enough to necessitate a long-barrelled weapon. The HK, without its screw-on suppressor, was just under seventy-one centimetres, which meant he had easily concealed it in his holdall. At this target distance, Akulov knew he could initiate a kill shot without the need for a specialist scope, but nevertheless that was not a chance he was willing to take.

At a little after eleven, a black Chevrolet Tahoe arrived, the size of the specially imported SUV made to seem monstrous on the narrow Argentinian street. A bulky man wearing a black suit exited from the shotgun seat and walked around to the passenger side nearest the kerb and opened the door. A tall, white-haired man climbed down from the SUV. He too was wearing a suit, yet his was light grey and accentuated by a bright blue shirt and cream cravat. Orosco waved back at the driver of the Tahoe who pulled back into the traffic and continued on past the café and around the corner. Orosco now walked with his head held high towards the entrance of the café. Before he reached it, a man wearing an apron opened the door and guided him along the pavement towards the wooden tables at the back.

Akulov tracked his target and cursed as first the waiter and then the bodyguard blocked his shot. Orosco sat and Akulov let out a long breath of frustration as now the café awning obstructed his view of the man from the waist up. Pushing his annoyance aside, Akulov scanned the immediate area for any threats, for any hidden security either watching out for Orosco or perhaps looking for him. It wasn't beyond the realm of possibility that he had walked into a set-up, it had happened in the past. However, he had not operated in Argentina before and had little reason to believe this to be the case. And then Orosco stood. Now all that could be seen of the man were his feet. Two more figures joined the table, but they had come from inside and Akulov had not seen them approach. All three sat. Both the new arrivals were wearing suits. Once again one of the pair, who was wearing a matching black suit to that of Orosco's bodyguard, was part hidden by the awning, but the second man was not. He was much younger than Orosco. His hair was jet-black, his frame rotund and he was dressed in a chocolate-brown two-piece suit and blood-red shirt. He'd taken the seat directly opposite Orosco, fully exposed to the sunlight. Akulov did not know the man. However, from the relaxed way he sat, Akulov presumed him to be either someone Orosco was well acquainted with or someone important enough not to stand on ceremony. The new arrival lit a large cigar and puffed a cloud of smoke directly up into the air. Akulov started to reassess his situation, yet he knew patience was key. He also knew that the longer he lay exposed on the rooftop, the higher the chance of him becoming compromised. Below, a waiter arrived with an order, presumably Orosco's usual as he hadn't seen him place an order. Orosco moved forward in his chair, placed his left elbow on the table and reached for his cup with his right hand.

Akulov started to increase the pressure on his trigger finger... and then there was a flash of movement.

A sudden popping noise, twice in quick succession, and repeated again.

The retort of suppressed rounds, two sets of two shots, a pair of double taps.

Akulov's eye moved away from the scope to take in the wider scene. The man in the brown suit was slumped sideways in his chair, his arms hanging limp. Orosco was frozen, seemingly unable to comprehend what had happened. His bodyguard was behind him attempting to lift him out of his seat. Akulov refocused, breathed out, and his finger started to contract again when the other man's bodyguard abruptly blocked his shot. This time it was Akulov who froze as he saw the bodyguard's face.

He recognised him.

But he was wrong.

He had to be wrong.

He could not believe the information his eyes were transporting to his brain, but before Akulov had a chance to comprehend what he was seeing there was another double tap and the bodyguard he recognised collapsed onto Akulov's target, knocking the pair of them into Orosco's own bodyguard who stumbled backwards and out of Akulov's line of sight, obscured by the overhanging awning.

Akulov removed his eye from the sight. He saw the second shooter. The assassin was dressed in a helmet and motorbike leathers and striding away from the café, weapon held at waist height, towards an idling bike. The pedestrians on the street cowered as the assassin calmly climbed onto the Yamaha, pushed the pistol inside a pouch and then with a chirp of tyres, tore across the paving stones and into the park causing those using its paths to scatter like pigeons.

Akulov continued to watch for what seemed like an eternity, yet in reality was no longer than a couple of seconds. The two bodyguards had managed to hustle Orosco inside the café, the one who had been shot seemingly still able to operate. The body of the man who had come to meet him had slipped from the chair and lay unmoving on the unforgiving tiled floor as a puddle of blood and brain matter spread on the tiles.

Akulov had missed his chance to take his shot.

Akulov had failed.

Akulov had failed because of the man who'd blocked his shot. Yet it was impossible for that man to be here.

Sirens reached Akulov's ears. Looking left he saw a police vehicle coming to a screeching halt, straddling the pavement. Seconds behind it the siren of an approaching ambulance added to the chaotic cacophony. Yet the police were too late, the assassin had escaped, and the medics had perhaps one life to save – that of the bodyguard. The first man shot was clearly dead.

Akulov had to admire the audacity of the other assassin. Close-up executions took determination; they were the riskiest of all. Inexperienced shooters invariably lost their nerve or at the very least paused upon locking eyes with their target. Yet this shooter had fluidly opened fire and then simply walked away, without hesitation, and without any outward indication of panic or fear. Akulov knew he had witnessed the work of a fellow professional. Yet what were the chances of two independent hitters being in the same kill zone at the same time to hit exactly the same target?

But had he and the biker been after the same person? Akulov played back the few seconds of action in his head. The shooter shot Orosco's guest first before targeting Orosco. So, was Orosco an afterthought or a secondary target of less importance? Then another aspect of the shooting hit him, six shots had been fired. The first four had been double taps whilst the last two had solely hit the man he'd recognised, the bodyguard, in the torso, a location which any self-respecting operator would have protected with a ballistic vest. So, were these not meant to be kill shots? Something did not quite add up.

Akulov pushed these thoughts aside because there was one upshot of the coincidental attack. He had not taken his own shot, he had not made his presence or his intention known. Franco Orosco was still breathing and within the café, and that meant Akulov had a second chance at completing his contract. Akulov decided he would sit, and he would wait, and then he would kill the man as he exited the café.

A crowd of onlookers had now gathered on his side of the street and those on the side of the café were being pushed back, marshalled by the ever-growing number of police officers arriving on the scene. A pair of black SUVs approached at speed. As they drew near, he noted the number-plate of the lead one, it was the same black Tahoe which had deposited Orosco less than fifteen minutes before. The driver exited from the Tahoe, and then a man appeared from the second vehicle. He was older, more squat, and had a mane of unruly grey hair. He was dressed in a police uniform. He barked out a command and the nearest police officer saluted him swiftly before he darted inside the café. A second officer now stepped forward and held out his hand to shake that of the senior officer, yet the man with the grey hair was having none of it. He held up his finger and pointed at the younger man in an accusatory manner, all but stabbing him in the chest. Before the reprimanded man could respond the café door behind him opened.

Akulov now looked down his scope and took a large breath, letting it out slowly as his right index finger started to take second pressure on the trigger of the long-barrelled HK416. The tall white-haired figure of Franco Orosco stepped through the doors accompanied by his own bodyguard on his left and the man Akulov definitely recognised on his right, who whilst moving was clearly in pain. Akulov now realised he must have been wearing a ballistic vest beneath his suit.

Wolf Six knew he had to be quick, or he would lose his shot. Once more, taking a breath and then releasing it, Akulov's index finger asserted more pressure and squeezed. A single suppressed round slammed into Orosco's head, striking him between the top lip and nose, obliterating his face and shredding his brainstem. Akulov knew his target was dead before he hit the ground. Firing a second shot was pointless.

He was on the move before those on the street below could comprehend what had happened. Stepping back from the edge of the roof, Akulov took a small IED from the custom holdall which had held the rife and carefully affixed it to the HK. He rechecked that the timer was set for six minutes and then started it. Pulling on a baseball cap and an oversized pair of aviators, he left the roof. He took the steps down, aware that at any moment armed police or residents could challenge or attempt to stop him. Akulov reached the ground floor and entered the foyer via a door next to the dual lifts. Baseball cap tugged down as far as he could to obscure his face, and sunglasses further masking the space between his eyes and his beard he crossed the foyer and headed for the exit. He took the steps down to street level and joined the growing group of gawkers who, despite having witnessed a second shooting, still stared like sheep at the scene across the road, watching the police and enjoying the commotion with, he imagined, morbid fascination.

Akulov heard the muted explosion from above, all but lost in the hubbub of the city street and certainly not noticed for what it was by the crowd around him. This was his cue to leave the scene. Akulov skirted the crowd and headed south and away from the double assassination scene as more sirens approached. He continued up Avenue President Manuel Quintana then took the first left onto Ayacucho. A hundred metres further on he ducked into an apartment store which he knew had an exit on the next street over. Akulov then walked the two kilometres to a bar he had scouted earlier, by a zig-zagging circuitous route, as he carried out countersurveillance measures to check for any tails.

The interior of the bar was dark even during the day, and its walls were stained nicotine yellow. He noted he was the youngest customer by perhaps two decades, yet no one paid him any attention as he took a stool at the far end of the bar and ordered a beer. The barman's chubby hand placed the bottle in front of him. Akulov nodded and pushed a couple of notes across towards him, he was not a fan of having a tab. He took a pull of Quilmes, enjoying the cold bitterness as it slipped down his throat. He never drank during an operation but knew that the one small bottle would not adversely affect his performance. Besides, he would have raised eyebrows ordering a Coca-Cola. As he sat with the rear exit in his peripheral vision, and the entrance directly in front of him, Akulov only now let his mind attempt to solve the puzzle it had encountered a little over an hour before. He recalled the old saying that everyone had a double, but it struck Akulov that this was more than a physical resemblance. Although he had only seen the face of the man via a magnified scope, he had felt the presence of another one of his kind, he had felt the presence of a brother Werewolf.

He took another long sip of beer then retrieved his burner phone, inserted the SIM and switched it on. He waited until it had logged on to the local internet provider then he accessed the latest Proton email account he'd set up for this operation. Using the draft folder he would leave a message for Tishina appraising her of the situation, that the contract had been completed but also mentioning the other shooter. Akulov looked up as another customer entered the bar, his threat radar did not ping and the man sat and unfolded a newspaper – something he imagined only a regular would do. Akulov drank again then opened the folder. He blinked. There was a message already there. It was from Tishina. Akulov stared at the draft message. Only he and Tishina had the password to access the account and the username itself was a randomised mix of numbers, letters and symbols. He had no reason not to believe it was from her, yet it was highly unusual. It read:

> Immediate new contract. Client fully vetted. Client will contact you at hotel. Usual terms plus 50%

Akulov deleted the message, then sent his own:

> Tell me about Wolf Nine.

Akulov closed his phone and removed the SIM. He finished his beer, nodded at the barman and left the establishment. Outside on the street, hand in pocket, he snapped his SIM into two then casually removing his hand, dropped the pieces into the gutter.

3

NURISTAN, AFGHANISTAN 2012

The Red Army had pulled out of Afghanistan in 1989, after what the rest of the world had called a stinging defeat, but what the Soviet Union had referred to as the end of a successful mission. Now some twenty-three years later a small element of the Red Army was back. However, it now had a new name and belonged to a new country – Russia. The small team of Werewolves were on a highly deniable and highly dangerous mission. Their target was a pair of brothers originally from Pakistan, who had attended university in Moscow. One training as an engineer and the other as a surgeon. Intelligence said the brothers had cultivated links with Islamic extremists in both Dagestan and Chechnya, whilst in Moscow. It was believed the pair had links to the 2010 Moscow subway suicide bombings, and were actively seeking to strike Russia again. Hidden away in the all but inaccessible Nuristan province of Afghanistan, the two Pakistani nationals were all but untouchable, or so they had believed.

Nuristan had seen some of the most brutal fighting during the Soviet occupation. Whilst the Taliban had taken control of the majority of the country after the Russians had pulled out, due to its narrow, craggy valleys and thick forests, Nuristan had become a stronghold first for al-Qaida and then Islamic State. The Americans too had been unable to tame the province and now it was still considered to be one of the unruliest regions of Afghanistan.

None of this mattered to Ruslan Akulov. His grandmother had been a victim of the earlier 1999 Moscow apartment bombings, and any chance he was offered to get back at the extremists who'd targeted innocent civilians he took without question or second thought.

* * *

Concealed amongst the produce in the three ageing trucks navigating the narrow, rock-strewn road to the town of Parun, the six-man Werewolf team waited. It was in Parun, in a shack of a coffee shop, that the brothers Arshad and Shahid Khan openly met with guests and associates. Satellite imaging suggested the town was nothing more than a single dirt road with low-storey buildings on either side, clinging to the bank of a fast-flowing river. Overlooked by towering cliffs on all sides, Parun was all but hidden from the outside world. The Americans, Akulov thought, would have just sent one of their many drones to the place and bombed the coffee shop and everyone inside, but the Russians had neither that ability nor opportunity. Russia did however have the Werewolves, and half of that unit was now on its way to liquidate the two terrorists.

* * *

Dressed in local clothes, with Pakols on their heads and thick beards obscuring their faces, all six Russians could pass as Afghani from a distance. Denis "Kizlyar" Petrov, aka Wolf Nine, sat on the opposite side of the truck to Akulov and whittled away at a small piece of wood with a sharp blade. It was one of several the Spetsnaz operative from St Petersburg was prone to carry, and this coupled with his unmatched knife-fighting ability was why he'd been given the nom de guerre "Kizlyar", after the place in Dagestan where the best combat knives in the Russian Federation were widely accepted to come from.

"Did you know that the province of Nuristan was only created one hundred and thirty years ago?" Kizlyar said, without looking up from his whittling.

"No. I did not," Akulov replied.

"It means 'land of light'. Previously this region was known as 'Kafiristan'."

"The land of Kefir?"

"No," Kizlyar replied, a half-smile now appearing on his sharp face, "Kafiristan. The land of the infidels."

"Then we should feel at home."

"I could live here, amongst the trees and the rivers. Just me, and of course my blades."

"In Afghanistan?"

"Why not, or you know where I've always wanted to visit?"

"Disneyland?"

Kizlyar sighed. "No. Canada. It looks just so, big. And green."

Akulov made no reply and peered out of the back of the truck. They were in the last vehicle, acting as tail-end Charlie. Wolf One, their commander Kirill Vetrov, was in the lead truck with Wolf Three, whilst Wolves Eight and Seven were in the middle one. The trucks were manned by local drivers who, used to the route, made the journey once a week with supplies for the shops and enterprises dotted throughout the sparsely populated region. They had been paid handsomely by a village elder at the mouth of the valley, to deliver the six passengers to town. None of them knew what the Werewolves were, and none of them had asked what their business was in Parun. Above the craggy hillsides on either side of the steep valley, the sky was a deep blue and cloudless, whilst the trees hanging on to the thin soil, interspaced between smaller bushes and rocky outcrops, were of a dark green. In essence it was an opportune place to hide, watch and set an ambush.

A gentle breeze blew down the valley. Akulov imagined that in the winter months the wind would not be so benign. Beneath his local clothes Akulov was wearing a chest and backplate which, while making him bulky, did at least offer some protection from small arms fire. He had an MP-443 Grach strapped to his right thigh, covered by the tails of his overshirt, and an AKS-74U lying across his lap. Although the sun was high in the sky, the temperature in the valley reminded him of a Moscow autumn and he imagined the weather here was just as capricious. He looked back at the road, which was nothing more than a well-used dirt track sandwiched between what appeared to be the muscled shoulders of a pair of giants. He imagined the Goliaths, watching and waiting, biding their time until they could strike anyone who dared to encroach upon their territory.

Akulov's eyes caught a sudden glint from behind a rocky outcrop, and then almost immediately the snap of a rifle round as it tore towards them. The round slammed into the step just past Akulov's feet with a ping.

"Contact rear!" Akulov shouted into his throat mic, as he pushed himself deeper into the truck amongst the crates of provisions.

More rifle rounds now struck the truck, accompanied by the

barking of Kalashnikovs. The truck came to an abrupt halt, causing a loose box to crash down onto Akulov's left shoulder.

Kizlyar clambered over and flung it aside. "Machine," Wolf Nine said, using Akulov's nickname, "you OK?"

"We need to exfil, this canvas is giving us no cover," Akulov said as he reached for his AKS-74U, which had fallen onto the floor of the truck.

"I agree."

There was a sudden whoosh, and a trail of smoke shot from behind a large outcrop. In his ear, Akulov heard Wolf One calmly state, over the radio, "Incoming RPG."

On instinct, rather than retreating further inside the truck, both Werewolves vaulted over the tailgate and crashed onto the rocky ground as the RPG tore a hole through the canvas of the truck before exploding against the sloping roadside. Showered with dirt, Akulov now rolled sideways and away from the truck. Kizlyar, Akulov noticed, was on the other side of the road. Both men's rifles, the short-stock assault version of the Kalashnikov, whilst boasting the same impressive round rate as the standard version, were less accurate over longer range. In short, shooting at the assaulters in the hills would be hit-and-miss.

Training and experience meant that the Werewolves were no strangers to operating under fire, and as Akulov pushed himself into a shallow ditch at the side track, he was already scanning what he could see of the hillside in order to plan his next course of action. He saw a figure step out of cover, with the unmistakable form of an RPG launcher resting on his shoulder. Akulov didn't target the man, but Kizlyar did. At the extreme range of his AK, the burst of rounds hit the man's legs and lower torso. The attacker juddered, collapsing sideways, and the RPG sailed across the narrow valley before slamming high into the rock face on the other side.

Akulov now saw a row of three, perhaps four men on a ridgeline, and they looked to be armed with rifles. Probably stolen Soviet Dragunovs, he thought bitterly. As the snipers opened fire, further down the hillside more men appeared from cover, assault rifles up, and charged towards the road, the three trucks and the six Werewolves.

As they came further into range, both Akulov and Kizlyar opened up with their AKs. Taking down a man each, and causing the remaining assaulters to dart and dive into cover. Akulov looked back and saw the other four members of the team also engaging targets. He knew the area was unstable, a place that even the Americans could not fully control, but yet he found it odd that civilian supply trucks would be targeted, unless this was some part of a turf war, or unless the fighters on the hillside had been tipped off and were targeting them. Under his own truck he could see the driver, face down and hands on his head. Surely if the man had been part of any collusion he would have quickly left the scene of the ambush?

"Exfil. Leave the trucks," Wolf One's voice again over the comms was calm, the words concise.

Akulov signalled to Kizlyar, and pointed to a narrow path skirting an outcrop of rock and disappearing into the hills. Kizlyar nodded, understanding. As Akulov gave covering fire, Wolf Nine – Kizlyar – hurried towards him at a crouch. He skidded to a halt, creating a cloud of dust and immediately went prone in the ditch a metre past Wolf Six's position. Akulov would move past him, leap-frogging the position. They would use this technique until they were both in the relative safety of the dead ground afforded by the outcrop. Akulov sprang to his feet as Kizlyar gave covering fire back towards the assaulters. Reaching a new position, Akulov now targeted the Afghans as Kizlyar sprinted past him. Both men paused, panting, and assessed the situation. Less return fire was coming from the vicinity of the trucks. Akulov saw the rest of the team moving towards a bend in the road and a further area with boulders affording cover. Kizlyar and Akulov were of equal rank, had been trained to work as a team yet could also operate as lone assets. Whilst it was important to reunite with the rest of the team, it would mean running back directly through the choke point of the ambush, which was something neither man would survive.

There was an all too familiar whooshing sound. Mortars!

Akulov looked on in disbelief as first one, and then another, landed behind them, and then the truck they had been travelling in exploded as a third shell hit.

Without sharing a single word or signal, both Wolf Six and Wolf Nine were on their feet and sprinting towards the overhanging outcrop and the path. Kizlyar was ahead yet Akulov was gaining as he heard a whistling in his ears.

Abruptly thrown from his feet, Akulov was slammed against the rocky hillside. Winded and dazed, it took him several long seconds to come to his senses. He blinked the dirt from his eyes and tasting blood, realised he couldn't see Wolf Nine. Behind him black smoke billowed from the last truck, and armed men swarmed onto the road.

Akulov staggered to his feet. Throat dry, he croaked, "Kizlyar... Kizlyar!"

Collecting his AK from where it had been hurled from his hands, he noticed a second rifle further ahead. He made for it and now saw that hidden from the road was a narrow gully, and at least thirty feet below this was a fast-moving river. As angry shouts sounded behind him, and the ping of incoming rounds snapped above his head, Akulov watched as the body of Wolf Nine was carried away by the water. Akulov felt disbelief and anger overwhelm him. There had always been twelve Werewolves, from the very start and now one was down. The violent tug of a bullet slicing through his sleeve awoke Akulov from his thoughts and he spun around, weapon up and firing a furious fusillade at three approaching Afghan fighters. They wore black turbans, and US-style field jackets. The first fighter dropped, Akulov's rounds destroying his face. The second fell to his knees clutching his ruined chest but the third, however, still came at Akulov. The AKS-74U clicked empty as an incoming round sliced into Akulov's left leg. He dropped the Kalashnikov, and dropping to his knees, pulled his pistol from its holster and as the Afghan fighter was close enough for Akulov to see his eyes, Wolf Six shot him directly between them.

Blood had started to soak the beige material of his left trouser leg red, and Akulov felt his head swim, but he had no time to staunch the flow now as more fighters were heading his way, and at least two of them carried RPG tubes. Turning, he grabbed Wolf Nine's AK and made for the outcrop no more than twenty feet away from him, as more rounds started to strike the earth around him and ping from the rocks ahead. Knowing he was outnumbered and out-gunned his only hope was to somehow get away.

An RPG sizzled past him slamming into the overhang, Akulov flinched as dirt and rocks exploded onto the path. But he had to push forward. He reached the overhang and saw that the path took a sharp left, winding between the undulating hillside. He knew he could be walking into a trap, yet he also knew he had no other choice. And then the second RPG struck, the shock wave pushed him against the rock face, a thunderous rumble travelling past him. This time when he opened his eyes, Akulov saw the path behind him was blocked by the overhanging rocks that had collapsed. Relieved at least that he could not be easily followed, he ripped off part of his left sleeve and tied it as tight as he could around his wounded leg as a tourniquet, realising as he did so that both his med pack and his canteen had been left in the now smouldering truck. He tried his comms network, already understanding that he would be out of range. He looked ahead and saw that the path angled down following the foot of the hill and, he hoped, eventually joining up with the river below. Akulov pushed back up to his feet and staggered onwards and downwards.

The sun had started to dip by the time he reached the river, and deep shadows formed amongst the irregular rock formations. He dropped to his knees, onto the wet stones, a dagger of pain reminding him of the wound to his left leg, and using both hands bathed his face, the icy water making him shiver before he started to take giant gulps. Coughing, he rolled onto his side and then his back and lay looking up at the dimming sky. The stars would be out soon, and with it the temperature would drop and the darkness, whilst hiding his approach from any enemy, would make his progress all the more treacherous.

He pulled himself up to a sitting position and leant against a rock as he prodded his leg. It could have been much worse, and the fact that he'd been able to put at least some pressure on it told him it was neither a permanent disability nor life threatening. But it was damn annoying. He was Wolf Six, he was the Machine, the Spetsnaz commando who could run forever over whatever terrain was placed in his way, and now here he was in the wildest area of Afghanistan forced to hobble like an old man. But he was alive. He thought back to Wolf Nine, Kizlyar, birth name Denis Petrov and he shuddered. He had lost friends before, during training exercises, before the Werewolves had been formed and he had seen more than his fair share of people die, but he had never seen that happen to one of his own, one of his brother Werewolves. Yet even now was not the time to grieve, it was the time to keep on moving; to follow the river and eventually hit, he hoped, the prearranged emergency rendezvous point in the shadows of the Pakistani border. Ruslan Akulov, Wolf Six, the Machine, got to his feet, gritted his teeth and started to walk.

4

BUENOS AIRES

Present Day

Akulov waited outside his hotel room door. The "Do Not Disturb" sign was still hanging over the doorknob, but the thin piece of Scotch tape he had placed across the miniscule gap at the bottom right of the door, between the door and frame, as a telltale, was creased. Someone had been inside during his absence.

Akulov slowly pushed his right hand inside his jacket and wrapped his fingers around the grip of his suppressed, sub-compact Glock 26, nestled in its custom-made holster. Using his left hand, he held his key card against the electronic lock, which bleeped annoyingly as it released. He pushed the door open and swiftly stepped inside, drawing the Glock as he did so. The obvious position for an ambush point would be the bathroom to his immediate right. However the door was closed. Akulov rapidly stepped past this, and dissecting the rest of the room with his handgun, quickly established that the room was empty. He turned back and, weapon up, walked slowly towards the bathroom. As he did so his eyes were drawn to something lying on his bed. He registered it as being a book but paid it no further attention. Shoving the door open, he swung into the bathroom. It was empty.

Once satisfied that he was the only living entity in the hotel suite, he holstered his Glock. Now carrying out a further visual inspection of the room, Akulov checked for any obvious changes such as fresh marks or indentations on the walls or cornicing. It would be clumsy and time consuming to drill into the plaster to place a camera or listening device, but not impossible. Any piece of equipment left by an intruder was much more likely to be hidden in the light fittings or smoke detectors. Akulov checked his watch, he'd be leaving regardless within the next half an hour.

Threat assessment complete, Akulov's curiosity took over and he crossed to the bed and visually inspected the paperback lying on his pillow, in place of a hotel chocolate. His eyes narrowed as he recognised both the cover and title. It was a Spanish language edition of *Dubliners* by James Joyce, and the exact same edition he had once read. He crouched down to make sure there was nothing under the book before he picked it up and opened it. There was an inscription inside:

To Wolf Six,

This is to replace the copy you lost when we last met.

R

Akulov frowned. He remembered faces, as well as other details most would forget, and this included where and when he had been reading this exact book.

And then his doorbell rang. Twice.

And then it opened as a key card was held against the lock.

There was no cursory call of "housekeeping" as a woman with long, dark hair, stepped into the room.

"May I?" she asked in English.

Akulov instantly recognised her and replied, in what he knew to be her native language, "Oui, entrez."

At the use of French, the start of a smile formed at the edges of her mouth. Shutting the door she said, "And now I have your name. It is Ruslan Akulov, aka Wolf Six."

Akulov had also learnt of the woman's identity since that day on the Spanish train. "As do I, Sophie Racine."

Racine gave the slightest of nods. "I suppose a girl has a reputation?"

"You are DGSE's most lethal operative, some say."

"And what do you say, Ruslan?"

"I say, why are you here?"

"You've not checked the draft folder of that anonymous web-based email you use to communicate with Tishina? She left you a message."

Akulov blinked on hearing the name of his broker, and then he understood. "You are the new client?"

"Yes."

"So why are you here?"

"I'm here for the same reason you are. To stop Orosco."

Akulov saw no reason to lie. "I was purely here to stop him breathing. This I achieved."

"Liquidating Orosco was only part of my mission," Racine stated.

Akulov took a beat to reply. "You are being extremely candid with me."

Racine's left eyebrow arched. "Candid? We are professionals, we both executed a man this morning. I am extending you my professional courtesy."

Akulov knew it was too much of a coincidence to be otherwise but said, "So that was you, on the bike."

"Yes. But you didn't see me when I came back. I saw you take the shot."

"I see."

"No, that's not quite true. I watched you leave that apartment building, but I'm an intelligent woman, I recognised you and put two and two together."

"I must try to be less memorable."

"Look, this situation is larger than just Orosco."

Akulov had become curious. "What were you here to stop Orosco from doing?"

Racine pointed at the armchair by the window. "May I?"

"Be my guest." He took a step backwards to allow the French woman to pass. He caught a waft of fresh soap as he did so, realising that she did not seem at all tense around him, which he found interesting.

Racine sat. "A gentleman would have offered me a seat."

"An independent woman would have not waited to be offered a seat."

"Bravo," she gestured to the second armchair, with her chin, "you don't want to sit?"

"I want to leave," Akulov replied, but sat anyway.

Without preamble Racine said, bluntly, "Orosco is attempting to recreate ETA."

Akulov blinked. "ETA?"

"The defunct Basque separatist movement."

"Thank you. I know what it was, I am just surprised."

"Then you must also be aware the Basque region straddles the French and Spanish border."

"I remember once opening an atlas," Akulov replied, thinly.

Racine continued. "Orosco's heritage is Basque. His parents

were active members of the Basque Nationalist Party. They fled Spain for Argentina when Franco took power in 1939. Twenty years later when ETA was founded, Orosco's father gave some financial assistance to the organisation. The man I killed today, Jorge Espinosa, was an important part of Orosco's overall plan. He was a conduit for untraceable funds originating from his illegal gold mining activity in Colombia. He used this to instigate the recruitment and training of a private army. Espinosa's head of security was in charge of this."

Akulov said, "I see."

"Five months ago, a local Spanish diplomat working at the Embassy of Spain in Buenos Aries abruptly resigned. Three months ago, his body was found in Colombia, in a Bogotá hotel room to be exact. He oversaw the department responsible for Schengen visas and Spanish passports."

Akulov joined the dots. "Are you telling me the Spanish and French governments believe this dead diplomat was working with Orosco and Espinosa?"

"No. They do not. I do. So does my department chief. We believe Orosco and Espinosa have created, near the town of El Bagre, a group of young, military trained men, who will be inserted into the EU to carry out terror attacks in the name of Basque independence."

"That is a large leap," Akulov said.

"It is. However, I am not wrong," Racine replied. "I'm rarely wrong."

Akulov appreciated her confidence. "The DGSE have sent you here to liquidate all bad actors at source?"

"That is a succinct way of explaining this. Yes."

"And you want me to do this?"

"I want you to help me. A second shooter would be valuable."

Akulov was puzzled. "Why didn't you shoot Orosco first?"

"He was an old man, he was slower, and he would have taken longer to react."

"But Espinosa's bodyguard did not?"

"No. He got in the way."

"Why didn't you shoot him in the head?"

"Because he was working for me."

Akulov nodded slowly, that made sense. He had been wearing a vest. "He is a DGSE asset."

"He is an independent contractor like you. In fact, he is very like you."

Akulov said nothing.

Racine said, "Why didn't you shoot Orosco?"

Akulov was embarrassed but nevertheless said, "I was distracted."

"By?"

"Your asset. I may have hit him."

"After all these years I'm cheered to see you still remain loyal to the Werewolves."

Was he being manipulated or was the man he had seen earlier that day really Wolf Nine? Akulov was uncomfortable, Racine knew too much about him and his former unit, so he said, "The man I knew died."

"Some of us have to die twice."

Akulov said nothing.

Racine asked, "Will you work for me?"

"Doesn't your organisation have its own resources?"

The skin around Racine's eyes tightened. "My department currently has cash but limited manpower. Besides, you are already here. And then of course there is your reputation as the world's most proficient assassin."

Akulov ignored the words, not caring if they were meant as a statement of fact or as flattery. "What happens if I decline?"

"I'd become upset. Wouldn't it be nice for you to have friends in French intelligence?"

"Does your 'asset' know you want to bring me into this?"

"Not yet."

"I would rather meet him unannounced."

"That is already arranged. In one hour. It will also be necessary for us to travel to Colombia, in perhaps two days' time."

"I see."

"Ruslan, this is the chance to liquidate an entire organisation before it has the opportunity to launch its first operation. We hit them here and we take them out there too. Innumerable lives will be saved by strategically taking those of a few. I know this appeals to your kill code." Racine checked her watch. "I need a decision now. Time is a luxury I do not have."

Akulov was not responding to being strong-armed, it was his curiosity which made his say, "Yes."

"Bon." Racine stood, took a small piece of paper from the back pocket of her jeans and handed it to Akulov. "Memorise this location. This is where you are meeting Denis. I will arrive after you and then brief you both in full on the mission."

Akulov took the note as Sophie Racine of the DGSE walked out of the door.

* * *

Jenner, California

The darkness brought the nightmares once more. The dreams had faded over the years yet, like a scar from a past injury, stubbornly remained. Although Torres's rational mind knew he was safe, sleeping in his daughter's house, that was not the part of his mind which was dominant as he lay, sweating in his fitful slumber. He had gone back in time, and was back in the army...

Torres's eyes were wet because of the whipping wind and the lashing rain, he told himself, remorselessly rolling across this South Atlantic island. In reality, however, he knew it was his own tears of despair. It was April yet the weather on the island showed no signs of spring, it was as barren and battered as any wasteland he had seen. Rolling grassy plains littered with outcrops of what he imagined was granite, stretched all the way to the mountains in the distance. During the day he had seen they still retained some snow cover. He was a nineteen-year-old boy, conscripted to complete his mandatory national military service, who had abruptly been sent to a troop ship and shipped across the choppy waters to the Malvinas. Two months before, the only guns he had seen were on television or at the movies. Then he was issued with a rifle and a bayonet, and was expected to kill for his country.

After a gruelling cross-country yomp, heads down to guard against the aggressive wind, padded coats heavy with rain and feet blistering in ill-fitting, cheap leather boots, Torres and his fellow conscripts, including two schoolfriends, Sergio Gomez and Ezra Kantor, had finally arrived at the farmhouse. Torres had dreamt of comfort, and expected warmth, yet he had found neither. There the gaggle of bedraggled teenage conscripts was greeted by their commanding officer – Franco Orosco, Captain Franco Orosco. It was a name and a face Torres and his friends recognised. They were from the same town, his family from the same street as Torres. Although a decade older, Orosco was someone Torres and his friends had known of and feared. He'd been a notorious bully, and a juvenile gang leader before somehow managing to get a place at the prestigious National Military Academy – "The Colegio Militar de la Nación" in El

Palomar, Buenos Aires. Now years later, his face was less boyish and his moustache had grown in. However, his eyes remained the same – coal black and pitiless.

And that was when Torres's troubles began.

He and the other members of his unit had been forced to drive four, thick poles into the earth opposite the front door of the commandeered stone-walled farmhouse. When Ezra had asked Orosco, politely, why they needed to place the poles into the earth, Orosco's barked reply was that he would be the first to find out. That night, before any of the men had eaten, the sergeant took Ezra to one side and ordered him to undress. Shocked, Ezra did not refuse but Torres now asked why, at which point Orosco stated that surely he knew that Ezra Kantor was not a real Argentinian? That he was a Jewish traitor whose father was a coward, and that Ezra would betray them all as soon as he could. Dumbstruck, and with the indignation of youth, both Torres and Sergio verbally leapt to Ezra's defence. However, this only landed the pair of them with the same treatment. That night the three friends found themselves hogtied to a pole each, wearing nothing but their underpants as the unforgiving South Atlantic darkness enveloped them.

The torment had continued. Torres and his group had been on the island for five days now, without seeing a single British invader or receiving any further information on the state of the conflict. That morning Captain Orosco had ordered the conscripts to dig trenches around the farmhouse. To Torres they looked like graves, and he imagined strangling Orosco and burying him in one of them. Despite the ground having been softened somewhat by the torrential rain, it was backbreaking work. After almost collapsing from exhaustion, the conscripts were instructed to go back inside, all except Torres and his two school friends. Orosco had singled them out for not working hard enough, which was a lie. Even in the freezing rain, Torres's blood ran hot, fuelled by the outrage at the accusation. The trio were ordered to strip, and once again were hogtied. This time, however, they were abruptly pushed into a trench each.

Torres found himself shaking uncontrollably, fearing he would either die from hypothermia or drown in the rising water. His mind began to wander. It seemed to always rain on the island. Perhaps this was because the Malvinas really should have been British. After all, Torres thought in his addled mental state, didn't it always rain in London? Why not just let the two idiotic islands remain occupied by Margaret Thatcher's voters and be done with it? This rain was of a type he had never experienced before, it felt like knives as it hit the exposed skin on his face, back and legs. Soon, however, he knew his body would become numb again, and then he would feel nothing as he drifted off into unconsciousness. The first time it had happened was several days before, when he had been tied to the pole. At the time he had not even realised it was happening and had woken up with the hot pain of the fire inside the farmhouse reanimating him like a corpse in that film he had watched with his friends, *Dawn of the Dead*. It was then and there that Tomas Torres resolved to make Orosco pay for his actions. He imagined that this was not the first time Orosco's brutality had been used against men under his command. Torres also understood that the Malvinas crisis had given the man an unparalleled and unchecked opportunity, as the sole officer in this part of the valley to unleash his full wrath against any of those whom he took issue with.

As Torres felt his eyes start to close, he noticed light spilling into the trench. The sergeant, Orosco's second-in-command, hopped down, his boots sinking into the mud as he landed by

Torres's side. A moment later, one of the other conscripts joined him.

The sergeant crouched down and tapped Torres's face with the palm of his hand, a gentle slap to rouse him. "We are to march in the morning. I have been ordered to bring you back inside."

Torres attempted to speak but all that happened was his mouth opened and closed; no sounds came out. Using a knife, the older soldier started to cut away at the bonds securing Torres's wrists and ankles. The two men then hauled him up to his feet and manhandled him out of the trench. As they attempted to move him towards the farmhouse, half dragged, half carrying him, there was an all but blinding flash of light as the door opened. Its frame was entirely filled by a tall, powerful figure wearing a long coat. In his right hand was a pistol. He advanced towards Torres and pushed the barrel of the pistol into the bare skin of his chest.

Orosco said, "You are much stronger than I imagined, and for that I give you credit. We are to march at daybreak, and I need every strong, able-bodied soldier I can muster. Now, I ask you, are you ready to undertake your patriotic duty?"

Torres managed to mumble. "Y... yes... s... sir."

"That is good, and as expected." Orosco pulled the pistol away from Torres's chest. "As for your two friends, however, perhaps they are less robust than you? I have no need of men who are feeble and fainthearted."

Torres attempted to understand the words of his commanding officer as the man strode towards the other two trenches. He raised his pistol as he reached the first and without hesitation, or a further word, fired a round at point-blank range at the man inside. The retort of the round was whipped away by the ferocious wind as were the anguished howls of Torres, and the second shot moments later.

* * *

Torres was shaking again, yet this time something was shaking him, it was a hand, and then he heard a voice calling him.

"Tomas, wake up."

Torres opened his eyes to see his son-in-law framed in the morning light.

"You were calling out in your sleep."

"W... what time is it?"

"A little after six."

"Was I loud?"

"Not at all, but I thought you'd like to hear the news."

Torres sat up. "What's happened? Is the family safe?"

"Everyone is fine," Christian reassured him. "It's the news. I thought you may want to see it."

Torres still didn't quite understand. "The news?"

"It made CNN, so it must have been verified."

"What did?"

"Your old enemy, Franco Orosco, is dead."

"Dead?"

"He and a Colombian businessman he was with were assassinated yesterday in a café in Buenos Aires."

"Really?" Why had his assassin shot a second man? Still, if that person had been an associate of Orosco, he probably deserved it. Torres decided to focus on the good news, "Tell me more."

"Two men killed within minutes of each other. The Argentinians think it was either the same assassin or a team of two."

Mind suddenly clear, Torres got to his feet. He felt giddy, a sense of excitement, exhilaration, yet most of all relief. Justice had finally been served, he had been both judge and jury, whilst the man he had contracted had been the executioner. "This we must celebrate!"

5

Sophie Racine's section of the DGSE was known as "The Department", and her particular section within this, specialised in clandestine, direct-action operations. In short, she worked as the Republic of France's assassin. It wasn't a title she would or could ever use or admit to, even when on those rare occasions she had to visit the office on the outskirts of Paris.

The secrecy was necessary as several years before, an outsourced hit team, operating under the orders of Russia, had attempted to destroy her unit. The existing director had been killed along with several other agents, and her former boyfriend and line manager Baptiste, had been left in a coma. Racine had told her director that she did not hold grudges. This was a lie. Racine held grudges, until the person she had a grudge against no longer drew breath. She saw nothing wrong with this. However, the world had moved on politically since the attack and France, via its commitments and military aid to Ukraine, was in a de facto state of war against Russia. This meant that those responsible for the Paris attack had scattered or been absorbed into Russia's war machine. Racine hoped they were already dead, but if not, she vowed to find them all and shoot them in the head.

Racine cast her eyes once more around her hotel suite, out of habit, to ensure she had left no unnecessary trace. As was her training, she had already wiped down all the surfaces she had touched with alcohol wipes to obliterate any fingerprints, although she reasoned if anyone really wanted her identity, they would come at her directly, or at least before the bedding was washed, reused and the room given to, and contaminated by, the next paying guest.

She moved to the window which looked out over the sprawling colonial style city. Some called it the Paris of South America, and she had to admit it did have its charms, and of course less dog shit decorating the pavements than the French capital. The vibrating of her encrypted iPhone drew her eyes away from the skyline. Racine dug it out of her jeans pocket and swiped the screen. A moment later she was engulfed by a wave of fury.

The message was from Richard Halbert, the French intelligence officer who had been given the task of overseeing the Bogotá safe house which was hiding Petrov's wife and child. The former Russian soldier's agreement with Racine was he would only work for her, luring his boss, Jorge Espinosa, to a meeting with Orosco in Buenos Aires, and provide intelligence on the organisation of the Colombian cartel if she agreed safe passage for him and his family out of Colombia. Halbert, with a team of two – a local couple – had been looking after the family for a little over a week since they had left their home in the gold mining town of El Bagre.

Whilst the message was from Halbert's phone, it was not from him, however. The first line read:

Hey French Puta! We have your traitor's puta wife and kid! You tell him to be on Avianca flight 154 tomorrow, if he wants to see them alive!

The message was accompanied by a video of the mother and child, with the men who had taken them boldly standing behind, making no move whatsoever to hide their faces. She didn't know the men but imagined that Petrov would, and that was the point of them showing themselves.

A second video arrived. It showed the three-person team. The local couple had had their throats slit and their tongues pulled down through the gaps as a Colombian necktie. The Frenchman lay on his front, with a pool of blood around his torso. The video moved back to reveal the face of the man who had been filming. Racine recognised him from her intelligence file. His name was James Botero and he was Espinosa's head of security. He spoke into the camera.

"Puta! You send him to me by tomorrow afternoon!"

Racine paused each video at points that clearly showed the faces of the men present and then attached these to an email to her DGSE section tech with the simple heading "ID Request. Colombia."

She clicked send, closed her eyes and took a long, calming breath. She'd instructed Petrov to get rid of his Colombian mobile, the one the cartel had given him, the one he had used under the name Jacob Greiner. Her only hope was that he had followed her order and not risked the chance of using it to call his wife. Racine then sent a copy of the horrific video to Paul Durand the DGSE station chief in Bogotá, with a brief summary.

Anger now threatened to engulf her, so she lay on the bed and started to "slow breathe". Racine was no stranger to revenge, it excited her, it made her feel alive, it was what she was built for. Her operation looked as though it had been in part blown. However, the two assassinations in Buenos Aires had happened and, the two more later that day, would end the Argentinian part of her mission. They had to go ahead, and now that she had two Werewolves at her disposal, she knew this would not be an issue. What was an issue, however, was how to get Petrov's family back. To do this both Werewolves had to get into Colombia, there was no way Petrov could take that flight. As she stared out over the rooftops a solution struck her. There was a pilot with a plane she could call, she just hoped he was in the area and wasn't on another of his gun runs to Cuba.

* * *

Buenos Aires

The bar was of a type that had started to die out in the Western world. It was dark, stank of tobacco and no garish music played. It was a place for men to meet, drink and occasionally also encounter a certain type of woman. Akulov was not in the bar to see a woman, but he was there to meet a certain type of man, in fact he was there to encounter a Werewolf.

Akulov sat at a booth located in the rear corner of the establishment and sipped from a glass of beer, ordering a Coke would have raised eyebrows. He didn't expect to encounter any immediate danger from his appointment, rather he hoped it would provide him with a few answers. Racine had arranged the meeting and would arrive later.

Akulov had questions. Not how Kizlyar had survived, but why he'd gone AWOL. This in the mind of most would have marked him out as a coward and a traitor, however Akulov knew Kizlyar well enough to know neither of these things were true.

The Werewolves had been the epitome of the American phrase "a band of brothers", yet the unit had been disbanded now for twelve years, and Akulov had left a year before that, sickened by the actions of the Russian war machine. In a sense he too could be considered a traitor, yet Akulov reasoned this was not correct. He had no loyalty to Russia, he was Ukrainian.

The door opened and a figure entered. Akulov instantly recognised the deceptively languid gait of Kizlyar. The man cast his eyes around looking for Racine, and then they locked on those of Akulov. He paused mid-stride, all but turning to stone, a statue, except for his eyes. In those, Akulov saw first incomprehension, then recognition, before finally the trace of a smile formed at the edge of the Russian's lips. Kizlyar gestured to the barman for two beers, then resumed his approach.

"Machine? Is that really you, Ruslan?"

"Hello, Kizlyar."

Maintaining eye contact with Akulov, Kizlyar sat. "Machine, I had hoped eventually we'd meet again. For a long while I thought you were dead, and then of course I started to hear the 'fairy tales' about this legendary assassin the underworld called Wolf Six."

Akulov said, "For a dead man you look remarkably well."

"And you look exactly the same, down to the beard."

"I grew it for a contract."

Recognition flared in Kizlyar's eyes. "Of course, I have been slow. This meeting is no coincidence; it was you who liquidated Orosco?"

"*Da.*"

"One clean shot, one clean kill." He cocked his head. "So, you too are working for Racine?"

"I was not, that was purely happenstance. However now I am."

"Where is she?"

"Racine wanted us to become reacquainted again before she joined us."

"That is wise, Machine."

"Why?"

Kizlyar nodded. "Because you deserve an answer."

"I do."

"You must think me a traitor?"

"Must I?"

"You decide." Kizlyar shrugged. "Back there, in Afghanistan, on that day, when I came to, I was helpless. I woke up, God knows where, being pulled out of the river by an ancient looking Afghan. I'd lost my AK, lost my pistol, couldn't walk and my left shoulder was banged up. I couldn't defend myself, but he somehow managed to get me to his place, a hut in a ruined compound. You know how much Pashtun I knew, even less than you, but he spoke Russian. It turns out he'd been a translator-cum-fixer for the Red Army back in the day. I stayed with him for a week before I left, and by then the rest of you were safely back in Mother Russia, or wherever the Kremlin wanted to send you."

"I was not," Akulov said, interrupting, "I was still walking out of Afghanistan."

"A stroll in the park for the Machine, surely?"

The barman arrived with the beers. Both men fell silent until he had retreated.

"You have told me the how, not the why?"

"The why." Kizlyar took a long swig before he continued. "Something changed in me, over there in the sand, and in the rocks. Receiving such kindness from that old man, seeing how he had been left to die in the dust when our predecessors, the Red Army pulled out, it made me wake up. Look, I understand this may make me sound foolish, idealistic or even selfish, but it made me realise I deserved more, that we all deserved more than Russia was going to give us."

"We were soldiers, we signed contracts."

"We were more than soldiers, we were Werewolves, we were brothers, yet we'd signed our contracts when we were still kids."

"So, you walked away."

"I did. Dying gave me the chance to live. Then look what happened to Mother Russia? She started to implode. It had already happened with the invasion of Georgia – remember when they sent us there? And then we invaded Ukraine, but for what reason? It is all pointless and it was mindless."

"I agree. I have no love for Moscow."

"What can I say, Machine? You know I was an orphan like you, all I had was the Russian army, and they had utter control over my existence. You were like a brother to me, hell all twelve of us were brothers, but I had to do something for me." Kizlyar let out a sigh. "Do you think me a traitor to my brother Werewolves or to Russia, Ruslan?"

"I don't care about Russia. To the Werewolves perhaps."

"I see. However, a long time has passed."

Akulov drank his original beer, it had become tepid and bitter. "During an operation in Syria, Wolf One made mistakes, some of us died. Tishina moved to a new program and took me with her. After this the Werewolves were formally disbanded."

"How many of us are left?"

"Including you and me, there are four of us."

"Four?" Kizlyar shook his head slowly. "Who?"

"Beast, Pushki, me and you."

"Of course, Beast made it! Can you imagine any bullet or bomb being big enough to get the better of that huge Chinaman?"

Akulov allowed himself a smile, as he imagined the face of the giant Burat reacting to his unofficial nickname. "I cannot."

"Are you in contact with them?"

"I have met with Beast. Pushki I have not seen since after Syria. He and his cannons could be anywhere."

"Where is Beast?"

"Kyiv."

"Kyiv?"

"He's adopted the city as his own. His says it has the best vodka."

"That does sound like Beast."

Both men drank their beer, Akulov now pushing his warm one aside and taking the fresh one.

"So, Machine, are me and you good?"

Akulov still saw lingering apprehension in the face of his old comrade. "We were never not."

Kizlyar visibly relaxed. "When I saw you, I thought that perhaps..."

"I was here to kill you?"

"*Da*."

"If I had wanted to, I could have killed you twice this morning. However, we are Werewolves, hence that I could never do."

"Thank you."

"Do not thank me, I am simply stating a fact."

Kizlyar took a long pull of beer and then let out an equally long sigh. "I have to get back to Colombia, I have a wife and a child."

"Congratulations."

"*Spasiba*. What about you?"

"I have no one."

"I'm sorry, Ruslan."

"Do not be, it is a choice I made a long time ago."

"Because of your line of work?"

"Yes."

"That was my thinking too, and then I met Catherine. Crazy right? I travel across the world just to marry a woman with a Russian name."

Akulov knew that the name had roots in several cultures but asked, "Is she Russian?"

"Of course not, she is Colombian. My son's name is Nairo. He's six."

Akulov didn't know what he was expected to say so he said nothing.

"This job for me was my way of cashing out, starting over yet again, and getting us all away from the corruption of Colombia. That's why I am working with Racine. They are in a DGSE safe house in Bogotá waiting for me."

"Where will you go?"

"Canada, of course, I have always wanted to go there."

"I remember."

"I've done my research. Some parts remind me of Russia, without the filth and poverty, of course. And you?"

"Me what?"

"Where do you live, Machine?"

"Nowhere," which technically was not true, "I roam."

"Like a nomad."

"It is easier."

"It is solitary."

"It is my choice."

Movement caught Akulov's eye. Racine had entered. She removed an oversized pair of jet-black sunglasses and strode towards them.

"You two are both alive and talking. I shall take that as a win."

"Oui, boss," Kizlyar replied.

"What now?" Akulov asked.

"There is a backroom here. Follow me."

Both Werewolves rose to their feet and followed the French intelligence operative through a door at the back of the bar, and then up a short flight of stairs. There was another door which she unlocked, and entered. She switched on a light and Akulov saw that the place had already been set up for a meeting. There was a long dining table, with six chairs and several cans of Coke. Questions ran through his head, but it would have been naïve of him to believe that she was operating without any assistance at all.

As if reading his mind, Racine said, "The owner of this place is a French asset. Occasionally it helps to have a nation behind you."

Last in, Kizlyar shut the door. Racine took a seat and without being asked to, both Werewolves did the same.

Kizlyar asked, "Have you heard from Catherine?"

Immediately Akulov could tell from Racine's expression that something was amiss. "No. We have a problem."

"What?" Kizlyar was almost out of his seat.

Racine explained, "The safe house has been attacked. Your family has been kidnapped by Botero."

Akulov knew it was not a time for words but for action, so he used only one. "Terms?"

Racine addressed Kizlyar. "He is demanding you return on a flight leaving here tomorrow at seven a.m., or he will kill them."

"You have proof of this?"

"Yes."

"Show me."

Racine retrieved her iPhone, unlocked it and handed it to the Russian. It was not advisable for him to see it, but she could not hide it from him. "One message and two videos."

Akulov made no attempt to watch the screen, but he did listen to the audio.

Kizlyar's jaw clenched, and he shook as though he was a muscle car straining at its parking brake. He handed the phone to Akulov before abruptly rising to his feet and slamming his fists against the table. "I am going to the airport!"

"No," Racine ordered, "you are not."

"Try and stop me."

"Wait," Akulov said, "listen to her."

"Denis, I don't know how you operated in the Spetsnaz, but I am in charge here. What I say, you do."

"This is my family!"

"I understand. But you cannot walk into Botero's trap."

"If I do not get on that plane he will kill... my family."

"The plane will not arrive in Colombia until mid-morning. You have until then."

"Botero will have men here, at the airport."

"They have men in Argentina?"

"No, Ruslan, they do not," Racine said, "which is why I will be on that flight to see who is waiting for Denis to land."

"Do they know you?"

"Only the cover name I used, not my face."

"And you are certain of this?"

Racine shrugged. "As far as I can be. I have to fly to Bogotá. At the safe house they killed three DGSE operatives, one of them was a French national. I cannot let that go unpunished."

Akulov understood the anger in her eyes, it burned in his own. "Who is Botero?"

"He is a dead man," Kizlyar seethed.

Racine addressed Akulov. "He is the head of security for Espinosa – the man I shot this morning, and now de facto in command of the Cartel – the Clan Del Oro."

"Blat!" Kizlyar swore in Russian, only now retaking his seat. "He is jealous of me, he could not accept an outsider being so close to Espinosa. And then of course when I married the boss's niece. If anything happens to either of them..."

Akulov said, "Your wife is Espinosa's niece?"

"Not by blood. She hated him, he married her aunt."

"Tell me what we know?"

"We?" Racine said.

Akulov nodded. "If this man has taken the wife and child of a Werewolf, then the Werewolves shall take them back."

"Thank you, brother."

Akulov made no reply.

"It is reasonable to assume," Racine started, "that Botero will be holding your family somewhere secure, which he feels is impregnable. Denis, where does he feel the safest?"

"On his country estate near the gold mines of El Bagre."

"A place you know well."

"I know the layout, and I know the staff."

"That is what I imagined. Denis, I have a plan, and I have a plane. It is en route and will arrive after three a.m. tonight. The pilot has agreed to fly you both into El Bagre."

"They will be watching the airports," Kizlyar said.

"You are Werewolves. You will be landing, the plane will not."

Akulov understood but asked, "What about the necessary equipment?"

"Already arranged."

"What if they have not been taken to El Bagre?"

"When I arrive in Bogotá I am going to ask the reception committee exactly where Catherine and Nairo are being held. We'll have a pair of Iridium handsets. I will message you if I have an update."

"OK."

"Denis, it appears the Colombians are already blaming you for the death of your boss, as we expected them to do. I'm sure the Clan Del Oro is scrabbling to understand what to do next. We have a short window where they will be in disarray, and it is this window we shall use to maximum effect."

"All I care about is getting my family back."

"And you will but you cannot get on that plane until it arrives. Until then we still have two more targets to liquidate."

"Two more?" Akulov's brow furrowed. He had been handed fastballs before but there was always a limit as to how little preparation was needed.

"Who?" Kizlyar asked.

"Orosco has two sons, both of them must be eliminated, but only one of them is currently in Argentina. The second man I need to put down is Orosco's younger brother – Luis." Racine collected her iPhone and swiped until she had found what she was looking for. She then handed it to Akulov.

It was an image of a man in a suit. "This is?"

"Hector Orosco, the eldest son of the man you shot. He is the leading candidate for Governor of the Buenos Aires region. Now swipe left."

Akulov did so and saw a second suited man, this one was at least a decade older than Hector with jet-black hair, and was fatter. "Luis Orosco?"

"Yes. This one is Luis. He has no political aspirations, he's a former police officer and a thug. A decade ago, when there were talks of pressing charges against Franco Orosco for alleged brutality during his command of a group of conscripts during the Falkland Islands crisis, Luis and Franco's second son – José, who was a member of a police tactical unit, were allegedly tasked with 'coercing' the witnesses. The eventual trial against Orosco was unsuccessful as three witnesses disappeared, and four others refused to give evidence. Leaving only two."

"And you know where Hector and Luis will be?"

"Oui. I have them under surveillance. What, Ruslan, did you think I would suddenly spring a 'fastball' on you without any intelligence at all?"

"Yes. I did. So where are they?"

"They are currently at Franco Orosco's house comforting his second wife, who incidentally is younger than them both. You'll see her photograph there in addition to those of two former military enforcers their father employed."

Kizlyar said, "José Orosco is in El Bagre. He is dangerous and unstable."

"More than us?" Akulov added.

Ignoring the comment, Racine stated, "He is overseeing training there of their militia, but the senior instructor is a man named Martinez. We believe he's former Spanish military, but it's a common name. Unfortunately, I only have a clear photograph of José, not Martinez. If you swipe again, you'll see it. You will need to liquidate them both."

"Only after we have rescued my family," Kizlyar stated resolutely.

"Of course."

Akulov said, "So no image of the second target in El Bagre?"

"Yes, but how hard can it be to locate a Spanish mercenary in a small town?"

"I have never met him, nor spoken to the men he has trained," Kizlyar stated, "but then I have only been to the training centre twice. Both times I was met by José Orosco."

"So, for targets one and two, in Buenos Aires, we go in tonight?"

"Tonight, Ruslan."

Akulov placed the phone back on the tabletop. "You just said no fastball."

"Ah, but this has been planned for a long time, it is only your involvement that was not. Now it will be even simpler."

"I see."

"Now we move out, we gear up. Then we hit them at one a.m." Racine stood. "Get up and follow me."

Akulov cast his brother Werewolf a look and said, "Do not worry. We will get your family back."

* * *

Palermo Chico, Buenos Aires

Known as the "Enclave of the Elite", Palermo Chico was the favoured place of diplomats, celebrities, and the country's wealthiest families. As such it had been the perfect place for a decorated, high-ranking military man to call his home.

The Orosco family house was on the same block as the José Hernández Museum of Popular Art, a synagogue, and the South Korean Consulate. It was an ornate townhouse with a swimming pool in the back garden, yet it was by no means an ostentatious structure, rather it reeked of old, respectable money. It was a distinguished residence for a serious, and powerful man of the people. And Orosco Senior had been just that. On the surface.

The original plans for the property had been held by a local government office, and Racine had managed to take a copy of them. From what she understood, due to the age of the building, nothing more than cosmetic renovation had been permitted, with the exception of the nineteen-eighties swimming pool, which she'd had to negotiate a week before when making covert entry into the house via the rear wall and the French window in the garden. It had struck Racine then, as it did again now as she watched on from the corner of the mature, tree-lined street, that for the father of such a high-profile politician, Orosco Senior had little security. He had what appeared to be a standard intruder alarm, and several motion sensors – all of which she had easily defeated. Perhaps, she imagined, Orosco had considered his fight to be over, but as she was all too well aware, war only truly ended when both sides agreed that it had. And the fact that both she and Akulov's client had not deemed it over, meant that he'd had to die.

Racine pulled up the feed from her miniature surveillance camera on her iPhone. It recorded movement, taking a five second video each time. It was trained on the front door of the house, and another had been set in an overhanging tree aimed at the back door. As far as she was aware neither the candidate for Governor Hector Orosco, nor his uncle Luis, had left the house since Hector had arrived to console his father's wife. Racine had no qualms about personally liquidating both men, and in fact had planned to herself before abruptly learning of Akulov's availability. She preferred working alone, but on this occasion had made an exception. The third member of the ad-hoc team – Petrov – was acting as the wheelman and waiting in a dull looking Volkswagen Passat, parked two streets over. Although he was a professional, she couldn't take a chance on his mental state since hearing of his family, perhaps impinging upon the operation. Time was tight and the trio would be leaving the country immediately after the double hit.

Racine checked her watch. It was time to go. Pressing a command on an app, she quickly disabled Orosco's security cameras again, making the feed freeze, before she stepped out of the shadows of the trees and crossed the street towards the front door.

* * *

Akulov dropped down into the gloom of the back garden, landing on a small area of grass up against the wall. He waited on his haunches, still and silent. He listened. Jazz music wafted from the target house through the open French windows of the lounge area. Illuminated inside, he could see a man standing holding what looked like a glass of wine. He was slowly swaying from side to side. Akulov recognised him from his photograph, it was Hector Orosco, the eldest son, the governor in waiting. Akulov retrieved his silenced Glock 19 and brought it up. He acquired the Argentinian. At this distance, for a marksman of his ability, it was an easy shot. His finger started to apply second pressure to the trigger but then another figure crossed the room. A woman in black. It was Gloria Orosco, the woman he had newly widowed twelve hours earlier. He felt a pang of remorse. She wasn't responsible for her husband's actions, he doubted she had even been born at the time he had tortured his men on the Falkland Islands. Yet she was now suffering because of it. Gloria was moving erratically. As Akulov watched on, she slammed both her fists into the chest of her stepson and started to scream. Immediately two large men, dressed in suits, entered the room and pulled her away. Hurrying her back out of the room. Akulov recognised them from both the photographs Racine had, and because one of them had driven Orosco to the café that morning. In the shadows, Akulov stood. He acquired Hector again. This time the squeezing action of his trigger finger was not interrupted. Two rounds, separated by less than half a second, raced towards Orosco, their retort minimised to a pair of muted thuds, reminiscent of a couple of heavy books dropping onto a tiled floor. Both rounds struck the man in his chest.

Akulov waited. Either the keening from the widow or the

wailing of the jazz had rendered his retorts inaudible within the house, as no one came to inspect the fallen man in the lounge.

* * *

Racine reached the front door. Earlier in the day, a pair of police officers had stood guard outside, warding off both members of the press and the concerned public who had wanted to pass on their condolences or lay flowers. Now at two a.m. the men in uniform had gone home leaving a collection of flowers and cards tied around, or resting against, the railings separating the house from the pavement. Racine found it highly peculiar that a nation could have collective amnesia regarding Orosco, forgetting the accusations made against him more than a decade ago, from former men under his command. She reasoned it had to be the millions he had donated to charity both before and after his unsuccessful trial, which had wiped memories or bought forgetfulness if not forgiveness from those affected.

Racine rang the doorbell. Twice. Two long bursts on the buzzer. The door was opened by a grumpy-looking large man in a black suit. Racine knew him as one of the thugs, former soldiers, employed by the brothers. A man whose hands were definitely dirty. Before he'd had the chance to utter a single syllable, Racine shot him in the head.

Stepping past, as the large man crumpled, Racine advanced into the marble tiled reception hall and was greeted by the trumpeting of a jazz ensemble. Immediately ahead of her an imposing wooden staircase led up to the bedrooms on the first floor. Weapon out and dissecting the space she skirted this and headed towards the lounge. As she did so she heard Akulov's voice in her earpiece, "Target one is down."

"Have that," Racine replied. "Entering lounge."

"Copy that," Akulov confirmed.

Racine moved to the body lying on the white rug. A vivid crimson stain had turned the plain item into something resembling a Jackson Pollock painting. She observed Hector Orosco for several long seconds before striking his head with a hard boot. Satisfied he was definitely dead, she moved across the lounge towards the library.

Loud footsteps clattered down the stairs, causing Racine to spin and refocus. It was the widow. Heavy, hurried, booted feet followed. Racine and the second heavy instantly made eye contact. The man's face flashing incomprehension and then imploding as she dropped him with a single round between his top lip and nose. In an act of hysteria, Gloria Orosco ran at Racine. Wailing and arms flailing. Racine transferred her suppressed Glock to her left hand and slammed her right fist into the widow's jaw. Gloria lifted off the ground before crashing down and onto a large, cognac coloured, leather settee. Racine stared at the woman for a moment and shook her head.

Akulov's voice spoke again in her ear. "I have movement from the library."

Racine didn't reply as she advanced towards the open door. She paused, then spun into the room, Glock up and assessing the space for targets. The room was dimly illuminated, causing shadows to fall on the French style boiserie walls. In one corner, a turntable spun a vinyl record. A man was sat at the desk immediately in front of the window. His head was down, as though he was asleep, yet his arms were waving frantically, seemingly at odds with the rhythm of the jazz. Racine couldn't see his face. She trained her Glock on his head, no more than four metres away, and said in a loud voice, "Buenas tardes!"

The man's head rose. His face was grey, his hair an unnatural shade of black, and his eyes were red. This was target number two – Luis Orosco, Hector's uncle, and the brother of Franco Orosco. He noticed the gun in Racine's hand and a look of anger flashed across his face. Right hand moving faster than Racine would have thought feasible for a man of his sixty-something years, he brought an object up from under the desk. A shiny, silver six-shooter. He started to rise, the barrel of the gun did so too, and the word "Puta" venomously flew from his lips.

Racine had been insulted enough for one day, so she shot him twice in the chest.

"Moving," Akulov said, in her ear.

Racine turned on her heels and left the room. She arrived at the lounge at the same time Akulov entered through the open French doors. Racine said, "Confirm, target two is down."

Akulov gestured back over his shoulder. "The widow is unconscious."

Racine looked the Ukrainian assassin in the eye, wondering if he thought she was incompetent, and said, "Exfil."

6

Akulov and Racine exited the house by the front door and walked away at a steady pace. The neighbourhood was quiet at this time of night and they saw no one else on the street, nor any other traffic. As they rounded the bend, the Volkswagen became visible on the corner of the next street, dimly illuminated by the moonlight. The driver's window was part open.

Racine spoke into her throat mic, "Approaching."

"Copy that," Kizlyar replied.

Akulov made eye contact with Wolf Nine through the windscreen as he stepped out from the pavement and onto the road, his old colleague gave him a nod. Akulov got into the rear on the passenger side, and Racine climbed in behind the driver's seat. Although the car bore no taxi markings, the three of them would look less suspicious if there were two passengers in the back.

The car slowly moved away from the kerb, as the Russian followed the turn by turn satnav directions away from Palermo Chico and then out of Buenos Aires. It was just over an hour to the disused former airfield which now housed a private museum, and Racine had assured them that it was a place her contact had used before to conduct business.

Akulov broke the silence. "How do you know this contact?"

"I have used him before. Genna is reliable, when of course he is expecting to be paid."

Akulov's eyes narrowed. "Genna?"

"He's Ukrainian."

"I see."

"A countryman of yours," Racine added.

"I see."

"He's in the area but usually based out of Moldova."

"And before the war he used to keep his ancient AN 12 at Chaika airfield."

"You know him?" Racine asked.

"We have met," Akulov stated, remembering their interaction a couple of years before in Cuba.

"The fact he's still alive shows me he can't be all bad," Racine added.

"Do you trust him?"

"I trust no one."

"Great," Kizlyar said.

"I do however trust his interest in making money. And transporting you two into Colombia in an illegal manner will make him a lot."

"Last time we met he was transporting weapons. Have you confirmed he has what we need?"

"That is taken care of," Racine said, "as are ballistic vests, and most importantly, parachutes."

"And if those fail to open?" Kizlyar asked.

"Then you will die, and I will never work with Genna again."

"Highly reassuring."

"Money talks."

Akulov leant forward in his seat and placed his hand on Kizlyar's shoulder. "We will rescue them."

"I know. I will need some knives."

They drove on for another half an hour before the satnav instructed them to leave the highway and take an exit south. After a further fifteen minutes they turned into a narrower road. There was a rusted sign advertising the museum affixed to a sagging chain-link fence. Next to this was a gap where the gate had once been.

"Drive on," Racine said, retrieving her phone, "I'll tell him we're here."

They carried on. Barely visible in the moonlight were a pair of hangar buildings, and just in front of these, illuminated now by the Passat's headlight, was the ancient prop driven Antonov.

"Pull up next to the plane," Racine instructed.

Kizlyar did as he was told. Racine climbed out, Akulov following a beat behind. Both assassins stood and listened to the stillness of the Argentinian night. A light breeze rustled the long grass at the edge of the concrete hardstanding. Light suddenly spilled from a door being opened at the nearest hangar, and a figure walked towards them.

Like the first time Akulov had met him, Genna's head was shaven and he was wearing overalls tied around his waist, whilst his chest was bare.

"Racine, I and my plane are here as is all you have requested," Genna's voice sounded strained.

"As it should be for the price we have agreed."

"Plane's need fuel to fly, and pilots need food to eat."

Akulov remained silent as he saw Genna's eyes widen as he suddenly recognised him.

"W... Wolf S... Six!"

"*Dobriy vechir*, Genna," Akulov said using their mother tongue.

"*Dobriy*," Genna replied, his voice sounding suddenly dry. "L... look, last time... I mean you know I had no choice... the Knife-Men... I owed them... Wolf Six."

"I know. We took care of it," Akulov replied, switching back to English.

Racine turned to Akulov. "You and Kizlyar need to go. I'll see you both in Colombia."

"You will."

Racine nodded and headed back to the car.

Akulov heard the car door open and a moment later Kizlyar joined them. "Is this him?"

"Yes."

"Can we trust you?"

"Yes, with your lives!"

"The issue is," Akulov said, "that we have no other choice."

* * *

Aeroparque Jorge Newbery, Buenos Aires

Racine was wired from the events of the past few hours. She could still feel the effects of the adrenaline in her system and knew that sooner rather than later she would crash. The Avianca flight to Bogotá's El Dorado International Airport was six and a half hours in length, and she intended to be asleep for its entirety. She had arrived at the airport two hours before take-off, not because she intended to shop or breakfast in the business class lounge, but because she wanted to check for anyone watching out for Denis Petrov, the man the Colombians knew as Jacob Greiner.

Greiner had initially been approached by a DGSE officer 'in country', to be cultivated as an inside man, a way into the powerful Clan Del Oro who controlled the entire area in and around the regional town of El Bagre, however it was Racine herself who had discovered the asset's true identity as a member of the twelve Werewolves.

Denis Petrov, aka 'Kizlyar', aka Wolf Nine, had not attempted to lie about his identity to her and had been frank about both his reasons for disappearing and his reason now for wanting out of the powerful cartel. His family's future.

Racine had never felt the urge to have children. When asked why not, if she'd had the energy to reply, had usually given the stock answer that she'd not met the right man yet. At the age of twenty-eight she understood she had the time to do so, but the peculiarities of her job aside, she knew deep down this was not the real reason. Racine preferred her own company. She cherished her solitude too much to share it with others. Perhaps, she thought, in a rare moment of introspection as the boarding pass was handed back to her, she was just selfish. The check-in staff took her ironic half-smile as courtesy, not knowing she was mid-personal critique.

But Racine's anger at the cartel prevented her from smiling. During the attack on the safe house in Bogotá, and in the process of snatching Petrov's wife and child, the Clan Del Oro had killed three DGSE personnel. In short Racine was livid, and although she was under no illusions that she herself would personally be in danger, had vowed the men responsible would feel her wrath for their actions. Paul Durand, the DGSE Bogotá station chief, had been in touch and ordered her, under no circumstances, to travel to Bogotá whilst hastily attempting to pin the blame on her. Such was the nature of intelligence officers who'd become too comfortable within their own fiefdoms. Racine had no physical proof that Durand was corrupt, but there had to have been a leak somewhere. She didn't trust him and hence had completely ignored his "request". If there was any music to face from those above, it would have to wait until she returned to Paris. If she returned.

Travelling with just hand luggage, she was quickly through the security checks and emigration and following the signs for the "business lounge". It was just a little over five twenty-five in the morning and even though the airport was mostly empty, she still carried out countersurveillance drills by looking at reflections in the windows of stores, and randomly stopping to check her watch and pockets. She saw no one paying her the slightest bit of attention. Of course, her cover name was known to the DGSE assets in Bogotá, which was why the passport she was travelling on was not. She was leaving Argentina as a Spanish insurance executive by the name of Isabella García.

She arrived in the lounge and settled into a seat with a glass of orange juice; they had no Orangina. She would have preferred a large glass, hell a whole bottle of merlot, but there was no way she was going to drink until the operation had been completed. From her seat in the corner, Racine had sight lines of the entire room. Without moving her head, she scanned the business lounge for anyone or anything that did not fit in. A pair of staff members tidied, a woman sitting in the opposite corner tapped at an iPad, and groups of businesspeople in dark suits drank or made small-talk in sumptuous chairs placed around low tables. She had no idea how many of her fellow business lounge users were on her flight, but none of them were paying her any attention. She rose and moved to the cold buffet counter and ignoring a croissant, which she knew would annoy her with its inauthentic taste and texture, took a beef sandwich, which given she was in Argentina, she decided would be a far more satisfactory proposition. Sitting again she ate her sandwich as she felt her body begin to tire. Once she had ascertained that she was indeed safe and on board the flight, she would sleep.

An hour later, Racine rose from her seat, collected her carry-on case and left the lounge. She had seen no threats, thus far.

7

COLOMBIAN AIRSPACE

Akulov usually slept on planes, it was the only time he felt safe from anyone attempting to attack him, but that was on commercial flights and private jets, not airframes that were older than he was. He knew he had dropped off for an hour, perhaps two, but as he sat in the uncomfortable cargo hold of the Antonov, he felt both tired and as though he had been wrestling a bear. He opened his eyes to see Kizlyar's were open too and fixed on his.

"Not long now," Akulov said, in a voice loud enough to be heard above the throbbing of the turboprop engines.

"You were asleep and nodding like a donkey."

"Even donkeys need their sleep." Akulov yawned then became serious. "Tell me more about Botero."

"Like what?"

"Anything you think will help us."

"What is there to say, he will die when I shoot him. No one is bulletproof."

Akulov nodded, he knew it was a difficult subject to broach.

Kizlyar said, with an unmistakable tone of anger in his voice,

"He and Catherine were together. A long time ago. When they were just out of college. She left him. He never accepted it."

"How long ago was this?"

"Ten, no, fifteen years."

"Seems petty."

"You have not seen Catherine."

"He has a grudge against you for this?"

"As well as being Espinosa's favourite and knowing more than him about security. I threatened Botero on all levels. You could even say on an existential level. But whilst I was Espinosa's favourite, he just had to accept it."

"And then you arranged for Espinosa's assassination."

"True, I did." A thin smile parted Kizlyar's lips. "Espinosa was the biggest piece of shit I have ever known, but the pay was good. When I found out what they were planning to do in Spain, that was it, I had to do something."

Akulov made no reply as he adjusted the zip of his jumpsuit and then checked the strap of his helmet.

"Racine has done well," Kizlyar commented, assessing his kit.

"Only if our chutes open."

Kizlyar waved away the comment with his right hand. "You remember the first time we jumped from an airframe?"

"I do. I was petrified."

"Do you remember what I told you then, Ruslan?"

"It only hurts if you hit the ground."

"And you said?"

"I said, if I hit the ground and it hurts, I know I am not dead."

"Exactly. If our chutes do not open there will be no pain, just time to say goodbye. Time to remember. I never used to fear death, during our training and our missions. I even used to wonder how it would all end for me. But now? Now I have something to live for. I have my wife; I have my son. That is why I refuse to die."

"Then continue to do so." Akulov smiled.

"Thank you, I shall." Kizlyar fiddled with his own straps before asking, "Do you even think about it?"

"Death?"

"Yes."

"No."

"No?"

"When it comes for me, it comes for me. I could choke on an olive tomorrow."

"You eat olives?"

"Only in my vodka martinis."

"We shall have cocktails tomorrow, one way or another." Kizlyar's tone had become grim.

Akulov asked, "You didn't tell me how you ended up in Colombia working for the cartel?"

"The Clan Del Oro?"

"Yes."

"I wanted to get as far away from my old life as possible, and of course the borders of South America were more porous than those further north – especially if you had money."

"And you did?"

"I picked up some work along the way. I managed to get a crew job on a Turkish cargo ship, did a few routes, crossings here and there, before I'd made enough money to get off permanently in Argentina. That's where I met Catherine."

"In Argentina?"

"She was over with a family group, and that included her uncle – Jorge Espinosa. Apparently, it was to celebrate the agreement with their Argentinian partners. Anyway, I found myself at the same bar

Catherine had escaped to, which was in a more downmarket area of town than her hotel, but the band was good. She heard I was a foreigner – attempting to speak Spanish and took pity on me."

"And gave you a job?"

Kizlyar smiled. "No, her uncle did. A pair of hoods on a scooter tried to steal her bag – it was one of those big Birkin things. I stopped them, and she told her uncle."

"I see."

"Look, I didn't want to work for them, but it was easy cash, and well, I had Catherine."

"Everyone has to eat."

"They do indeed."

Akulov felt the pressure change in the cabin and checked his GPS device. "We're just over five minutes out."

"Good." Kizlyar stood.

As Akulov clambered to his feet, he saw Genna leave the cockpit. He held up his right hand, fingers splayed and shouted across the Antonov's cargo bay, "Five minutes, then I lower the ramp."

Akulov gave Genna an exaggerated thumbs-up.

For the next few minutes both Werewolves didn't speak, each man retreating into himself in preparation for what they were about to undertake, which would start with them placing their lives in the hands of Genna and his parachutes.

And then the cargo ramp started to groan and the air pressure in the cargo hold changed again. A ferocious, wailing wind whistled into the Antonov's interior, attacking the two Werewolves as the An-12's cargo ramp lowered. High above northwestern Colombia, Akulov and Kizlyar stood patiently awaiting the signal from Genna that they were over the correct drop zone. Dressed in jumpsuits and masks, with packs held between their legs, both men felt and looked as though they were back in the Spetsnaz.

A light next to the ramp changed colour from red to green.

Led by Akulov, the two Werewolves shuffled forward and without hesitation stepped out into the howling abyss.

Free-falling at a terminal velocity of one hundred and twenty miles per hour, Wolf Six and Wolf Nine plummeted towards the drop zone. As they hit eleven thousand feet both men deployed their chutes, feeling the instant, violent, deceleration punch them in the guts. From here on in they would rely on GPS waypoints and terrain features to navigate. However, in the rainforest of Colombia, the latter were few. Here and there orange scars of barren earth caused by illegal gold mining broke up verdant forest, and according to Kizlyar these were all either controlled or run by Clan Del Oro. As two dark specs against the South American morning sky, they were visible to anyone who happened to stare skywards through the gaps in the tree canopy. Akulov had to assume the worse, that they would be spotted by someone, perhaps lookouts for a cocaine lab, or for one of the mines. However, as their insertion point was ten clicks from the target address, Akulov just had to hope that this was far enough away not to link them to Botero's estate. But he knew hope was a tool of fools.

The trees and scrub at the edge of the rainforest rushed up to meet Akulov as he landed. He took two steps, grabbed his bellowing canopy and then went static next to a large bush. A moment later Kizlyar landed, being dragged until he managed to get to his knees. Both men waited in silence for several minutes before they dared remove their harnesses, change out of their jumpsuits and bury their canopies in the red, Colombian soil. They were now on their own with the clock ticking.

"You OK?" Akulov asked.

"Yes, I guess I'm just a little out of practice."

"What can be easier than falling out of a plane?"

"Landing in one, Machine."

In the mid-morning light Akulov smirked. He checked his GPS. They were on target, the estate was exactly ten clicks to the south. A further ten clicks up the river would take them to their exfil point. "Less than an hour until Racine arrives in Bogotá. We're cutting this fine."

"If anyone can make it, Machine, it's you. The Werewolf who never tired. Thank you again, my friend."

"There is no need to thank me, we are brothers," Akulov stated. "Now, we need to move."

* * *

El Bagre, Colombia

José Orosco became aware of sounds and shapes around him. He slowly snaked his left hand out from behind the bed covers and fumbled for his watch. He opened his eyes and in the dull, dawn light saw from the lume on the Rolex's dial that it was almost five a.m. But what he could not read in the dark was the date. He fumbled again and found the light switch. The weak bedside light turned the room from a dull grey into a rich maroon. The heavy velvet curtains at the window absorbed the daylight whilst the heavy pile rugs on the floor deadened the footfall. He checked the date. Monday morning. Another weekend gone, and the last thing he remembered was mid-afternoon Saturday when he'd gone back to Angie and Dora's place. He looked to his right; both women were still slumbering on the huge bed he had paid for. He pulled the covers back and leered at their naked forms for a while before deciding he needed to use the bathroom. He swung his feet out of bed and planted them on the rug, and as he did so the hammers of pain started to strike his temples. He heard a moan from Dora and, being a gentleman, threw the covers back over her buttocks. Pushing himself to his feet he felt unsteady, as he always did after a weekend of booze and Colombian narcotics. He looked back at the table and realised his phone was not where he usually left it. Scanning the room, he saw it face down near the window. Shuffling over, he picked it up to find the display was blank. He held the power button, and nothing happened. Grunting with annoyance José looked for a charger, he knew the women had one for the iPhones he had bought them. Finding it on the other side of the bed he plugged his phone in and made for the bathroom.

He sat heavily on the toilet seat and urinated, satisfied that his flow was long and hard, before loudly passing wind. He now moved to the sink, washed his hands and splashed water on his face, noticing the two-day growth of stubble and his bloodshot eyes. From the cabinet above the sink, he took a small plastic ziplock bag of white powder, opened it, wet his finger and slipped it in. Making sure his digit was nicely covered. He then thrust it into his mouth and rubbed the amphetamine across his gums. Instantly feeling the rush, more narcotics banishing the booze and drug hangover. He heard his iPhone bleep as it came back to life from the other room and waved a dismissive hand at it, then stepped into the shower. As he washed, he felt like a new man, and what better for a new man at the start of a new week than to enjoy the physical delights of two women.

Towel dry, and ready for action, he re-entered the bedroom. As he lowered himself down on Dora's side of the bed he noticed his iPhone screen. Puzzled and somewhat annoyed he pulled it away from the charger and inspected it. He had a list of missed calls, voice messages and texts. There was also a news alert with both his father's name on it and his brother's. Brow furrowing, he opened the alert.

As the words and then the images from the news report registered in his brain, an abrupt wave of nausea overcame him. Turning away from the bed, José Orosco vomited across the rug and up the purple, painted wall.

8

EL DORADO INTERNATIONAL AIRPORT, BOGOTÁ

It wasn't Racine's first time through Bogotá's El Dorado International Airport, but it was for the legend she was using. As a business class passenger, without any hold luggage, she was one of the first to complete immigration with nothing more than the usual formalities and a smile from the moustached official who she could see was taken with her chest. Once past immigration, she did her business suit jacket up and popped on a pair of oversized, eyeglasses. They were clear lensed and altered the appearance of her face to a casual observer.

The airport was a modern glass and concrete structure and, if she squinted, it reminded her of Nice Côte d'Azur. Except here the two most popular languages were Spanish of course, and English, although the only people she heard speaking that were an elderly tourist group and a pair of young backpackers. Colombia was trying hard to reinvent itself as a tourist destination, though it was still not a place she would have chosen to visit.

In the entrance hall a crowd of people stood behind barriers, including chauffeurs and private drivers with the usual name cards for their rides. There were also signs for "Taxi Imperial", the only company legally allowed to solicit rides at the airport. Past the crowd a group of men stood. From experience she knew they were trying their luck as "gypsy cabs", approaching travellers as they passed to offer their cheaper services.

Racine ignored all and followed the Taxi Imperial signs, and then she saw them. Two of the known associates of James Botero, two of the men who had been with him in the video. They were hustling from the main entrance towards the oncoming new arrivals. Racine paused, moved out of the stream of travellers and, for effect, retrieved her iPhone from her handbag. She swiped at the screen as the men drew nearer. Their gaze did not fall on her for any more than a second, as they scanned the increasing stream of arriving passengers looking for the man they knew as Jacob Greiner. Racine wondered how long it would take for them to realise Greiner was not on the flight. She doubted it would be too long as neither of the scruffy, heavyset men looked like the patient type.

Racine moved towards the coffee shop and took a seat, she watched on, watching the watchers. She was in an international airport and logic suggested that even if she was recognised, they would not abduct her here. However, she was unarmed and unless she could get a tactical pack from Durand at the French Embassy, she would have to find something. She ordered a coffee and sipped it as she watched. The two men initially seemed calm but as time passed, they became visibly agitated. After forty minutes they turned away, and the thinner, taller of the pair put a phone to his ear and made a call.

In an ideal world, Racine would have followed them, she would have then made covert entry to wherever it was they ended up. She would have checked that Petrov's family were not there, but she knew she had an even more extreme course of action to pursue.

She followed the pair, with her eyes, out of the terminal building, before leaving money on the table for the coffee, getting to her feet and following them. Outside, the sun made her squint, and she removed the clear lensed glasses, which were accentuating the glare. She saw the two men were heading for the parking lot directly outside the entrance doors. It was a simple, large concrete lot and cars were arranged in rows, dictated by neat thick painted lines. The two men headed for the third row and a Mazda sedan which was parked between a pair of Toyota SUVs. For a moment Racine wondered if these were also part of Botero's crew, but the men ignored the vehicles. The one with the phone then blipped the locks open.

Racine had no time to be subtle. She saw a man approach her, car keys in hand. He was older, perhaps in his fifties, and was wearing baggy slacks and a shirt which seemed a size too big. He asked her, in a voice which already sounded as though he expected a negative answer, "Chauffeur?"

"Sí," Racine replied.

"Where to?" A smile now formed on the man's lined face, and he seemed to be standing taller.

"I don't know the address, but I'll pay you two hundred US dollars to drive me for the day. OK?"

The smile on the driver's face was so large it seemed to split it in two, as Racine had just offered him the equivalent to two weeks wages for one day. "Sí."

"OK, where is your car?"

The driver pointed to a Renault Duster parked illegally on the side of the road. Further ahead she could make out Botero's reception committee had reached the car in the third row of the open-plan car park. One of the men was inside, and behind the wheel, whilst the other was leaning against the driver's side and lighting a cigarette. Racine pointed at the car. "You see those two men?"

The driver turned his head and squinted. "Sí."

"They work for my husband, and I need to follow them because he thinks they are also working for our competitor. So, I need to see where they are going."

"Sí," the driver said with some uncertainty in his voice.

"I hope you understand."

"You want me to follow that car?"

"Yes. Then when they stop, you can stop too, but not too close by."

"Like in the movies?"

"Exactly."

"Are you a cop?"

"No."

"A spy?"

"If I was I couldn't tell you." Racine winked.

"OK. Money up front?"

"Yes. I'll pay you when we get in the car."

"Sí, OK." The driver turned and walked towards his car and opened the passenger door for Racine. As she approached, she kept her gaze on the Mazda. The smoking man took a long drag then flicked away the smouldering butt before opening door. Racine climbed into the Duster.

"My name is Jairo," the driver said, now handing her a creased business card.

Racine took the card and then fished her hand into her bag, found her cash and handed Jairo his money. "Here is your two hundred dollars, Jairo."

"Gracias." The driver turned his head, looking at the rows of cars in the official airport car park. "OK, they are moving. I shall follow, but not too close."

"Very good," Racine replied.

Slowly the small Duster SUV pulled away from the kerb and headed towards the exit of the airport complex. Ahead, the Mazda exited a manned pay barrier, parallel to the route Jairo had taken.

"If they are going into the city they will not turn off for a while," Jairo said, "so you can enjoy the ride a while."

"Thank you," Racine replied. Retrieving her small Iridium satellite handset from her bag, she tapped out a message to Akulov:

> Reception committee left airport. Suggest Botero knows Denis not on plane. Following Botero's men. Will update with any new intel.

By the time both cars were on the access road heading towards the Avenue El Dorado, Bogotá's main thoroughfare, Jairo had allowed three other cars to get between them. Racine sat back and attempted to look relaxed. In the distance, below the cloud-heavy sky, she could see the Cerros Orientales – the Eastern Hills, the natural barrier, hemming in the Colombian capital like a wall. In the right light, and of course the right angle, some would call it picturesque but these thoughts were not on Racine's mind. What was running through her head was the task in front of her. Somewhere to the north, in Al Bagre, the two Werewolves would be assaulting Botero's villa and she sincerely hoped Denis's wife and child would be rescued.

As they continued on, housing blocks started to appear on both sides of the highway, and they started to grow in height.

Up ahead now was an intersection. Jairo said, "He's taking the turn for Kennedy. That's not the best area for a foreigner."

"I'll be fine," Racine said. Amongst the municipalities of Bogotá, Kennedy had the second largest number of low-income residents and was home to both commercial and industrial areas. It was to the south of the city centre, and not somewhere that was highly recommended for tourists to visit.

"*Dar Papaya,* when you get out, just hold on to your bag."

"I will, thank you."

They continued for another ten minutes, the high-rise apartment blocks giving out to older, concrete buildings, many with storefronts on the first floor. A few of these were three or four storeys tall but the majority were just one or two. Ahead, and still with at least one car between them, the Mazda changed lanes, took turns and eventually pulled into the parking lot of an Éxito supermarket, the shop's canary yellow signage competing with the reds and blues of the surrounding smaller shops.

"You want me to follow them in?"

"Yes."

The Duster turned right and continued to follow the Mazda. The car park was large but mostly full. The Mazda made its own space at the end of a row, whilst Jairo manoeuvred the Duster into a space three rows behind, and up against the boundary railings.

"And now?" Jairo asked.

"We sit and watch them, until they move."

"Like a stakeout?"

"Exactly like a stakeout."

"Are you sure you are not police? Perhaps Spanish police? Interpol?"

"I am just a businesswoman."

"Do you sell to the supermarket?"

"This chain not yet."

"What type of products are they?"

Racine knew her cover was thin so she replied with an answer which would hopefully curtail Jairo's interest, "Female sanitary products."

"I see."

They sat in silence for several minutes and watched the car on the end of the row, three cars ahead. The driver was on the phone, the passenger was just sitting. Then both men exited the car and walked towards the car park exit.

Racine said, "Stay here, wait for me."

"Of course," Jairo replied.

Racine transferred her leather laptop bag into her right hand and bunched up the strap as she stepped out of the Renault. She was wearing a navy-blue trouser suit and flat sensible shoes, which whilst not wowing anyone on the Paris catwalk, did enable her to move as quickly and freely as she needed. But she would have preferred boots, preferably ones with steel toecaps. She drew level with the Mazda to see the two heavies walking onto the street and waiting for a gap in the traffic to cross the road.

They crossed one side, reached the grass verge in the middle and then crossed the other. Racine hung back until she could see which direction they were heading in and then walked parallel to them, and several steps behind, heading South. Feeling conspicuous in her navy business suit, she slipped her bag across her body, to free up her arms. Racine's side of the street was taken up by the exterior brick wall of the supermarket, which, after the intersection with another street, gave out to a respectable looking arrangement of five-storey brick apartment blocks sitting in their own fenced-in territory. The other side of the street, where Botero's men were walking, was definitely the scruffy side. Dirt and litter lay in the gutters and the pavement space was taken up by kiosks and stalls in front of small, local stores. The two men paused outside a building whose ground-floor shop displayed racks of sports shoes whilst its first-floor store displayed mannequins and an inflatable doll, dressed in revealing leather clothing, in its windows. The men then continued on past a mini-mart, a shuttered restaurant and a dentist to a narrow, navy-blue painted, boxy-looking five-storey building. A large Union Jack had been painted on the brickwork of the third floor and a banner with large lettering below proclaimed "English Language Courses". Outside, two men in their twenties, wearing matching black tracksuits, stood with mobile phones in hand. They nodded and shook hands with Botero's men, before the pair of thugs entered the building.

Racine crossed the road and walked directly past the two men in tracksuits, assessing them as she went. They were athletic looking, and had short, no-nonsense haircuts. Definitely a pair of low-level lookouts. Both men not too subtly gawped at her as she turned left into a small store next door selling snacks. Inside Racine bought a glass bottle of Coke, using Pesos from her pocket. Back outside now, she took a swig and looked back up the street in the direction of the Éxito supermarket, and of course the language school immediately next door. She wasn't dressed like the locals and although her long dark hair was tied back, she didn't look like them either, and the more she stood still, the more attention she would attract. This was exactly, for the moment, what she wanted. She saw the two tracksuits turn to face her now. One nudged the other, who then edged forwards. Walking towards her with an upright gait, in order to extract an extra inch or so from his average height frame, he suddenly smiled.

"What's your name?" he asked in Spanish.

"Claire," Racine replied, "Claire Kenmuir."

There was confusion on the tracksuit's face. "You are a foreigner?"

"Only here."

"Where are you from?"

"Wales."

"Wales?"

"The UK. I am an English teacher looking for a job."

The tracksuit looked back at the language school behind him, before he replied, "That is why you are here? You want a job?"

"Yes. I was working in Quito but I wanted a change, so now I am here looking for work."

"You are alone?"

"Yes. Why is that a problem?"

"No. No, not a problem, in fact easier, for work. We have a school," the tracksuit waved his arm back at the building behind him, "I can take you to the director?"

"Please, that would be good of you."

The tracksuit turned and started to saunter towards the entrance of the language school. Racine followed a pace behind and gave a quick "Hola", to the second tracksuit who was still staring at her. The glass, hotel-style double doors parted, and the tracksuit entered. There was a reception desk on the left, a row of plastic chairs on the right and a staircase leading upwards next to a corridor Racine imagined led to a backroom. A man was standing behind the reception desk. His eyes widened on seeing Racine.

"You wait here. I will get the director," the tracksuit said.

"Thank you," Racine replied.

The tracksuit headed to the corridor and disappeared towards the back of the narrow building.

"Hello. Please have a seat," the receptionist said.

"I prefer to stand," Racine said, flashing a quick smile back at the bemused man. He smiled quickly and, blushing, focused on his desktop computer. Racine looked around at the space. There was a plastic map of the world on the long wall next to the reception desk. To her annoyance, it was the type with the US in the middle but, she reasoned, that it made more sense here in Latin America. Off to the back she could hear voices, although the words were indistinguishable. Racine raised her bottle of Coke that was still half-full and took a sip, noticing the receptionist staring at her as she did so. Men were so obvious, and so predictable that it was simply irritating. However, it did work to her advantage.

"Do you have many students here?" Racine asked.

"Er yes, we have here perhaps twenty. Different classes."

"How many teachers do you have?"

"Just the one – Professor Sanches. He used to teach at the Universidad de Los Andes Colombia."

"That is impressive," Racine said.

"He will be here later."

"Please come this way," the tracksuit called, reappearing from the hallway.

Coke bottle in hand, Racine made for the hallway. At one end of this was the rear door of the building and on the right were two doors. The tracksuit beckoned her into the first. Inside, a man sat behind a simple desk on which was a laptop and a mobile phone. Racine immediately recognised him as the third of Botero's men who had been present on the video. An instant anger rose within her and she felt her left hand clenching around the Coke bottle.

"This is the teacher," the tracksuit stated.

"You can go now," the man behind the desk said, as he rose from his seat, "and shut the door."

Racine remained still, eyes fixed on Botero's man as the door clicked shut behind her.

"Hello, you are a real British, English teacher?" He extended his hand, as his tongue darted across his upper lip, like a lizard.

Racine took the man's hand, jerked him forward by it, and then slammed the bottle of Coke into the side of his head. It exploded and he instantly went limp. Stepping over the unconscious man, Racine moved to the computer and looked at the screen. It was paused on a YouTube video of a popular Spanish language soap opera. She sat and quickly opened the hard drive then, taking a USB stick from her bag, downloaded its content before shutting the laptop and transferring it and the USB stick, into the empty laptop section of her bag. Opening the desk drawer, she found a Glock 19, a suppressor and an extra magazine. She'd had no doubt the man was one of the three killers with Botero, and the suppressor was an added, and unexpected, bonus. She threaded the suppressor onto the barrel, put the magazine in her left pocket and holding the now suppressed Glock in her right, she stood. Picking up the man's iPhone, she saw that it was conveniently locked but took it anyway.

The man on the floor started to stir, slowly raising his head. Racine launched a heavy right foot into his face, hearing the cartilage of his nose crack as his face imploded. Satisfied he was not getting up anytime soon, if at all, Racine walked towards the door, Glock trailing at her right side. Anger had gotten the best of her but at least she was now armed. She doubted the pair of heavies she'd been following had exited whilst she'd been in the room, and the incapacitating of the third man had been almost soundless. She opened the door and walked back up the hallway, as quietly as she could. The receptionist was now talking to a pair of young woman who were standing by his desk and didn't look back in her direction. Racine took the stairs up to the next floor. Here a hallway linked two rooms, one at the back and the other at the front. Both had no doors, but what they did have were arrangements of desks and a whiteboard. Both rooms were empty. Racine climbed again. The next floor had the same layout as the one below, and this too was empty. Taking the stairs up again, this floor yet again had the same layout and the front classroom was empty whilst in the one at the back two middle-aged women sat behind a desk studying a single, thick textbook. Neither looked up as Racine continued, quietly, upwards. The top floor was different. The floorplan was the same but the room at the front seemed to be a library of learning resources and the room at the rear a common room. The door was open.

And in the common room, were the two heavies.

One of them was perched on the end of a padded armchair, cup in hand, peering down at an iPhone lying on the coffee table, whilst the other was standing with his back towards Racine by an open window, smoking. Racine needed only one of them to talk. Raising the Glock she fired a single round, striking the smoking man in the back of the head. He was propelled forward and came to rest hanging half in, half out of the window.

The other man's head jerked upright, confusion flashing across his face as he now looked directly into the end of the suppressor trained directly on him. His mouth started to open, and his right hand began to move towards his pocket.

"Don't," Racine said, quietly, "if you want to live."

The man raised both palms slowly. "P... please..."

Racine wanted confirmation, so she asked, "Where are they?"

"W... who?"

"Greiner's wife and child."

"I... I... don't know w... what do you mean?"

"Your boss sent the video to me. You and Tony tobacco over there were in it. Where are they?"

The goon went tight-lipped and shook his head.

Racine sighed. "You have no idea who I am. You have no idea

who Greiner really is, and you have no idea what is coming for you all. Tell me where they are and I may let you live. Where is the mother, and where is the son?"

"I... I can't... Botero will... will kill me!"

Racine fired another round; this one missed the man's right ear by a millimetre.

"El Bagre! El Bagre! We took them to El Bagre. They are at Botero's country place."

"Thank you. Did you tell your boss Greiner was not on the plane?"

"Sí."

"What were your instructions?"

"To return home tonight."

"By car?"

"Yes."

"A ten-hour drive?"

"Sí."

"Liar." Racine waved the pistol. "Which leg is your favourite?"

"Wh... what?"

"Would you like me to shoot your left leg or your right?"

"No! Please... Okay... There is a private air strip."

"Is that how Botero transported them to El Bagre?"

"Sí. We drove them to the airport."

Racine gestured at the iPhone. "Show me on a map where it is."

"OK." He slowly reached for the phone.

"No. Keep it flat on the table."

"OK."

"Do not try to send a message or make a call."

"Please," the man pleaded, "I have done nothing."

"Nothing?"

"Sí. Nothing. I am just a driver."

"With a Glock in your pocket?"

"H... how did you know..."

"X-ray eyes," Racine replied flatly.

"Y... yes. Colombia is a dangerous place."

"Tell me, then, Mr Driver, who slit the throats of the man and woman looking after Greiner's family?"

"Diego. That was Diego."

"Where is Diego?"

"You shot him."

"How convenient. And the Frenchman?"

"The Frenchman?"

"Who killed the Frenchman?"

"Killed? But the Frenchman... he... he is not dead."

Racine felt a chill travel down her spine. "Explain."

"He was Botero's man. He let us into the safe house."

The Frenchman, Richard Halbert, was a traitor. An icy calm in her voice, Racine asked, "Where is he?"

"He is in Medellín."

"Where?"

"At the boss's place."

"Which boss?"

"Espinosa."

"Why?"

"To get his money of course."

"Thank you," Racine said, and sent a round between the man's eyes.

Taking out her satellite phone, Racine sent another message to Akulov:

> Family confirmed at Botero's El Bagre villa.
> Good luck.

Racine moved to the window and pulled the dead man away

from it, then searched the bodies of both men she had killed. Each had a Glock 19, which she preferred over the larger standard seventeen. She removed the magazines from each and put them into her bag. Retreating from the room, she shut the door and casually took the steps down. The two women who had been studying on the floor below were no longer there. Perhaps they had finished, or perhaps they had heard the commotion from above, either way, unless she climbed out of a window, Racine had no choice but to continue down the stairs the way she had come. She met or saw no one until she reappeared on the ground floor. The two middle-aged women were now standing by the receptionist. Had they heard what had happened upstairs? Racine slipped her hand, holding the suppressed Glock, into her trouser pocket a second before the trio at the desk turned to stare at her. It stuck out slightly, she had to hope they didn't recognise what it was.

"Thank you, it was a good meeting," Racine said breezily as she strode past them.

Outside on the street, the two tracksuits were still hanging around. The one she had spoken to before attempted to block her path. "Wait, Claire. We can go for a drink."

"No thank you. I am not thirsty," Racine replied, as she started to walk away.

Unperturbed, tracksuit jogged after her, and grabbed her left arm. "I insist. I like you. You are a beautiful woman, and well, I am a man."

Racine pivoted, turned and using her right leg swept his out from under him. Hand slipping away from her jacket, tracksuit landed with a heavy thud on the grey pavement. In English now, Racine said, "Piss Off!"

With her hand still concealing the suppressed Glock in her

pocket, Racine continued back towards the supermarket car park, leaving tracksuit nursing his bruised feelings.

"That's it! You'll pay for this! No job for you in Bogotá!" Tracksuit shouted angrily.

Racine ignored him and crossed the road. Quickly, she reached Jairo and climbed back into the car.

"Business conducted OK?" Jairo asked.

"Yes. I got what I need to know."

"Good. Where to now?"

"Now," Racine said, "I need you to drive me to the French Embassy."

9

NEAR EL BAGRE, COLOMBIA

Kizlyar went down on one knee in the damp leaves. A moment later Akulov joined him.

"Which way?" Akulov asked.

"The right fork is the direct route to the house, but it's mined to dissuade uninvited visitors." Kizlyar took a long sip of water from his camelback.

"Mined?"

"Not my idea, Botero's. The left is a longer route, but much more open. Anyone in the house can see all approaches. So, we go right."

Akulov nodded, sending droplets of sweat to the rainforest floor. "The people inside, how well do you know them?"

"I was here a lot with the boss. The domestic staff I have no issue with – the cook and the gardener. The rest are local kids with guns, but if they are holding my family they are fair game."

"I understand."

"I know you do, Machine."

Readjusting and tightening the straps of his small day pack, Kizlyar rose to his feet and scurried across the dirt track which, in this part of rural Colombia, passed for a road. Akulov followed.

Kizlyar said, "I'll take point. And I'll try to remember where the tripwires are."

"You'll try?"

"I'll try hard." Kizlyar moved forwards in the treeline, scanning the path to his left as he advanced. Akulov looked back, a suppressed, sub-compact, HK416 A5 11" in his grip ready to repel anyone who attacked them from behind. Thus far they had encountered no one on their ten-kilometre advance to target, however now they were on the final, most sensitive stretch. Akulov turned and followed Kizlyar, stepping exactly where he had stepped. His brother Werewolf was moving fluidly, his own weapon up, when he abruptly dropped to his haunches. Akulov went static and did the same. Ahead he saw Kizlyar push his HK on its strap behind his back and retrieve his weapon of choice – a combat knife, from his chest rig. Akulov heard a voice. It was a conversation in Spanish, but only one of the sides was audible. Kizlyar abruptly swung his right arm and launched the knife. The conversation halted mid-word followed by a subdued thud.

Kizlyar stood and moved forward. A moment later, Akulov joined him as he inspected the dead man.

"You've kept up your training."

"You know me and knives." Kizlyar crouched down and removed the knife from the man's neck. "I know him. He was a miner who turned enforcer. Not a nice person. His nickname is Samsung, as he's always on his phone. He's one of Botero's inner circle. And if he is here, Botero can't be too far away."

Akulov saw the man's phone, it had skittered into the middle of the track. At that moment it started to vibrate as it received a call. Akulov noted the slight raise in the ground around it, it had landed on top of a mine. The weight of the phone and the vibration from it should not be anyway near enough to set off the mine, regardless of type or specification, however Akulov was not eager to hang around to find out.

He said, "How much further?"

"Half a click."

"On you."

The two Werewolves continued their advance. The path widened and then split into two forks around a grassy island, on which was a wooden command post. In the shadows, and behind the verdant foliage, both Werewolves were hidden as much as they could be from view. A hundred metres past the island, was a two-storey whitewashed, concrete, boxy-shaped building. It did not look like the architecturally aesthetic villas or mansions Akulov had infiltrated in Europe or North America; it seemed crude, unfinished. Rural.

Akulov felt the Iridium phone in his pocket vibrate. He pulled it out and checked its screen. There was a message from Racine:

> Reception committee left airport. Suggest Botero knows Denis not on plane. Following Botero's men. Will update with any new intel.

"The cat is out of the bag," Akulov stated.

"What about my family? Are they here or there?"

"Racine is going to find out."

"OK," Kizlyar said, the apprehension on his face clear. "But we can't wait. I can't wait, Machine. I can feel them. They have to be inside."

"So, we go in."

"Agreed. The path to the river is directly opposite the back door. We're going to need to check if the boat is there."

Akulov nodded. During the flight, Kizlyar had explained the

layout of the villa and the surrounding land, including the jetty at which, more often than not, a Zodiac inflatable was moored ready for Botero to whizz downriver.

They continued to watch the house and the guardhouse. The sun was now high, its rays casting deep shadows in front of the guardhouse. And then there was movement. A figure stepped out from the guardhouse. He lit a cigarette and walked forward, gazing down the driveway, past Akulov and Kizlyar. The house was in the middle of nowhere, several clicks from a small provincial town and surrounded by rainforest. Akulov doubted the guard was particularly skilled, but then again that meant he would be more likely to shoot first and ask questions later.

"Cover me," Kizlyar said, as he placed his HK on the ground and then stood.

Akulov understood what Kizlyar was up to, but it didn't mean he approved.

Kizlyar stepped out of the heavy cover of the trees and called out, "Luis!"

The guard recoiled with shock and dropped his cigarette. "Jacob?"

"Yes, it's me," Kizlyar replied in Spanish as he continued to advance casually towards the guard, still hidden from view of the house by shadows cast by the hut.

"What are you doing here..." the body language of the guard changed, and he started to reach for his Kalashnikov.

Akulov had a clear shot, so took it. A pair of suppressed rounds propelled the guard backwards and onto the grassy ground. Akulov collected Kizlyar's HK and jogged towards him.

"And that's all the usual security they have here," Kizlyar said as he took his HK back. "We need to drag him inside."

Akulov agreed, and the two Werewolves easily carried the smaller Colombian into the hut. The interior smelled fetid with the sweat of a thousand hours of boredom and greasy food. A second mobile phone started to trill. It was an old workhorse Nokia, used for its extreme battery life and not its "smart" features.

Kizlyar picked it up, pressed the speaker button and effected an accent. "Sí?"

"Luis, you seen Samsung? He's not answering his phone."

"He went to check the path, probably having a piss."

"Go find him. It's urgent."

"Will do."

The call ended. Akulov said, "Who was that?"

Kizlyar spat out the name, "Botero."

"Something is up. We need to hustle."

"If we skirt the drive via the trees to the right, we can get to the river, check the boat, then we should be able to take the path and enter the house through the kitchen door. As long as no one is looking out of the windows."

"Agreed."

Still in the lea of the guard hut, the two former special forces operators darted back into the treeline and then began to slowly and stealthily skirt the front of the house. The sound of rushing water reached their ears, and they diverted through the trees to intersect the path leading to the river to check for the boat. Both men stopped again once they had a visual on the dock, and the grey shape floating in the water next to it. Akulov flashed Kizlyar a thumbs-up.

As they changed course towards the house, the mid-morning sunlight threw ever starker shadows across the lawn at the front of the house and the white gravel which had been spread over the orange, earthy soil. Akulov knew assaulting the house without any intel on the number of opposition inside, or the exact location of the hostages was highly risky, yet on their side they did have Kizlyar's knowledge of the building's layout. Akulov felt a vibration against his right thigh, and unclipped the Iridium phone from its holder. It was a message from Racine:

> Family confirmed at Botero's El Bagre villa.
> Good luck.

Akulov passed the phone to Kizlyar, who let out a sigh of relief. Pocketing the phone once more, Akulov tapped Kizlyar on the back. The duo started to move again. They drew level with the kitchen door as a figure pushed through it backwards. It was a plump, middle-aged woman carrying a huge metal pot. She turned as she exited then took several steps before tipping the contents of the pot on the grass away from the house. As she turned her back, Kizlyar exited cover and jogged towards her. He snaked his left arm around her neck and then placed his right across her mouth and spoke into her ear. The woman struggled for a second and then relaxed, before speaking to him in a low yet animated voice. Kizlyar beckoned Akulov forward as the woman stood staring at him.

"She says Catherine and Nairo are in Botero's guest bedroom. She understands what is happening and she is sorry."

Akulov nodded; the woman looked petrified.

"Who else is inside?" Akulov asked.

"Three men, one in the kitchen and two upstairs," the cook replied, her voice shaky.

"Where is Botero?" Akulov asked.

"He went. He went to the school."

"School?"

"The training facility," Kizlyar explained to Akulov, then addressed the cook. "Go. Get away back to your family."

The woman nodded and, turning, started to walk and then run back down the drive.

"On me," Kizlyar said, a tone of determination now in his voice.

Wolf Nine entered the kitchen first through the door, with Wolf Six a beat behind. Both Werewolves had their suppressed HKs up, quartering the room. On the stove a large pot boiled and next to this stood a man eating from a china bowl. Kizlyar sent a double tap directly into his chest and he dropped, the bowl smashing onto the tiled floor. Using his left hand Kizlyar now motioned towards the far door, which Akulov knew from looking at the basic plan of the house Kizlyar had drawn on the plane, led towards the lounge and wide staircase up to the villa's first floor.

Akulov followed Kizlyar through the door and along the short, narrow hallway. On reaching the lounge, both men again dissected the space with their HKs, seeking out threats and finding none. Akulov motioned to the stairs. Kizlyar gave him a decisive nod and moved past him and started to climb. Two steps between them, to lessen the chance of both men being hit by the same burst of gunfire, they tactically advanced upwards until Kizlyar reached the landing and paused. To the right was a long banister overlooking the lounge below, on the left there were two doors and a third lay directly ahead at the far end of the landing. Kizlyar cocked his head, and then Akulov heard it too, voices, two of them. Kizlyar started to edge forward again, and now Akulov reached the landing. Kizlyar held up his left fist, the universal combat signal for "halt", and then he pointed at the first door on the left. Akulov trained his HK on the door as Kizlyar advanced towards it. Reaching the door, he paused before standing to one side with his back against the wall. Akulov took up position on the other side. Kizlyar nodded then wrapped his left hand around the handle, turned it and pushed the door open.

Both Werewolves bomb-burst into the room, Wolf Six on the left side of the room and Wolf Nine taking the right. In the middle, a large bed used up much of the space and on the left of this, sat a man wearing nothing but boxer shorts. In front of him on the dresser was a bag of white powder. A second man was bending over the dresser with a straw protruding from his nose. Both men were unarmed but a pair of AK47s were leaning against the far wall under the window. Akulov hesitated no further and sent a suppressed three round burst at the one who was standing, whilst Kizlyar targeted the other. Both men dropped, landing on the carpeted floor with a pair of heavy thuds.

Kizlyar moved to the door then spun quickly out of the room and back onto the landing. A moment later Akulov followed. The only internal threats now came from the two remaining doors, one leading to the master bedroom at the very end of the landing, and the next door which, according to the cook, was where Catherine and Nairo were being held.

Kizlyar tried the door whilst Akulov kept his HK trained on the door of the master bedroom. Although the cook had said there were just three men in the villa, he didn't want to risk being surprised. Botero was not in the house, but that did not mean the room was unoccupied. Unable to open the door, Kizlyar took a step back and then launched a powerful stomp-kick at the wood immediately next to the lock. The wood cracked, and the door groaned. From inside the room both men heard a scream.

"Catherine!" Kizlyar yelled and delivered a second stomp which exploded the door inwards. He flew into the room, with Akulov on his heels. This room was far more opulent than the previous one and looked as though it had been recently redecorated in preparation for important guests. There was an even larger bed than in the last room and also a second, single one to one side. On the huge bed was a young boy and sitting with her arms draped around him with anger in her eyes was one of the most striking looking women Akulov had ever seen. Her long hair hung down around the boy like a shield. Kizlyar dropped his HK and rushed towards the bed with his arms held out.

"Catherine!" he called, and for the first time in their long history together, Akulov heard Kizlyar's voice crack. Kizlyar wrapped his arms around both his wife and son, his chest heaving as though he was struggling for breath.

Akulov understood love. What he remembered of the love he felt for his parents as a young boy, the love he had felt for his grandmother who had raised him after their deaths. Yet what he was seeing now was a type of love he had no reference to. It was perhaps the purest love, he reasoned, that of a father to his son and the mother of his child. It was also something he knew he would never experience. Akulov watched on for several seconds before he averted his gaze and moved to the window. This all felt too easy to him, as though Botero had wanted Kizlyar to rescue his family, but he was being paranoid surely? Akulov checked his watch, a rubber strapped Casio G-Shock. It had been an hour and a half since Racine's plane had landed in Bogotá, which was ample enough time for Botero to act on the information that Kizlyar had not arrived. And that would mean what exactly? Had Botero really been serious in his threat to Kizlyar's wife and child? Or were those empty words which nonetheless gnawed at his fellow Werewolf's very being?

"Nairo," Kizlyar said to his son, "this is Uncle Ruslan. You can call him 'Machine'. He helped me find you."

The little boy detached himself from his mother and looked up at Akulov. There was a quizzical expression on his face. "Machine? Are you a Transformer?"

Akulov frowned and then a large smile split his face. “You can call me Bumblebee.”

“But you are not yellow!” Nairo, said, adamantly.

Catherine got to her feet. For a Colombian she was quite tall. She extended her hand formally and locked her, deep brown eyes onto Akulov’s. “Denis has often spoken about you, thank you so much for helping us all.”

Akulov took her hand, it was soft and warm. Before he could reply she stepped forward and turned the handshake into a hug.

Akulov said, “You don’t need to thank me. Kizlyar is my brother.”

“So you really are my uncle?” Nairo asked.

“Yes, he is,” Kizlyar replied, scooping his young son up into the air and swinging him around.

Akulov extracted himself from Catherine’s embrace and said, “We have to go. Botero could come back at any minute, and I doubt he’ll be happy to see us.”

Kizlyar said to his wife, “The cook said he went to the school?”

“Last night he made us both eat with him, like we were guests, not prisoners. At dinner he said today was to be a very important day at the school. Graduation day.”

“Graduation?”

“Yes.”

As Akulov started to realise what the implication was, he said again, “We need to get out of here.”

Kizlyar nodded.

A phone trilled. It was coming from the room next door, the one they had already entered, the one with the two cocaine users. This time Akulov went to answer it. The iPhone was lying on the bed, in between the pillows.

“Sí?”

"Don't you 'sí' me! Now you get your act together. Shit is about to go down."

"Sí."

"How is the woman and kid?"

"In their room."

"Well you go to them, and you make sure they stay there, you understand?"

"Sí."

"Sí? Is that all you can say?"

"Sí," Akulov replied, ended the call and dropped the iPhone on the floor.

Out on the landing he joined Kizlyar, Catherine and Nairo.

"Who was that?"

"Their boss. He said something about 'shit' going down."

"Had to be Botero, that's his favourite phrase."

"Where are we going?" Nairo asked.

"We're going on holiday," Kizlyar replied to the boy in his arms. "To Canada."

Catherine said, "He took our passports, and all our things when they attacked..."

Kizlyar shook his head, and swore in Russian, "*Blat!*"

"He has them in his room; he was taunting me with them."

"Then I shall get them."

Kizlyar moved with Catherine to the master bedroom. It was locked and he again broke it open with his boot, then they both disappeared inside. Nairo looked up at Akulov and smiled. He approached Akulov and prodded his ballistic vest with his finger. From behind Akulov, the discarded iPhone rang again and, this time, a second phone joined in, the phone of the other dead man. The trilling was then joined by an external noise. The rumble of tyres. Moving back into the room occupied by the two dead men, Akulov looked out of the window.

He saw two white vehicles moving quickly, a pair of Toyota Hi-Lux pickups. They were the double cab variant which, in addition to the driver, could easily fit four passengers, more if they were crammed in. Yet from this distance Akulov couldn't see how many were in each truck, so that meant a minimum of two and a maximum of perhaps ten unfriendliest were inbound. Then racing up behind them, on raised, beefed up suspension was a Mk1, metallic green, Porsche Cayenne. It looped past the two Toyota's bouncing across the grass and continued towards the house. The Cayenne came to a sliding halt on the gravel. All but immediately, four armed men burst out, one of which Akulov could now see was Botero. Each of the men had an assault rifle, either an AK47 or an M16. They started to run towards the house. The two Toyotas stopped in the same manner and disgorged their passengers, four more armed men from each vehicle in addition to the four from the Porsche gave a total of twelve armed hostiles heading their way.

"We have company! Kitchen door, now," Akulov commanded. "Go."

Appearing back on the landing, Kizlyar scooped up his son and handed him to his wife, before he raised his HK and jogged towards the stairs. Akulov moved back to the window. There was nothing else for it, he had to slow down the advancing men. Putting his own HK on the floor he collected one of the dead men's Kalashnikov, aimed it down at the drive and opened fired, shattering the glass of the window and causing the incoming men to scatter. He had missed Botero's party, but the two groups of men from the Toyotas scattered. Below, inside now, he heard gunshots, and then Kizlyar shouted up, "Machine, get here now!"

Akulov fired another burst from the Kalashnikov into the drive before he collected his own HK and ran out of the room. Glancing down at the railings as he took the stairs down, he saw a pair of men sprawled on the cold, marble tiles. And past this he could see the forms of Kizlyar, and Catherine carrying their son, in the hallway leading to the kitchen.

Akulov reached the bottom of the stairs as another pair of gunmen entered through the front door. Pivoting and dropping to one knee, he engaged them with a pair of snapped three round bursts, before sprinting across the lounge area and towards the kitchen. Return gunfire sounded behind him, rounds zipped past and one slammed into his back, impacting with his ballistic vest and making him stumble forward. Fighting to stay on his feet, Akulov continued to race down the corridor before he entered the kitchen. He saw Catherine still holding Nairo, crouching behind the large island whilst Kizlyar took on targets outside the back door. He turned back and gave Akulov a nod. "Let's go."

Akulov held out his hand and pulled Catherine to her feet as rounds suddenly ricocheted off the marble-topped island. Nairo screamed and Akulov felt his blood run cold. He spun around and cut the gunman, who'd appeared in the corridor, in half with a three-round burst.

"Go! Go!" Akulov yelled at the family.

"Machine!" Kizlyar shouted back.

"Go!" Akulov repeated, as he now took on more targets advancing along the corridor. Another man went down, and Akulov tried to remember how many more there were, four more, or two? He turned and ran to the back door. Outside he saw Kizlyar and the family disappearing into the rainforest, using the path that led to the river. More rounds struck Akulov in his vest, making him judder and fall sideways against the wall of the house. There was a sudden growl of an engine and a vehicle slewed around the edge of the house and flashed towards Akulov, forcing him to dive out of the way as its front bumper missed him by millimetres. This was another Hi-Lux, a single cab version this time, and its flatbed was packed with armed men. It skidded to a halt to his right and immediately the driver and passenger jumped out, closely followed by the six men from the back.

As the barrels of eight weapons were trained on him, Akulov felt a sudden sense of relief, not of panic, nor one of fear, but a serenity he could not explain. Around him there was no more gunfire, and through his ringing ears he heard the sound of an outboard motor cough into life. Kizlyar, Catherine and Nairo had reached the water. If he was to lay down his life to protect that of a woman and her child, then was that really such a bad way to go out? Akulov didn't fear dying, it was living that scared him. He had always known that his own death would come one day, and it would be violent, and it would be at the hands of a stranger. He had a choice to make, did he raise his weapon, and try to take as many of the men as he could with him, or did he drop his weapon and wait to be enveloped in the black, painless abyss of death? In the end it was neither. There was a sudden grunt from behind him, and the chirping of rubber-soled boots on flagstones and then a monumental force slammed into Akulov's back, propelling him forward and into the grass and red mud. Winded, and seeing stars, Akulov's hands were dragged behind his back and tied together. A voice speaking in Spanish said, "Throw this bastard into the cellar."

10

JENNER, CALIFORNIA

Cup of strong, black coffee in hand, Torres leant against the balcony railings and breathed in the fresh, sea air. He had been responsible for the death of another human being, yet unlike on the television or at the cinema, he was not wracked with guilt, he had not been lying awake at night after experiencing nightmares. He did not see the face of Franco Orosco. In fact, his sleep had been better than ever. He was now visited in his dreams by his wife, and even though he was asleep at the time, he knew he had been smiling. He felt good. He felt relaxed and, finally, he felt at peace. His grandchildren were playing on the lawn below and his daughter was in the kitchen preparing lunch. The decking behind him creaked and Christian appeared. He was holding two glasses of Scotch.

"Drink?"

"It is a little early, but why not?" Torres took the tumbler with his left hand.

Christian sipped from his own then let out a sigh as he too leant against the railing, "That's better."

"You seem troubled?"

"I'm having problems with my supplier," Christian admitted.

"Of gold?"

"Yes. There is going to be a delay in the shipment."

"Can't you buy from someone else?"

Christian shook his head. "Not at this price, for this quantity."

Torres was puzzled. "How much do you need for a few wristwatches?"

"That is the exact issue. Not enough for the larger suppliers to make it worth their while. And of course, my partners would not be happy if I were to go elsewhere. They are not the easiest of people to conduct business with. The issue is that I have already paid them for a product I do not have."

"Ah, I see. Do you need me to lend you some money?"

"No. But thank you."

Torres emptied the dregs of his coffee onto the grass, placed the cup on the decking and then transferred his whisky to his right hand. As he did so, the twenty-four-carat face of his watch sparkled in the sunlight. It was a nice item, and an unusual one. It was an automatic dive watch which Christian had designed and manufactured. Whilst its mechanism was Swiss – just like a Rolex, Christian had boasted – everything else had been fabricated and assembled in California. Torres drank. Collecting wristwatches had been his son-in-law's hobby, much as his late wife amassed a museum of shoes, his daughter hoarded handbags, and his granddaughters created a menagerie of dolls. Yet without warning, Christian had abruptly decided to sell his insurance business and become a watch manufacturer. Torres thought it was a brave move, if a little foolhardy, and he worried about his daughter's financial security.

"We will need much more gold in the future; I'm getting a lot of positive feedback about the *Pacheco Urre*."

Torres examined his wrist. "It is a very nice watch."

"Thank you."

"No, thank you for giving it to me."

"It's about making those first big or high-profile sales. If I could just get the watches out there and seen by the people who mattered."

"Do you mean 'influencers'? I didn't think youngsters wore mechanical watches?"

"Generally, they don't, and that is one target audience, but perhaps for a cheaper Japanese movement. What I really want to do is to get Pacheco perceived as a luxury brand, at the moment we are just 'boutique'."

"It will happen, Christian, you just need to have faith."

"Perhaps I'm being foolish, wanting to take my own personal funds to invest in a watchmaking business? But I have to tell you, Tomas, the insurance industry was killing me with boredom."

Torres gestured around at the house and garden with his spare hand. "Do not be too hard on the insurance business, it did pay for all of this."

Christian sighed. "Yes it did."

Torres studied his watch again. "Perhaps you should call this model the *'Pacheco Oro'* as no one knows what '*Urre*' is."

"As I told you, Tomas, *'Urre'* is Basque for gold. It's back to my heritage."

"Ah yes, I remember now. Keep it as *'Urre'* then."

"I think I will."

Both men drank. Torres then said, casually, "Did you see the latest news from Buenos Aires?"

"What news would that be?"

"Hector Orosco has also been assassinated."

"What?"

"The day after his father."

"B... but," Torres noted Christian sounded stunned, "wasn't he the one running for governor?"

"Yes. Luis Orosco, his uncle, was also killed at the same time; he was the younger brother of Franco."

"That's shocking."

"Perhaps. It is as though someone has targeted the entire family. And I for one do not blame them at all."

"Tomas, that is a harsh statement to make."

"I agree, yet it must be said. That man was a monster, and my belief is his sons were too."

"How many children did he have?"

"Two boys. The youngest – José Orosco – is a dangerous man. A gangster."

"C... come on, really?"

Torres noticed Christian looked noticeably shocked, more so than someone reacting to an international news headline. "Yes, really. His father put him in charge of the illegal trade coming and in and out of the docks in Bahía Blanca. Not my ships, I hasten to add. It is common knowledge, yet it is also commonly ignored. Then of course there was his involvement with his father's trial." Torres felt again the icy dagger of grief stab at his heart, his wife's death and then the memory of the death threat he had personally received, directly from José Orosco. It had not prevented him from giving evidence into the Malvinas prosecutions, but he knew that others had been less brave. But it had forced him to live in exile with his daughter. "Yet, such is life, and now of course death."

"So why has this killer spared José?"

"That is something I do not know, and to be blunt I do not care about. I am just happy that the man who tortured and murdered my friends, is now also dead." Torres had never told his daughter and Christian that he believed the Oroscos had murdered his wife, and he doubted that he ever would. He raised his glass, "This revenge tastes rather good."

"For you it is revenge, for me it's Scotch."

* * *

Buenos Aires

José Orosco was panting for breath and sweating heavily as he reached the very top floor of his father's house. He'd had to climb to escape the assembled mourners attending the rushed wake for his three dead family members. After arriving back in Argentina two days before, he had been stuck in the house. First the place had been swarming with police searching for evidence and taking photographs, then it had been fumigated and cleaned and scrubbed by a team of professionals and now it was full of both business and political elite, or those who deemed themselves to be so, of Buenos Aires. He didn't know if it was his weight, his lack of sleep, the narcotics fuelling him, grief or a mixture of all four which was making him sweat. He removed a handkerchief from his pocket and mopped his brow. Looking out at the garden he remembered a time when he and his brother had played, jumping in the pool having fun with their mother. But never with his father. He had been a cruel and distant figure. José had been told by his father that he had been a drunken mistake, and he knew his father had never liked, let alone loved, him. He had done all he could to make that man love him. He had sold his soul, committing the most heinous act of all – murder – to save him. Not once, but several times, including disappearing those who had sought to speak out against him in court. Then he had planned and carried out the "hit-and-run" on the wife of Tomas Torres, although murdering her had still not shut that one up. He had become a murderer for his father, and the man had simply not cared. Over time José's longing for the love of his father had turned into an indifference, and that had metamorphosised into hatred, both at the man and at himself, for what the man had made him become, and that hatred had been decidedly mutual. This, of course, had made plotting the man's murder all the easier. In his mind it was justice. The man who made him blacken his soul would now himself become the victim of the abomination he had created. He also had no love for his uncle, the man who was fifteen years his senior yet dyed his hair to emulate him, or so he thought. He'd called his uncle "The Penguin" after the comic book villain. His death was not an issue at all. Yet his brother, the only person he truly loved, had been ripped away from him, and that was who José Orosco felt real grief for.

Pulling his iPhone from his sweaty, trouser pocket, he swiped the screen then called the number of the man in California. Christian Pacheco answered on the third ring, "Yes?"

"Was it him?"

"Was what him?"

"Do not treat me like a fool, Christian. I want you to tell me if Torres also paid for the murder of my brother?"

"As far as I know he did not."

"As far as you know?"

"I am not his keeper."

"Oh, but you are, Christian. Remember who came to your financial rescue when your insurance business tanked after those massive claims? Remember who bailed you out? That would have been my father."

"Whom you despised."

"That makes no difference. I am now the head of the family. I now have the money, and the power. It is that which enables you, a failure, to live like a business tycoon in California. Now tell me, you *puta madre*, did Torres kill my brother?"

"No. I mean, I don't think so."

"You don't think? Oh yes, that is exactly that. You do not think. You must not think. You follow my orders. You get that?"

"Yes."

"Yes what?"

"Yes, I do get that."

"Good. Now listen, I am going to come over there, and I am going to ask Torres directly, do you understand?"

"To my house?"

"Sí."

"My family house?"

"Sí. Is that a problem for you Christian?"

"My wife and children are here."

"Send them to the cabin, that one I know you have by the lake."

"She won't go on her own."

"Tell her to take a *puta* friend, they can have a girls' night, or she can stay, meet me and I can show her what a real man can do to her."

"Now you listen to me. If you lay one finger on my wife I'll..."

"You'll do what?"

"You just better not even think about it."

"Sí, I apologise. I forgot you were a big man. Such a scary man with your failed insurance company and your worthless watches."

"When?"

"When? I'm going to get on a flight tonight. But before I arrive, I want you to find out if he did it or not. You understand?"

"I understand."

"So, what are you going to ask him?"

"I am going to ask him if he paid for your brother to be murdered."

José ended the call; a wave of grief abruptly engulfed him. In the attic room, he opened the top drawer of a dresser and then exposed a secret compartment. From this he took a small, ziplock bag of white powder. He unsealed it and wet his finger before plunging the damp digit into the contents. Pulling out his coated finger, which now reminded him of some childhood piece of candy, he rubbed the powder caked digit against his gums. He repeated this twice until he felt invincible. Using his iPhone again, he dialled a new number. This one was Spanish, and it was answered on the third ring.

"Sí?"

José did not use the name of the man who had answered, to mitigate the risk in case the line was being monitored, or maybe intercepted. "Are you getting ready for the party?"

"Sí."

"The party is postponed for a few days. I will give you the new date. You understand?"

"Sí."

José ended the call. The events in Spain would still take place, it was after all what they had planned and trained for, and he was damned if he was going to miss it. José wiped his nose on the back of his hand, sniffed then left the room. He headed downstairs, the grieving brother, whilst pretending to also be the grieving son and nephew.

* * *

El Bagre, Colombia

Akulov leant against the wall, breathing deeply as he assessed his situation. He had given up his own chance of escape in order to save Kizlyar and his family, and he sincerely hoped all three of them were miles away by now, speeding down the river. Kizlyar had told him of a truck he had hidden for the exfiltration some thirty miles away, far enough not to be tied to either him or the house. Meanwhile Akulov was a prisoner again. The only aspect of the situation that gave Akulov any hope was that they had not killed him yet, which usually meant they wanted something from him. And he guessed what they wanted was information on where Kizlyar was going so they could be stopped. Despite the stifling heat outside, the bare concrete floor of the cellar was cool against his stockinged feet. At gunpoint his boots, body armour and watch had been taken, leaving him both unarmed and unable to tell the time. He tugged at his shackles, and at the ring cemented into the wall. Both were unyielding, secure, escape-proof.

He imagined it had been less than half an hour later when he heard the rattling of a bolt echoing across the cellar as the trapdoor from the kitchen was raised. Moments later there was footfall on the steps. The door opened and one of Botero's men entered, cradling a Kalashnikov. He sneered at Akulov, spat at his feet and then peered at the shackles. The man shouted back up the stairs and less than a minute later there was more footfall, lighter this time yet faster. A second man entered. Akulov immediately recognised him from Racine's briefing photographs. It was Botero.

The wiry de-facto cartel boss rapidly made his way across the floor to Akulov. His movements jerky, as though he had too much energy or was on edge. The veins in his neck and forearms were bulging from under his fatless skin.

He stopped a metre in front of Akulov and looked him up

and down. Speaking in Spanish he said, "You are a gringo? Or perhaps you are another German like Greiner? To be polite, *cabrón,* I'll switch to English."

"Gracias," Akulov said.

Shaking with anger, Botero screamed, in English, "You tell me where he took her!"

Akulov made no reply.

"You tell me, or I'll kill you!"

"If you kill me," Akulov said flatly, "I definitely will not tell you."

Botero's right fist rose quickly and snapped at Akulov's jaw. "*No me jodas!* You have a death wish? Huh, *pendejo?* Now you tell me where Greiner has taken her."

"Just her or the boy too?"

"What? You being funny with me, *cabrón*?"

Akulov said nothing.

"Now, where is he taking THEM? OK, is that clear enough for you?"

Akulov said, "They are going on holiday."

"Holiday?"

"Vacation."

"The way I see it, *cabrón*, you have a choice. You either tell me where he is taking them, or I can kill you."

"We all eventually die. I imagine you will soon."

Botero swung his fist at Akulov, who did not give him the pleasure of flinching. The fist hit him in the jaw again.

"Now you tell me!"

Through the stinging pain, Akulov said, "If you break my jaw I won't be able to tell you."

"*Puta madre...*" Botero jabbed Akulov in the stomach. "I know they took the boat. Where are they going?"

Akulov frowned, as though the answer was obvious. “Downriver.”

“I KNOW!” Botero screamed, losing control. “Tell me where!” He launched a flurry of jabs into Akulov’s stomach and then when he drew his right fist back for a headshot Akulov decided he had had enough and swung a hard, right kick into the smaller man’s abdomen. Botero folded over and fell to the floor.

The man with the AK was wide-eyed, the end of his assault rifle wavering. “You want me to shoot him?”

“No! Not in here, you’ll make us all deaf!”

Akulov remained still, remained calm. Something told him Botero was used to being feared and when he was not, he had no idea what to do. “I have a suggestion,” Akulov said in a neutral tone, “why don’t you unchain me. I’ll forgive you and walk away.”

“Hijueputa!” Botero swore and pulled out his phone. “Killing you would be too easy, but I have a better idea.” He raised the phone and snapped a photo of Akulov. “Let’s find out who you are and where you flew in from.”

“That is a great idea,” Akulov said.

Botero pointed his finger again, then abruptly lunged at Akulov with his own kick. Akulov tensed as the boot connected with his gut, causing minimal damage.

“Malparido pendejo!” Botero spat at Akulov, kicking him twice more before turning on his heels and stomping back up the stairs. “Next time I see you, you talk, or you die.”

11

EMBASSY OF FRANCE, BOGOTÁ

To Racine's eyes, the exterior of the French embassy looked as though it had been made from giant Lego blocks by a studious teenager. It was a square, six-storey building, with visible horizontal and vertical lines where each block of concrete had been connected in an attempted tiled pattern. It occupied a corner plot and most of its front facing façade was protected from the first to the fifth floor by an iron grille. It was surrounded by a security fence made up of thick bronze-coloured bars. This colour scheme continued on to its official signage and the roof of the secure entrance area. Even for a lover of brutalist architecture, as Racine was, it was an ugly building which would win no prizes.

Once through the security cordon Racine had been shown to a meeting room by a severe looking Frenchwoman who made no attempt at conversation. Racine sat at the head of the long meeting table and took a bottle of complimentary Perrier. Unlike the outside of the embassy, the meeting room had been decorated with an artistic flair. A large line-drawn mural of the Paris skyline took up the entirety of the wall on one side of the room, and two large windows took up the other. The wall at the other end of the table was blank, and this she presumed was used for either charts, or to view projected images. The air conditioning was cool, and she started to shiver.

She glanced at her watch. The Bogotá DGSE station chief had thus far kept her waiting for twenty-three minutes, this was in addition to the long, slow process of passing through the security cordon at the main entrance. Racine knew she was being tested, and she knew she was being watched. It was all a game, a way for Paul Durand to assert his seniority and his dominance, but she had no time for games and he would soon learn that his rules did not apply to her.

She watched the door handle turn and then Durand stepped through. He was a hawkish looking man, with a large, sharp nose and greying hair which was swept back from his large forehead with what she imagined was hair wax. He was wearing burgundy-coloured slacks and a camel-coloured cardigan over a pale blue shirt. To Racine, he looked as though he had just stepped out of his Chateau in Normandy. He came to a halt by the chair at the opposite end of the table with his hands clasped behind his back.

"Racine, I cannot say that this visit was unexpected. I knew you would come here sooner or later and attempt to justify the utter mess and chaos your one-woman show has created."

Racine was surprised by his tone yet did not allow this to show on her face. Instead, she retained a neutral mask. In her opinion it was always best to let fools have their say and then once they were done, correct or silence them.

His brow furrowed at Racine's calm. "Have you nothing to say?"

"Have you finished, Durand?"

"Finished? I have yet to start! I cannot believe Colonel Grillot would allow such a reckless and ill-thought-out plan to go ahead.

He did not ask for my permission, rather he ordered me to provide you with every possible assistance. Yet to what end? What has been the result of this? Two dead local assets and one dead French DGSE officer whose body has been stolen by the Clan to be, one imagines, strung up later. You deserve to be thrown out of the service at the very least. Richard Halbert was an intelligent, courageous officer with a highly promising career ahead of him."

"Richard Halbert was a traitor," Racine stated.

For a moment Durand seemed so surprised, he was dumbstruck. His mouth started to move and then, as if catching up, his body started to shake as what Racine imagined was outrage, bubbled within. It was as though she was watching a live version of one of the old Mickey Mouse cartoons she used to watch with her dad, where the boiler of a steam train was about to explode. Eventually Durand spluttered, "W... Wh... what did you say?"

"Richard Halbert was a traitor. He was working for the Clan Del Oro. He told them exactly where to find Petrov's family, and he is in Medellín awaiting his payment."

Durand only now sat. He reached for a bottle of water, slowly unscrewed the top then poured a measure into a glass. Once he had finished drinking he said, "Even if I were to believe all of this, what proof do you have?"

Racine let her eyes bore into his before she replied, "Why would the clan have killed Richard and then taken his body? What possible purpose would that have served? Would they not want to ransom him or use his life for leverage?"

"Again, Racine, what proof do you have?"

"The statement of one of the other men in the video Botero sent me. I did send you a copy."

"When did you, I shall rephrase that, *how* did you get a statement from one of the men in the video?"

Racine gave the short version. "They were waiting for Petrov at the airport, when he didn't show they left, and I followed them to a language school. Once there, I simply asked them."

"What exactly did you ask them?"

"I asked them who murdered Richard Halbert."

"Of course, each of these thugs said 'it wasn't us'. Really, Racine, are you that naïve?"

Racine took a deep breath; Durand was right to be sceptical, but his condescending tone grated on her. "They said he was alive and in Medellín to collect his payment."

"You have no proof of this. They would have told you anything. Now, where are these men? Have you handed them over to the Bogotá police? Justice will need to be served."

"Justice has been served."

"What do you mean?"

"They won't be hurting anyone else again." Racine swigged directly from her bottle.

"What did you do to them? Racine, answer me!"

"Look," Racine sighed, "I came here to give you a 'head's up' that you have had a traitor working within your station for the past two years. I suggest you take all necessary actions to mitigate whatever damage he has caused. For all we know he may not be the only informant within your team."

"What? I have personally vetted my entire staff. Wait, are you accusing me of somehow being involved with all of this? That is an outrageous statement to make!"

"Durand, I am merely stating that a formal investigation into Halbert's activity and work here will now have to be conducted."

"You, a woman who is nothing more than a glorified street thug, has the audacity to tell me I will be investigated? You will be the one who is the subject of a formal investigation, Sophie Racine, and not me! I am going to make an official complaint against you to Colonel Grillot and to our director general! It is you who has been the cause of all this. Two confirmed deaths, and now according to you a missing DGSE officer?"

"He is not missing. He is hiding in Medellín, and I expect to find him."

"You expect to find him? You, Racine, will do nothing of the sort! You will stay here, and that is an order, until I get directions from Colonel Grillot."

Racine stood and, even though Durand was at the other end of the table, he flinched. "You seem to be under the misguided impression that you exert some type of authority over me."

"I am the Station Chief for Bogotá!"

"Exactly, but I am not actually here."

Racine strode past Durand, opened the meeting room door and headed back down the long, narrow corridor towards the entrance of the building.

"Racine, stop!" Durand ordered, getting up and following her.

Racine ignored him.

"Stop her! Do not let her leave!" Durand now shouted at the two security officers on the front desk, and he hurried into the hallway.

The first officer got to his feet and held out his right hand in the "stop" motion.

"Move," Racine ordered.

The guard stepped forwards and attempted to grab her. Racine in turn grabbed his right arm, twisted, dropped her shoulder into him and threw him over her back and to the ground in a quick, clean motion. She pointed to the other guard who was standing, stunned, behind the desk. "Open the door."

The guard shook his head. Racine sighed, reversed her course and as Durand caught her up, grabbed his throat with her left hand. She squeezed and he started to flap his arms in panic. "Tell him to open the door or I'll crush your larynx!"

Durand frantically waved at the guard. There was a click. Racine dropped Durand on the hard, tiled floor, and rushed forward.

"Y... you are a... maniac..." Durand croaked.

Outside Racine turned, and shouted back, "I am France's maniac!"

Racine ran around the street corner, crossed the road and then climbed back into the waiting Renault Duster, with Jairo at the wheel. "Drive."

"Where?"

"To the airport."

"You are leaving so soon?"

"It was a flying visit."

The car pulled away and joined the traffic. Racine sat back in her seat and closed her eyes. She was tired, in fact it was more than that, she was exhausted. A smirk formed about her lips as she pictured Durand attempting to explain to both his and her superiors what had transpired at the embassy. She didn't believe Durand was involved with Clan Del Oro but she did believe that he was an imbecile. She understood that she was the very sharp tip of the DGSE spear, whereas Durand was an intelligence officer, who acted as though he worked for a multinational banking conglomerate.

Racine sighed. She had been the operator who had been sent in some five years before, on a kill/capture mission against a French traitor hiding in Russian occupied Eastern Ukraine, and now she found herself doing the same in Colombia. As her fatigue weighed heavy on her eyes, Racine found her thoughts drifting back to that mission and the Englishman from the British Secret Intelligence Service whose own assignment had intertwined with hers. She wondered where Aidan Snow was now. She imagined he was embedded somewhere in Ukraine aiding the Ukrainian intelligence service. Racine realised her life seemed to be riddled with encounters with men whom she either had no time or little desire to get to know, on a personal level. What now of this Ukrainian assassin, widely considered "the best in the world"? Who was Wolf Six really, and what type of man was he? She wanted to find out...

A sudden trilling made her eyes snap open. Taking a moment to understand where she was, Racine dug her satphone out of her bag and studied the screen. It was the number she had given Akulov and Kizlyar.

"Give me an update?"

"Racine, it is me – Denis. I am with Catherine and Nairo. We are en route to Medellín. Akulov did not make it out. He stayed in order that we could escape. I am sorry I had no choice; I had to choose my family over my brother."

Racine's eyes narrowed, and not because of the strong, Colombian sunlight now streaming in through the Duster's windows. "Is Akulov alive?"

"He has to be. Wolf Six cannot die."

But you have no idea of knowing that, Racine thought. "Continue to the airport, get out of the country. Your commitment to me is over. Go and live your life."

"What about Wolf Six?"

"I'm sure he can take care of himself."

"Goodbye, Racine..."

Another voice sounded on the line. "Papa says you paid for my vacation."

Racine suddenly had a lump in her throat, "Is this Nairo?"

"Yes. I am six."

"And I am thirty-two."

"Mamma is older than you... Mamma wants to talk to you."

Catherine now spoke. "Thank you for helping us. We can never repay you."

"I am sorry about what has happened, Catherine."

"Men will always be men," Catherine replied.

"Goodbye, and good luck."

"Thank you."

Racine ended the call. She noticed Jairo looking at her via the rear-view mirror.

"Your eyes are wet," he said. "Are you OK?"

"Goodbyes can be hard," Racine replied, realising that for once she had shown emotion without feeling embarrassed.

The car slowed then came to a halt. Racine looked around and realised that she didn't recognise the road. Something was not right. "Where are we? Is this the way to the airport?"

"Yes. There was an accident, we had to take another route and now we have hit the traffic. Everything will be OK. You will make your flight to Medellín."

"Thank you." Racine knew she had not told Jairo where she was going, so was it a guess or had someone told him, and if so who? Who knew she was headed for Medellín? The only person who knew was Durand, but that had to mean...

Racine waited until Jairo's focus was on the car in front, whose driver he now berated for being a donkey, before she reached forward and removed the Glock and silencer she had surreptitiously stashed in the front passenger seatback pocket before visiting the embassy. She rethreaded the suppressor and then sat with the 9mm pistol under her right thigh. Something was going to happen but at least now she was prepared.

The Renault edged forward in the gridlocked traffic for another seven minutes before Jairo indicated and took a left turn onto a much smaller street. "This is a short cut. We will be there soon."

"I hope so," Racine said, "there will be hell to pay if I miss my flight."

Jairo looked back, worry now on his face. "You will make it."

The street was lined with two and three-storey concrete buildings, and these ones seemed to be the most decrepit of any Racine had seen so far. The car passed a white van, slowed and then turned again, and that was when it happened. Another van moved out from its parking space and blocked their path, whilst the one they had just passed now turned into the road to block them from behind.

Jairo stopped the car and removed his hands from the wheel. "I am sorry. I had no choice, they said they would kill me. I have a sick sister to look after."

"Who are they?" Racine asked, but it made no difference.

"Clan Del Oro, of course." Jairo opened his door and stepped out of the Duster with his hands raised.

Racine looked around. There was no one on the narrow street, and the shops on both sides looked deserted or shut. The front passenger door of the van ahead of her opened, as did its sliding side door. Three men in total clambered out, each wearing a black balaclava. One of them had a handgun, two had knives. She knew which one she would shoot first but before she dispatched any of them, she had to be certain that she was not being sneaked up on from behind. As the men advanced the ten or so metres towards the Duster, Racine turned in her seat to see two men climb out of the back of the second van, the one blocking her rear. Both wore balaclavas, and more importantly, both had guns.

She waited until all five men were nearer her car. She noted none of the handguns were raised, they were simply held by the side of their owners, seemingly an explanation of their power. This made no difference to Racine. She took a long, calming breath then drew the suppressed Glock from beneath her thigh, and acquired the first of the men approaching from the rear. She fired a quick, single round at the gunman. It hit him in the head, dropping him instantly. The second man had no time to react before Racine's next round slammed into his throat. He spun to his left and dropped. Racine spun too, now she faced the front and the three incoming men. The one who had the gun had started to raise it. This time she fired a double tap, the rounds arriving so closely to each other that the gunman visibly jerked before he fell.

Weapon up, Racine opened the door and got out of the Duster as the two knifemen ran back to their van. Two more rounds made quick work of the man on the left, whilst a single well-placed round in the right thigh of the second man caused him to crash to the ground. Looking backwards, then to her sides, Racine checked for any other targets. There were none. Satisfied it was just her and the single, injured knifeman, Racine advanced towards the man. He had rolled onto his back and was desperately trying to drag himself back towards the van he had arrived in.

Racine crouched down and pulled off his balaclava. She momentarily froze as she saw the face of the teenage boy beneath. He had a wispy moustache on his upper lip. "Who sent you?"

"D... don't kill... me!"

"Who sent you?"

"It was... the Frenchman..."

"The old Frenchman?"

"No... the other... one... please... I have a mother..."

"So do I, but mine is a lunatic who left me when I was a teenager."

"Please... it hurts..."

"I will let you go if you tell me all you know."

"All... I... know?"

"Yes."

"Okay... I will tell..."

Racine felt the disturbance of the air and then the crack as the high velocity round zipped past her left ear. It slammed into the boy's face, instantly turning it into pulp. Racine threw herself to the right as a second round sparked against the tarmac where her left foot had been a millisecond before. On her haunches now she pushed up to her feet and sprinted for the cover of the van. A third round missed her by the smallest of margins and punched a hole in the bodywork. Crouching behind the nearside wheel, she chanced a glance back and her jaw all but hit the floor. Jairo was standing in a first-floor window with a rifle. He saw her and raised the weapon. Racine scurried towards the back of the van and then around the other side. From here, due to the overhang of the nearest building, Jairo did not have a visual on her. Getting to her feet, she did the one thing she knew he would not be expecting and counterattacked. Unseen by Jairo, Racine ran towards the building he was in and pushed through the gap in the corrugated iron sheeting which had been used to close the open doorway. Inside the building was unbearably hot, wet and stank of rotting rubbish and urine. Racine slowly, and silently, took the bare, concrete steps upwards. She paused as she reached the first floor then swung right and into the nearest room, the one she had assessed Jairo was firing from.

The taxi driver stood, rifle raised facing away from her. Racine shot him in the right leg. Jairo howled, dropped the rifle and fell onto the dusty concrete floor.

"You almost made me miss my flight," Racine said.

Lying on his back and clutching his leg, Jairo's eyes were no longer friendly. Racine kicked his wounded leg. "I know you like to talk. Tell me everything you know."

"*Es una*, shoot me now."

"OK." Racine put a round in Jairo's other leg. "Happy?"

"*Puta Madre!*"

"You'll lose a lot of blood, but you'll live, if you answer my questions. Where is the Frenchman?"

"Medellín."

"Where?"

"He went to the boss's villa."

"He is at Espinosa's place?"

"Yes."

"Thank you." Racine turned and started to walk away.

"He will kill you. He is a professional!"

Racine paused, looked back, raised the Glock and put a round in Jairo's stomach. "He is a traitor, and like you he will die, slowly and painfully."

12

Akulov had a headache, in part he reasoned from Botero's punches to his face, but mostly from dehydration, the Colombian hadn't hit him that hard. The room they'd left him in was a wine cellar, an empty one. There were two sets of manacles on the wall opposite him and on the simple concrete floor were stains, which he identified as blood and urine. His own shackles seemed newer, they glinted in the harsh light cast by the overhead strip light. His wrists were cut and throbbed from where the shackles had been clamped. It wasn't serious, yet he knew it was only a matter of time before infection would set in to the broken skin. He knew by then he would have a decision to make. He was alive because they wanted something of him, or perhaps because the person who was allowed to kill him was not yet present and able to do so. And Akulov had an idea who that person might just be – Orosco's remaining son. But would the gangster risk coming to Colombia? Perhaps then, and this was more likely, someone would be sent in his place, a trusted aid, or perhaps his execution would be Zoomed?

Akulov snapped away from his thoughts and back to the here

and now as he heard footsteps approaching outside. They descended the stairs, two sets of boots. As they arrived at the bottom, Akulov got to his bare feet, the metre of chain allowing him to take a single step away from the wall. The door opened and the two goons entered.

Akulov, hands raised, wrists shackled together but with his palms splayed, made direct eye contact with the two thugs as they entered the room. He'd had enough of being compliant. He had both legs free which, in his opinion, was a mistake, but he was grateful for it. He knew if either of the guards came within reach, he'd be able to strike, incapacitate them and grab their weapons. As before, the first man, the one who had opened the door, was carrying a handgun, and a respectable, simple one at that. It was a Glock 17.

The second man had a standard AK74, probably ex-Soviet and certainly not the best weapon to be using in such a confined space.

"Gringo, you stay still. You move, I shoot." The key man spoke in guttural, accented English.

Akulov made no reply, as the man with the AK74 moved sideways, rifle up, finger on the trigger, squarely aimed at Akulov's chest.

Glock man now pointed it at Akulov with his right hand as he waggled a key in his left hand. "You come with us."

Akulov remained statue still as the pistol was slipped into the jailer's waistband before both of his hands undid the iron shackles. Akulov sensed and saw both jailers tense. This was the most dangerous time for them, the instant they expected him to attack, to make a break for freedom. In the corner of his eye Akulov noticed the end of the AK74 quiver.

"Hands on your head!" Glock man said.

Slowly Akulov raised them, noticing the AK74 tremble again.

He wasn't going to make a move now, whilst they expected him to do so, he'd wait until they believed they had him under their full control, and then he'd kill them both.

AK74-man now gestured towards the door with his barrel, and said, "Moving!"

Glock-man stepped out of Akulov's path and pointed his pistol at the door. "Walk!"

"Moving, walking!" AK74 said.

Akulov padded towards the door, his bare feet slapping the coarse concrete. Once through the door he immediately turned left and slowly started to take the stairs up. Both men were behind him and, as far as he could tell, there was no one waiting for him at the top. It was ten steps up to the kitchen, and after four he felt the cold end of the pistol barrel press into the small of his back. It was meant to warn him, to keep him controlled, but it would do exactly the opposite.

Five steps, six steps, seven steps and Akulov's head now rose above the hatch. Quickly scanning the room, he ascertained it was empty. As he took the ninth step he jerked to his left, feeling the 9mm Glock lose contact with his back as the pressure applied to it made it slip sideways. A round exploded from the barrel and Akulov felt the gasses scorch his skin as the lead projectile raced parallel to his body and slammed into the far wall of the room. Akulov rolled away across the flagstone flooring, and came up behind the hatch. He could have closed it and locked the two men below, but he was unarmed and wanted their weapons. He stood and, from the heavy wooden worktop behind, grabbed a meat cleaver from the selection of chef knives.

As he knew he would, Glock-man bellowed angrily and rushed up and out of the entrance, pistol up. Akulov waited until he was clear of the steps then unforgivingly, slammed the cleaver down on the top of his skull, all but splitting it in two. As he began to sink forward, Akulov dropped the heavy knife and grabbed the pistol. Unwilling or unable to stop, the one with the AK74 was half out of the entrance when Akulov shot him in the back of the head.

The retort of the round was just as thunderous as the first, and anyone else in the villa should now definitely be alerted. Akulov took the AK74 from the second dead man, and moved into the corner of the room, the furthest part away from both the back door and the door leading into the large living room. Anyone following up on the gunshots would arrive from either of these two entrances, and he'd rather they came to him than he run into them. He listened, and he waited. Two minutes passed and no one came. There was no rapid footfall or concerned shouts, just something distant... a beat. Somewhere from within the house he could hear the rhythmic thump of music. It was time to move.

He could have taken the back door, he could have escaped by using the path to the river, but he didn't. Akulov wanted closure. He wanted to finish the job and liquidate the one running the operation, the one who had kidnapped Kizlyar's family. So, he headed for the internal door, AK74 across his back, Glock up, steadied in a two-handed stance.

He followed the narrow hallway, staying in the middle of the space before spinning to the left and into the large, open plan living area. It was empty and the floor-to-ceiling French doors were closed. He became still, obscured from anyone on the first floor by the large, wide staircase that joined the two. Akulov edged forward then swung a left and pointed the pistol up the stairs, this was where the music was coming from.

Yet, again, he saw no one.

Akulov started to take the stairs up, his damp, bare feet sticking to the marble steps. The marble gave way to thick piled, orange carpet which hugged his feet with each step as he reached the landing. As he passed the first room, he cast a cursory glance inside. The bodies of the men he had killed earlier had been moved, but the blood had not yet been mopped up. Now he passed the second room, the one that had been a gilded cage for Catherine and Nairo. It too was empty, and the bedsheets rucked. With each step, the music became louder as he neared Botero's lair, the huge double bedroom taking up one third of the upper floor, which doubled both as bedroom and study. Silently Akulov stood at the door, he counted to three then booted the door open and entered the room.

The music hit him like a wave, it was heavy rock, although he didn't know the tune nor the artist. Botero was standing at the window, a large cigar in his left hand, with his back towards the door, seemingly completely unaware that Akulov had entered. Without hesitation, Akulov shot him in the back of his right knee. Botero shrieked as his knee collapsed, and he fell forward, collapsing onto the windowsill. Akulov crossed left towards an old-fashioned style CD tower and pressed the off button.

The room was plunged into silence before he heard the sound of a door opening and a familiar voice with a Texas twang said, "Ruslan, put down your darn gun!"

Akulov spun around. From the en suite a powerful figure entered. He was in his late fifties, wearing khaki slacks and a dark blue polo shirt, and his thick grey-blond hair floated across his forehead. Akulov was confused, "Casey?"

"Lower the Glock," the veteran CIA operator's hands were held aloft in a placatory fashion. "It's just you, me and laughing boy."

"My men... will kill you!" Botero spat.

Akulov said, "The two men who took me from the cellar are dead. Do you have any more?"

"There was no one else around when I arrived," Casey confirmed.

Akulov let his eyes scan the room once more before he complied with Casey's request and lowered his Glock. "Explain?"

"Casey? You... know this... *puta?*"

"We go way back, but I had no idea he was here. Clamp your hand on that wound Pablo, and you may live," the CIA deputy director said, before addressing Akulov, "It just so happens that Pablo here and I have a 'working relationship'."

"Are you telling me that he's an agency asset?"

"I am... a partner!" Botero said through gritted teeth. "A... valued partner! And you... you are a dead man!"

Akulov ignored the threat. "Casey, did you know about the woman and child he kidnapped?"

"I did not."

"They... were guests."

"You kidnapped my brother's wife and child and killed the three-man team who were guarding them."

"Brother? Three-man team? That's a hell of a lot to unpack there Ruslan."

"I... I don't know... what he's talking about, Casey! You gotta help me here! This man shot me!"

Akulov said, "Did you know about the passports?"

"Passports?" Casey seemed confused. "What passports?"

"The Spanish ones."

"Hey, Pablo, what the hell is he telling me?"

"Casey... please! I need medical attention!"

Akulov continued. "A Spanish diplomat was selling passports to Botero."

Casey met Akulov's eyes. "Would this be the same Spanish diplomat who was found dead the other month in a Bogotá hotel room?"

"It would."

"Pablo, why are you buying Spanish passports?"

"For... options. We... all... need options."

"His private army were going to use them to conduct terror attacks in the EU."

"His what now?"

Akulov made a mental leap, as his mind started to make connections. "He has a place called 'The School', it is where he trains his militia."

"Yeah, I know about 'The School'."

"Then you... you know... they are my... personal protection team... security for the mines!" Botero said, through gritted teeth.

Akulov now understood he was on the right track, so he continued, adding what Racine had told him. "He has been training a team to infiltrate the EU and attack targets in both Spain and France."

Casey's brow furrowed. "Spain and France?"

"The Basque country."

"Now that is interesting," Casey's eyes narrowed, "and you never thought to tell me about this, Pablo?"

"Wh... what? Lies! He... is lying! Casey, are you gonna... gonna take the word of this... this American assassin over... me?"

"Firstly, he's Ukrainian and secondly, he's the world's best assassin. Isn't that so, Wolf Six?"

"W... Wolf... Six!" Botero's eyes became wide as the realisation of whom he had been punching registered. "I... I had... I did not know..."

"Listen," Akulov said, ignoring the flattery, "Botero and his boss Espinosa were working with Franco Orosco to resurrect ETA."

Casey said, "You whacked him yesterday in Buenos Aires,

didn't you, Wolf Six?" Akulov made no reply, so Casey continued. "You have proof of this accusation, Ruslan?"

"I do not. The French do."

"Let me guess, Sophie Racine?"

Now it was Akulov's turn to be shocked. He saw no reason to lie, so said, "Yes."

Casey crossed his arms. "I heard some low-level chatter, but nothing actionable. It seems Racine and her boss Grillot were right."

"Casey... wait... you can't believe... this..." Botero attempted to drag himself up to his feet, but his knee gave way, making him howl.

"Pablo, I'm disappointed. Highly disappointed."

"Casey... please... please!"

"Hey, Ruslan, if I toss you a dollar as a down payment, can the CIA contract you to shoot this Colombian clown for me?"

Botero was now sobbing. Akulov imagined it was a mixture of pain, fear and frustration, a heady cocktail, which was why he'd targeted the man's knee. "W... what? N... no! Please!"

"No need, the French have already offered me a euro, but this is personal." Akulov raised his Glock.

"Please! It was not my idea! I am just here for... the money! It was... Espinosa!" Botero blurted out.

"Ruslan, hold that thought. Pablo, how many passports?"

"Twenty-three."

"Twenty-three?" Casey repeated. "That's a considerable number to go missing. Is that for twenty-three men, or spares or what?"

"Twelve men... plus Martinez."

"Who is Martinez?"

"He is... their leader. He trained them. He is... a Spanish soldier."

"The trainer at The School? I've never met him but I thought he was a local?"

"He's... Spanish... Spanish. He has a house in El Bagre... he has two women there."

Casey's tone became stern. "You give me his full name, now."

"Ángel Martinez."

"How old is he?"

"I don't... know. Perhaps thirty-five?"

"Thirteen men, in total," Casey cocked his head. "So the eight other passports are what, extras?"

"I don't know."

"That's Toro-crap, Botero. You tell me or Wolf Six will shoot out your other knee."

Akulov moved the Glock.

"Wait! Yes... thirteen men... thirteen passports. Three of them have two each."

"Why?"

"They are the team leaders."

"So, it's three groups?"

"No, two groups... of six men, and Martinez has an... extra one also."

"Yes."

"So that's two targets?"

"I don't know. Espinosa told me I did not need to know."

"What about the remaining six passports?" Akulov asked. "Where are they?"

"Espinosa took one and gave one each to Orosco and his two sons."

"That's four."

"I have one too."

"Five."

Casey was incredulous. "You were going on the operation?"

"No, I was going on vacation."

Akulov said, "And the last one?"

"It was given to the Frenchman."

Casey looked at Akulov, then back at Botero. "The Frenchman? Who the hell is the Frenchman?"

"My informer at the DGSE."

"The one you murdered in the video," Akulov said, as a statement of fact.

"Y... yes. Him. The one we killed."

"Show me your passport," Casey commanded.

Botero's eyes darted to his desk. "Top drawer."

Casey nodded. "Keep that Glock on him, Ruslan."

"It is not going anywhere," Akulov replied.

Casey moved to the desk and started to open the drawers. From one he removed a bottle of tequila and a pair of shot glasses. "You didn't even offer me a drink?"

"H... have one..." Botero stammered.

"What have we here?" Casey retrieved a large brown envelope. He sat at the desk and tipped its contents onto its padded leather top. A plastic document sleeve slipped out, from this Casey pulled out a burgundy-coloured passport with the words "Unión Europea España" and coat of arms on the front cover. Casey inspected the document, "This is as real as they come. Now tell me, Pablo, where are the twelve men and their passports?"

"They... they are not here."

Casey sighed. "Ruslan, shoot him."

"Wait! They have already left."

"When?"

"Two days ago. That was why Espinosa was meeting with Orosco. They were going to celebrate the success of the mission together."

Casey shot to his feet, grabbed the smaller Colombian by his shirt and pulled him off the ground. "When is the attack, where is the attack, and what is the target?"

"I don't know!"

Casey growled. "Damn it, man. Tell me!"

"It was a... secret. Only Espinosa and Orosco knew."

"Shit." Casey let go of Botero, who grunting, struggled unsuccessfully to steady himself on his shattered knee, before he fell back against the wall, whimpering.

Akulov said, "Do you know the names in those passports?"

"I don't know them! I don't... have them."

Akulov waggled the Glock. "Who does?"

"Espinosa."

"Espinosa is dead."

"He has photocopies... of the passports... in his villa."

"I'm guessing," Casey said, "this is not in the little place he keeps near El Bagre?"

Botero shook his head. "No. His main home in Medellín."

"Of course, it is, where else for a cartel boss to call home?"

"All his important papers... are there."

"Where in his villa exactly are the photocopies?"

"He has a grandfather... clock in his study."

"Yeah, I know, remember he invited me there once."

"It has a secret drawer... at the bottom. I was with him... when he put them in there."

"Really?" Casey raised his eyebrows. "Very Agatha Christie."

Akulov asked, "Who knows about this drawer?"

"Just me, and his bodyguard... Greiner."

"Where is Greiner?"

"He was here; he came for his..."

"Family. We rescued his family," Akulov said. "He is now hopefully halfway to the airport at Medellín."

"Can you contact him?"

"No. Racine can."

Casey sat again. "I think Pablo is about finished here."

"I am?" Botero said, hope suddenly appearing in his voice. "I mean I am... Look I have helped you... the CIA. And you, Wolf Six, I am sorry."

"I am not sorry," Akulov said and fired a single round into Botero's forehead.

Casey watched as the Colombian slid backwards down the wall before he reached the floor in a crumpled heap. "Cold, as ever."

Akulov moved back to the entrance, peered outside, making sure no one was approaching, then shut the door and took the guest chair opposite Casey. "We need to find those men."

A smile appeared on Casey's face. "So, you and I are a 'we' again?"

"For now."

"Welcome back, I have no problem with that. But why is this your fight?"

"They are terrorists."

Casey said, "Where is Sophie Racine, I need to talk to her."

"Bogotá."

"Of course. You have her number?"

"No."

"What about Greiner, do you have his number?"

"No. Racine has that; he has a satphone. He was her asset."

"And I missed all this?" Casey retrieved his own Iridium from his pocket. "I'm calling her boss."

Akulov waited and watched as Casey dialled his contact at the DGSE.

"It's gone to voicemail. Damn time zones. Hey, Grillot, it's Vince Casey here. I know Racine is in Colombia, Bogotá to be precise. I need her number. Call me back on this one. This is priority one. Merci." Casey ended the call and sighed. Then tapped out a message on the keypad. "Never in when you need them. Now I need to get this name over to Langley, if we can get a face for this Ángel Martinez person, we can use facial recognition on anyone who has left Colombia or entered Spain in the last two days. Now we wait for our ride. I've requested a chopper to Medellín."

Akulov said, "Why are you here, Vince?"

"Espinosa was our asset, not this bottom-feeder Botero. His codename was 'Target Echo'. As soon as I heard Espinosa had been taken out, I had to personally fly into this green and orange asshole of a town to make sure Botero was going to honour his dead boss's agreement with us."

"Which was what, to give up a percentage of their takings to be ignored by the CIA?"

"Jesus Ruslan, that's cynical even for you." Casey yanked the cork from the bottle of tequila and poured two shots. Without waiting for Akulov to take one, Casey raised the nearest to his lips and downed the fiery liquor. "Look, we messed up in Colombia last time, big time. We learnt our lesson with Escobar way back when. But now the game has moved on. They've been mining gold in this region for over a hundred years, but cocaine was always number one. Then it all changed. A curious thing happened. In 2011 the price of gold shot up from twenty US dollars an ounce to almost two thousand. That brought opportunity, for everyone. The prospectors, the local businesses, and of course the gangs. I mean the gold trade had become more profitable than cocaine. The population of El Bagre rocketed from five to thirty thousand, yet here's the kicker. To open a mining operation, you need to apply and pay for a permit, have your equipment and staff certified, and then lose thirty-two per cent minimum in tax on whatever you turn in. Start an illegal mine however and all you need is a bucket and a spade, then find a part of the riverbank that no one else is digging up. Then when you've finished, you take your nuggets to any exchange store in El Bagre where, as soon as they cross the counter, they are automatically legalised, checked for purity and, as if by magic, you've got your cash. Here's the catch. If you go down that route you've got to work with the gangs, and that means you pay a tax to them."

"I'm guessing that the largest of these is the Clan Del Oro." Despite himself, Akulov took the shot and necked it.

"Exactly. Now these guys have a great thing going on. Ninety per cent of the region's economy is from illegal mining."

"So, the CIA wants a cut."

"In part – every penny helps the black ops budget." Casey refilled the glasses. "Look, putting it crudely, you see what the government gives the people in this region? Hell, Antioquia is an area with huge potential and natural resources, but it's also got huge unemployment amongst the young, who get minimal schooling and less spent on them than in all neighbouring Latin American countries. So, what do the little kids, and the big kids do? They turn to farming coke or working in the mines, or they join a gang. Or a mixture of all three." Casey drank his tequila. "Now these people, 'the Clan', it's a dangerous entity, but its leader is clever, people are generally accepting of working under him, so he realises that he can be more than just a cartel boss. I don't know how he met Franco Orosco, but he did and suddenly you've got Espinosa taking notes from the Orosco family on how to move from the shadows into the bright lights of politics. Now at this point, Espinosa piques our interest. He's different to all the other crime lords. He becomes someone we can nurture, someone who could lead the region, if not the entire country. It's a long game. So, we're thinking, if we help him now, he then helps us in the future."

"Except Espinosa and Orosco had grander ideas. They wanted independence for the Basque country."

"Which is way out there in left field. It is the wildest thing I have ever heard."

"I agree it is."

Casey blew out his cheeks, and rubbed his face. "Tell me about your 'brother'?"

"Greiner is not my brother by blood."

Casey sat up straighter in his seat. "You are telling me another Werewolf was here?"

"Yes."

"Working for Espinosa as his personal bodyguard."

"Yes. You didn't meet him when you met Espinosa?"

"I've not had an in person 'face to face' with the man for two years. His bodyguard then was Colombian." Casey shook his head. "So, the German wasn't German."

"You knew of him?"

"We checked him out, found no records, presumed he was former Bundeswehr or something. Who was he?"

"Wolf Nine."

"I thought I knew all the names of the Werewolves?"

"He vanished in Afghanistan, officially he's been dead a long time."

Casey closed his eyes, as if trying to access a memory. "Denis Petrov?"

"Yes."

"He went AWOL?"

"If we all hadn't believed he was dead, then that is how it would have been classified. I came here to rescue his wife and child from Botero."

"Who Botero had kidnapped because what, he thought Wolf Nine had been responsible for the death of his boss Espinosa?"

"Yes. In part."

"Ah, so you were both in Buenos Aires!"

"I was not the one who killed Espinosa."

"Orosco then?" A thin smile appeared on Casey's lips. "Racine?" Akulov made no reply, so Casey continued. "She then takes out Espinosa at the same damn meeting? I was going to say that his death really set us back, but now it looks like the Agency has had a fortuitous escape."

"It did."

"Hmm, I've got an idea." Casey retrieved his phone and dialled a number from memory. He pressed the speaker button and Akulov could hear it ring at the other end, and then a voice he recognised answered. It spoke in English, a home counties accent to be precise.

"Who is this?"

"Valentina, my dear, how are you?"

Valentina Tishina sounded calm if a little surprised. "I am well, thank you, Vince. To what do I owe this pleasure?"

"You're on speakerphone, and I'm sitting here in a villa, in the middle of the Colombian rainforest with a very dead cartel boss and your boy Wolf Six."

"Ruslan is there with you?"

"Hello, Valentina."

"Ruslan," Tishina said, "why are you with Vince? What type of compromising agreement have you got us into now?"

"I haven't," Akulov replied, and realised immediately that he sounded like a petulant teenager.

"Listen, Valentina," Casey said, "I called you because I need a favour."

"Well, this is quite the occasion, Vince Casey of the CIA needs a favour from me?"

"That is correct."

"Very well, I am listening."

"Do you know a Spaniard by the name of Ángel Martinez?"

"Should I?"

"Do you?"

"That name does not ring any bells. Who is he?"

"We think he is former Spanish military, a contractor. He is leading a terror cell which we believe will imminently be launching one or more attacks on mainland Spain."

"So, you would like me to put my feelers out to my network to see if anyone knows of him or has heard from him?"

"Very succinct. Yes, I do. I don't need to tell you that this needs to be done in such a manner that he doesn't get spooked."

"No, Vince, you do not."

"Thank you, Valentina, you can contact me on this number."

"Fine. Now, can you explain to me why the pair of you are there, in the middle of the rainforest, together?"

"Kismet," Casey said.

Tishina sighed. "Goodbye, Vince."

"Bye. Ruslan?"

"Yes?"

"Say goodbye to Valentina."

"Oh yes. Goodbye, Valentina."

"Goodbye, Ruslan."

The call ended. Akulov noted Casey had an amused expression on his face. "You have Valentina's number memorised?"

"Yep. You mean you don't, Ruslan?"

Akulov shrugged. "I don't have her number."

Casey smirked. "I still can't figure the pair of you out."

"What do you mean?"

"Ah, nothing." A harsh trilling sounded. Casey picked up his satphone. "Grillot, mon ami!"

13

CALIFORNIA, UNITED STATES.

In theory it was a two-hour drive from San Francisco International Airport to Christian Pacheco's family home in Jenner, California, however the traffic around the airport had been heavy and this had only lessened once they had left the city proper. Now travelling North on the coastline hugging Shoreline Highway, José Orosco was letting himself enjoy the views from the back of the highly padded Mercedes S Class sedan. The greenery reminded him much of parts of Argentina but what he enjoyed was seeing the waves crash against the rugged shore.

He had stepped off a fifteen-hour indirect flight from Buenos Aires and even though he had been in business class, there had outrageously not been any first-class seats available; he was tired. This was also due to the amount of free-flowing alcohol he had consumed on the flight. The flight attendants had been young and pretty, however his mind had been elsewhere. A week before his brother had been poised to win the election to become the governor of Buenos Aires yet now, he was dead, gunned down in his father's house. Orosco knew Torres – by way of the assassin he had contracted – was responsible for his father's murder, because it was he who had been instrumental with the plan to use Christian to persuade him to put out the contract on him. In fact, it had been an informer of José's who, working at the docks, had been approached by Torres all those years before when he had been looking for someone who may be able to assist him in securing a contract killer. That same man had reached out to José less than a month ago, and this time José had given him the name of a broker to hand to Torres. José allowed himself a smile as he relished the simplistic wickedness of his machinations. Torres was the perfect suspect. Someone who had a grudge against his father, someone who had been denied justice and someone who now had the financial means to take direct action.

Torres was a highly bitter man who had vowed to get justice for the families of his fellow conscripts. José had to begrudgingly admire the man, who had not been intimidated by his threats, like the other witnesses had. The man who had carried on the fight, in spite of his family tragedy – the coincidental, accidental death of his wife. Torres had held fast in his conviction, and this had made it all the more delicious to see the expression on his face when eventually the trial had been dismissed due to lack of evidence against his father. In fact, José had deemed it fanciful that he would be able to get the outwardly straight-laced, but acrimonious, former businessman to take such a step without using his final piece of persuasion, but he had, and that was surprising.

Perhaps when all of this was over, he would ask Christian to set out step by step exactly what he had said and done to make it happen. Perhaps, José mused, Christian was not as useless as he had previously believed, his company had continued to be a safe way to launder clan cash, and now he had even started to import their gold – albeit in miniscule amounts.

José sighed, his father had deserved to die. He had cast a long shadow, and even he believed Orosco Senior was very capable of the charges put against him. However, he knew that if his father had been found guilty, that would have been the end to his brother's political aspirations. But now all that lay in ruins regardless. His brother had been murdered, and José would not stop until he had wrought his own form of justice on those responsible, not for him, or even for his brother, but for his brother's sons, the boys who would one day command the business. He knew he had to start his trail somewhere, and that somewhere was Jenner, California, where he would confront Torres face to face like a man and ask him outright if he had put a contract out on his brother.

José became aware that the driver of the Mercedes was looking at him in the rear-view mirror. The driver asked, in his Mexican accented English, "Is everything OK, señor?"

"Yes," José replied.

The man was a sicario. A hitman from Juarez. He was on the payroll of Clan Del Oro to be utilised whenever they had an issue with anyone within the West Coast area. In the last year, his services had been called upon twice, and each of those calls had resulted in the deaths of those making the problem. In normal times it would have made José feel powerful, invincible, alive to know that his Colombian partners had hitmen he could call upon at his whim. Today, however, the man was being used as a tool to provide José with a suppressed 9mm handgun, and then to ferry him to his target in Jenner.

Taking his eyes off the view for a moment, José took one of his two Spanish passports out of his jacket pocket and inspected it again. It was faultless, and it had been the basis for its bearer to receive an ESTA and be admitted into the United States. José had to appreciate the foresight of the man who had supplied the passports in getting the US entry visa because, without that, José would not have been able to clear the scrutiny of the US Customs and Border Protection officials back at the airport. José Orosco had entered the US as José Perez, a teacher from Madrid, and no one had batted an eye. He studied his unflattering passport photograph. He really needed to do something about those chins, perhaps he'd get some of that diet drug all the celebrities used – Mounjaro? Yeah that was it, and he'd supplement it with his usual uppers.

Putting the passport away he now turned his attention to the hard-shell case on the seat next to him. He opened it to inspect its contents. This included a standard Glock 17, which was reliable if nothing fancy and, next to the handgun, in a space of its own, was a suppressor. He casually removed both items from the case and gave them the once-over. He'd been trained in firearms when serving as an active member of the Grupo Especial de Operaciones Federales (the Federal Operations Special Group), with further specialist training carried out by the US FBI Hostage Rescue Team. So, shooting an old man in daylight was not an issue at all. Satisfied that the tools of his trade looked serviceable, he screwed the suppressor to the barrel of the Glock. He felt the weight of the suppressed pistol in his hand and liked it. Now that he was safely away from the airport, he switched his Colombian iPhone back on, realising that he really should be using a burner, but loathed to give up his phone with its treasure trove of hidden spicy videos of himself with the two El Bagre women he supported. Of equal importance, of course, was his WhatsApp number, which he too could not go without. As the device switched on, he groaned at how little battery life it had left. He did have a charger, but that was in his case in the trunk. The Mercedes was fitted with a charging socket, but he had read stories of vehicles being hacked to steal the contents of anything plugged into them, and he did not trust the killer driving the car enough not to sell his data, and photographs, to the highest bidder. His phone had started to lose battery power at an alarming rate, but it was so small an inconvenience in light of recent events that he had overlooked it. Even now, mere minutes after turning on, his phone decided to display the "20 per cent low battery" warning message and then proceeded to lose a further two per cent of its juice as it first searched for a network and then downloaded his email and messages. In addition to the standard "Welcome to the US" text from the service provider his phone had chosen, there was a one from a number he did recognise. It was from the Frenchman in the Bogotá embassy, Durand. He opened it:

Racine knows about the operation. My cover is blown. Further, she is responsible for the killings in your father's house.

José blinked and rubbed his face, as he felt indignation and anger rise from within. The Frenchwoman had murdered his brother, not Torres? Really? But she was an intelligence officer, not a sicario. Wasn't she? This was something he found hard to believe. He sent an immediate message back:

What proof of this do you have?

José stared at the screen willing the man to reply to his WhatsApp as the Mercedes continued on to Pacheco's family home. Five minutes, nothing, ten minutes, nothing. At the half an hour mark, José was about to send another message when the driver spoke.

"We are fifteen minutes away from the address, boss."

"Thank you," José replied.

José continued to breathe in the passing landscape, the

myriad of lush trees hanging on to the rocking hills on their immediate right and the sea on the left. Every now and again the road would bend, nearer to the hills, then push back out again towards the sea as it followed the coastline. Large, mostly wooden clad houses were dotted here and there on the side nearest the sea. José imagined himself living in such a place and, as he did so, he became angry at Christian for doing just that. The Mercedes slowed and took a turning left, and downhill onto Ninive Drive, the small road which granted direct access to the eight large houses making up Christian's neighbourhood. Each of the sprawling houses were hidden by thick trees and foliage offering the residents privacy from anyone who passed. This was beneficial to José Orosco and the sicario at the wheel of the black Mercedes. The car slowed to a speed which would not raise any concern if they were spotted, before finally coming to a halt just shy of the entrance to Christian's driveway, purposefully concealed behind the dense foliage.

"Do you want me to come in?"

"No," José said, "this is something I must do alone. You will wait here, to ensure that we leave smoothly and quickly."

"Understood."

"Good."

Placing his iPhone back into his pocket, José clambered out of the large sedan. The suppressed handgun was in his right hand and he held it in line with his right leg. He was not expecting any trouble, therefore did not need to advertise the fact that he was armed. However, if trouble attempted to come to him, well, he was ready. He passed the last tree and turned into the drive, gravel crunching under the soles of his expensive dress shoes as he did so. The house was a long, low wooden structure which reminded him of the type of hunting lodges found in the movies when rich Americans would go big game hunting in Africa.

"Me Tarzan," José mumbled to himself.

He kept his eyes on the various windows facing in his direction, imagining that at any moment he would be spotted, and the front door would be opened by a curious Torres or nervous Christian. Yet, as he neared, he saw no one but he did hear voices, excited voices and screams.

"Monkeys," he muttered.

Moving onto the front lawn he skirted the house, passing a wooden bench set up to admire the view of both the house and the sea, and now saw movement at the back. He froze. Christian had not listened to him. The wife and children were there, and standing, watching them with his back to José was the old man – Tomas Torres. He looked greyer than José remembered, and his back was a little bent, but it was unmistakably the same person. The family had not spotted him yet, but if he stood there for much longer, they would, and the person who did see him would be one of the two little girls who were whirling and twirling on the grass like mad things. José stepped back, putting the edge of the house between him and those in the garden. All he had wanted to do was talk to Torres face to face and to put the question to him. To look him in the eye so he knew for sure if the old man had, or had not, ordered the execution of his brother. But he had not wanted that exchange, and the resulting consequences of it, to take place in front of Torres's daughter and grandchildren.

A vibration came from his pocket. José realised it was his phone. He transferred the Glock to his left hand and dug in his trousers with his right for his iPhone. He swiped the screen and saw a WhatsApp notification. It was a one word reply and a video attachment. José clicked on the link and the video started. Turning so that the phone's screen was not in the sunlight, José watched as, in view of a neighbour's CCTV camera, a woman entered the frame, crossed the road then rang the doorbell of his father's house. She waited for perhaps ten seconds before she rang again and then knocked on the door. As José watched, he saw the door open and then the woman with a shockingly fast draw, raised a handgun and shot the man who had opened it, whom he knew had been one of his brother's bodyguards. That clip ended as the front door was shut, but then the image jumped as the camera caught movement again, this time the door opening and the same woman exiting with a man.

A new message arrived. It was a photograph, a still image from the second part of the video clip. José could tell it had been enlarged and enhanced. The woman's face could be made out, but the man's could not. There was a caption underneath it: This is Sophie Racine of the DGSE.

José started to shake, and he felt the blood rushing in his ears. He realised his heart too was pounding, it was a curious sensation to be experiencing. Was he having a heart attack? He took a series of deep breaths, stumbled back towards the wooden bench and sat. He placed the Glock on the bench next to himself and holding the iPhone now with both shaking hands, sent a reply:

Who gave you this footage?

The reply was all but immediate:

My contact within the Buenos Aires police department. He wishes to know if he is to delete this or share it as evidence.

José replied:

Destroy it. I will handle the Frenchwoman.

"So, this is how it is to be?" A voice he recognised called out.

Looking up, José saw Torres striding up the slight incline towards him. "I... I've..."

"You have what? Come to murder me?"

"Yes," José replied, his hand grabbing the Glock and raising it.

"Do it! Do it!" Torres snapped back as he continued to make his approach, only stopping when he was no more than ten feet away.

José held the gun, trained on the old Argentinian. "Did you pay for a contract killer to assassinate my father?"

"Yes," Torres replied, without hesitation, "I did. And I would do it again!"

"Did you?"

"I don't understand?"

"Did you do it again? Did you also hire an assassin to murder my brother?"

"Your brother? No, I did not."

Maintaining eye contact with Torres, José lowered the gun. "I believe you."

"Why would I not tell you the truth, and live with the indignity of being a liar?"

José put the gun back by his side, on the bench. "That is what I respect about you, Tomas, you have always been a man of principles."

"First name terms now, is it?" Torres sat at the other end of the bench; the Glock rested between them. "There is nothing I respect about you, José."

"That I am well aware of. My father was not a good person. I know what he was accused of, and I believe he was guilty. I apologise for what he has done. He has tortured innocent men, and he has turned you, one of the most honourable men I have ever encountered, into a murderer. He was a poor parent; he pushed me away. He and I never had any love for each other. Some may say that the apple does not fall far from the tree, with myself that is undoubtedly true, but that is not so with my brother. Whatever his faults were, he was trying to make the lives better for the people of our hometown and far beyond. I can accept, even thank you, for my father's death, but I will not accept the death of my brother."

"I do not know who killed him."

"I now do."

"So, what will you do?"

"I will find the woman who killed him, and I will kill her."

"Woman?"

"Yes, they are the deadliest."

"What about me?"

"What about you? Our story is finished, Tomas. You have had your justice."

"Finished? You think the assassination of your father, the man who killed two of my friends, and who ordered the murder of my wife, is justice enough for me?"

José let out a sigh. "My father did not order the murder of your wife."

"What, are you going to sit here and lie to me?"

"It is not a lie. It was my idea, and it was I who was driving the car." In the corner of his eye, José saw Torres flinch and then his arm start to move. José grabbed the Glock and stood. "You really think you could pull the trigger, Tomas? You really believe you have what it takes to look into the eyes of another and end their life?"

Torres fists were clenched, and his body had started to shake. When he spoke his voice had become hoarse and not much more than a whisper. "You took her from me? You killed her to protect your father?"

José met Torres's eyes. He saw pain, he saw hatred, he saw himself. "Your wife, and the others, died not to protect my father or me, but to save the family name, to save my brother."

"Your brother's life was more important than the lives of all of those you killed?"

"Yes. It was. But what has it brought me now? I killed your wife. I would kill her again if I knew it meant safeguarding my brother, and I would kill you too."

Torres pushed himself to his feet. "Do it. Do it now."

"Too much has been destroyed; it is time to rebuild. My nephews are without a father, and your daughter is without a mother. I will not take her father too."

"How very noble."

"Nobility has nothing to do with it." José pocketed the Glock and started to walk back up the driveway. He paused, turned around, and said, "I envy you. This is a family I will never have. It is over between us."

"I am going to kill you."

"Perhaps, I deserve it. Send your assassin, the man you paid to kill my father, maybe he'll agree a repeat customer discount. We shall not see each other again."

* * *

El Dorado International Airport, Bogotá

In an overpriced airport shop, Racine had bought a pair of stretch jeans and a denim jacket. She had then paid for and entered the domestic lounge as her fifty-five-minute flight did not have a business class cabin. The lounge, she discovered, was devoid of any shower facilities, so Racine had been forced to change and freshen up in the bathroom. The lounge did, however, have light snacks and alcohol. Racine took a couple of unidentifiable sandwiches and allowed herself a glass of merlot. It was cheap, and it wasn't French, which annoyed her, but at least it was wine.

She sat in a corner and attempted to relax whilst she waited the hour for the next flight to Medellín. The flying time was just under an hour, which was annoying as it meant she would have little time to sleep, but the upshot was she would soon be in Medellín and searching for the rogue DGSE officer, Richard Halbert. It would have been easier if she'd had a laptop, but the only computer she had, she had taken from the language school, and she wasn't going to attempt to open it, that was a job for a techie back at DGSE headquarters.

So, using her satphone, she had managed to locate Espinosa's villa via Google Earth. It was more than a single building, it was an estate in the exclusive area of San Lucas, El Poblado. The house itself had been extended twice, with each new wing adding half again to the size of the existing structure, with the flat roof of one wing tiled as a rooftop terrace. At one side there was a standalone guesthouse and, at the other, a pool house and barbeque area surrounded a large, custom-shape swimming pool. The entire group of buildings was painted in a startling terracotta orange. It was anything but subtle, especially when compared to the neighbouring homes in the rest of the street which were strictly painted white.

Racine imagined that Halbert would have been put in the guesthouse, as, like Botero, Espinosa did not have an immediate family to disrupt, he would still not want a business associate poking around his private possessions. Zooming in on the Google image from above, she noted an older model silver Audi Q7 and a white Toyota Hi-Lux pickup were parked in the large, tiled courtyard at the front of the sprawling house. The imagery however was not live, it had been taken, according to Google, eleven months before, so the cars didn't necessarily belong to anyone at the house. The place was secluded as there was a single entrance for vehicles via an access road, and both a wall and mature trees hid the entire complex from their neighbours on all sides. It wasn't a bad hideout for a bad guy, but she had seen better, and as Medellín was inland, it was nowhere near a beach. Racine raised her hand to her mouth to stifle a yawn and realised she had finished her wine. Wine was her thing, it was what she drank to unwind, and occasionally to also forget, and even though the one she'd just had was crap, she already yearned for several more glasses. But she wouldn't.

A message appeared on the screen of her phone. She frowned as she did not recognise the number, in fact, as far as she was aware, the only person who had it, apart from whoever held the Werewolves satphone, was Colonel Grillot. Yet this was not his number. She tapped open the message and read it, with mild surprise:

> Racine it's Vince Casey, I'm with W6. Call me on this number. Extreme urgency.

Racine knew who Casey was, even though she had not met the CIA Deputy Director in person. Was it a trap, a rouse to track her? But then, she reasoned, her phone was on so if someone knew the number, they would already be tracking her. She looked around the lounge, ensuring that no one was paying her any undue attention, then tapped on the number in the message.

"Sophie Racine, I presume?" The voice had a discernible southern twang, Texas perhaps.

Racine replied, "Who is this?"

"You know who I am."

"How did you get this number and, more importantly, why did you get this number?"

"Listen, I've just come off a call with Grillot. He has explained to me what you told him, about the ambush in Bogotá and the two possible traitors."

Racine didn't believe him. "I doubt that."

"Listen, Racine, I know where you are and where you are going. Can you meet us there?"

"Yes." Racine was not going to give anything away regarding her location. She wanted to ensure that the man was who he said he was, and not someone working for Durand or the Clan. "Put him on the line."

"You mean your Ukrainian friend?"

"I would not call him a friend."

"Odd, that," Casey said.

There was a rustling and then another voice spoke. "Racine, it is me, Akulov. Casey was at Botero's place."

Racine was almost convinced it was Akulov, but had to be certain. "What was the name of that book I gave you?"

"The one I lost on that Spanish train?"

"Yes."

"*Dubliners* by James Joyce."

"I had to ask."

"I understand," Akulov replied at the other end.

"Why?"

"Why what?"

"Why was Casey at Botero's place?"

"I will let him tell you."

"I'm glad you made it out, Ruslan."

"Thank you. What about Kizlyar, Catherine and Nairo?" Racine noticed for the first time since she had known him, a sense of concern in Akulov's voice.

"Yes, as far as I am aware they are still headed to their extraction point."

"Medellín airport."

"Yes."

"I will pass you back to Casey now."

"Racine," Casey said. "Espinosa has twelve men, two teams of six heading to the EU on those stolen Spanish passports."

"Heading? They have already left?"

"Yes. Look, Botero assured us Espinosa made photocopies of the passports and has them hidden at his villa in a grandfather clock."

"A clock? A bloody clock?" In the lounge a man in a suit gave her a confused stare, in return she smiled.

"Yes. We need to find the copies so we can stop the team."

Racine understood, the photocopies would have each man's face, in addition to the passport number and name they were using to travel under. "Rendezvous where?"

Casey said, "You'll recognise us."

The call ended, and Racine realised that she was no longer tired. On the information screen she saw that her flight had started to board, so she collected her bag, grabbed a bottle of complimentary water and headed to her gate.

* * *

Manzanares el Real, Spain

Manzanares el Real was a forty-five-minute drive north of Madrid. At the foot of La Pedriza, a part of the Sierra de Guadarrama, and hugging the Santillana reservoir. It had two castles, one ruined and the other extremely well preserved and made famous by the Charlton Heston film *El Cid*. It was a place the man using the identity of Ángel Martinez had visited many times before just to wander around, to breathe in the history, and of course to conduct business with his contact.

Leaving the M608 at the roundabout, Martinez turned into the small town and a minute later was directly outside the address of his contact on Calle de Lavapiés. The picturesque area was visited by enough tourists and day trippers that one more anonymous Seat hatchback with a sticker on the rear windscreen identifying it as a hire car, aroused no suspicions. Martinez stepped out of the car and rang the bell for Sancho's apartment. As he waited, he stared at the distant castle. He remembered the first time they had met when Sancho had told him he often felt himself like "El Cid" as he too fought for both the Christians and the Muslims alike. Martinez hadn't pointed out that whereas the Castilian knight, Rodrigo Díaz de Vivar had attempted to broker peace, Sancho was an arms dealer who brokered war.

The door was opened by a man with tight black T-shirt and a bushy beard, "My friend! How good to see you! Do come in!"

Martinez made a show of looking happy to be greeted in such a manner, just in case anyone was watching and listening to them, and entered the building. Inside, whilst remaining cordial, both men became more businesslike and didn't say another word until they'd climbed the steps to the first floor flat and entered.

Sancho asked, "Do you have it all in cash, like I said?"

"Do you have all the goods, like I asked?"

"That is a yes from me."

"It is a yes from me also." Martinez tapped the thick wad of euros in the pocket of his jacket.

"Then walk this way, my friend."

Sancho led him through the hallway and into the living room. The room was bright, with sunlight reflecting from the new looking laminate flooring and smooth, cream-coloured walls. Two settees had been arranged in an L shape, and there was a long, wooden table between them that looked as though it had been made from cuts of reclaimed railway sleepers. On top of this was a long, black kit bag.

Sancho pointed to the larger of the two settees. "Take a seat, inspect the goods."

Sitting Martinez said, "It all fits in there?"

"No," Sancho sat on the second settee, "that is bag one of two. Bag two is in my car in the underground car park. I'd rather not bring ordinance and live rounds into my home."

"But firearms are fine to have at home?"

"Sí, because they do not explode. But I have made an exception. There is a sample grenade in there, just do not pull the pin!" Sancho flashed a smile, it was insincere.

Martinez zipped open the bag. He could instantly smell the gun oil and gunpowder. "These are used?"

"Sí, mostly. For the low price I charged you, and the quantity you required, it would not have been possible."

Martinez took out a cloth covered handgun and started to unwrap it. There was an issue with used, unlicensed firearms. They had a ballistic rap sheet. Each firearm had its own unique ballistic fingerprint, a set of marks and scratches it left on the cartridge casing, and the bullet itself, in the process of spinning the round out of the barrel. Once a handgun, assault rifle or machine gun was used, any round fired could be traced back to it. Which meant that if a firearm had been used during a criminal act, and either the round or the cartridge casing retrieved, that weapon became forever linked. This was why a new, unused Glock 19 commanded a premium over one which had been fired in anger once or one that had been used twice or more. Yet Martinez cared nothing for this. If the weapons were in working order, he could not care less who and what they were connected to, in fact that would even muddy the waters of any potential investigation as to who the shooter was and where the weapon was from. "You can guarantee that these work?"

"As much as anyone can guarantee any product. I have cleaned each and every one of those. I saw no damage, and the magazines are full, but obviously here I cannot test fire them but that is why you choose a Glock, is it not? It is the most reliable, if not the most elegant 9mm handgun."

"It is." Martinez unwrapped each and every handgun in the bag. They were mostly "nineteens" with a few "seventeens". "OK," he opened his jacket pocket, "here is your cash."

Sancho took the wad of cash and gave it a cursory glance. "I trust you, and what is a friendship without that?"

"A business agreement."

"That is right and, in this business, it is the friendships that keep us all above ground and breathing. C'mon, we will go to the car park and get the second bag." Sancho stood.

"Can I use your bathroom?"

Sancho cocked his head. "Sure, whatever. It's the second door on the left."

"Thank you." Martinez stood and left the room. He found the bathroom and shut the door. Now face to face with his own reflection in the mirror, José Orosco grinned at himself. He had done it. His deception had been complete. In Colombia he had assumed the identity of a man he had met in a bar in Buenos Aires a year before, a man who had subsequently gone missing, and here in Spain, once again he had become the former Spanish soldier. He removed a small plastic bag of white powder from his pocket, wet his finger and rubbed it across his gums. Instantly feeling revived, he then put the remainder away, washed his hands and headed back into the living room of his business associate.

Sancho had zipped up the bag. With a grimace, he hefted it up and off the table. Although each loaded Glock was not heavy, at roughly nine hundred and fifteen grams each, thirteen of them, plus the grenade was a noticeable weight. "Here, it's yours."

José took the bag. "Thanks."

"Let's go." Sancho led them out of the room, through the hallway and then shutting the front door, down two flights of stairs to the metal door leading to the garage. He tapped in a code and pushed the door open revealing the subterranean space, which was surprisingly bright, due to its whitewashed ceiling and even lighting. There were eight bays and five of them were taken. On one side, nearest the corner was a large BMW motorbike, then two spaces along from this a grey Peugeot hatchback. On the other side of the car park, and facing these, three vehicles stood side by side, the first a Fiat 500, the second a Cupra Leon, and the third a Porsche Boxster.

"Which one is yours?"

"Have a guess my friend."

"Given that I know you appreciate craftsmanship I would say the Porsche, but I doubt you would keep anything that could go boom in that. The Peugeot?"

"Sí, you are correct – but the Porsche is also mine, I use it to 'entertain', if you understand me."

"We all need to entertain once in a while."

They crossed to the Peugeot, which José now recognised as a 308. Sancho popped the boot and the large rear window raised bringing with it the rear lip. He reached inside and José heard the sound of a zip opening, "Have a look."

"I will." José peered into the large boot. The bag was identical to the one in his hand, yet this one contained boxes of ammunition and other larger boxes which he knew contained grenades.

He zipped the bag closed, then with some considerable effort hauled out the bag out. “Can you take the lighter one?”

“Sure. We’ll walk up the ramp; it comes out just past your car.”

“Bueno.”

José shut the boot; Sancho locked the car with his key fob and then both men took the access ramp up towards the street level. They turned right, passed a car parked half on the hash lines by the entrance to the underground garage, then a second car before arriving at José’s rental. All the while they saw no one. It was a little after one p.m. so José imagined most locals were inside, even though the summer heat had long dissipated. He opened the boot, gingerly placed his bag inside, then took the second one from his contact.

Sancho didn’t hold out his hand but said, “Thank you. I hope to see you again, my friend.”

“You will,” José replied, although he knew that was a lie. If the operation went to plan, he would never have the need to see low level suppliers such as Sancho ever again. And nor would he need to play act at being Ángel Martinez.

14

JOSÉ MARÍA CÓRDOVA INTERNATIONAL AIRPORT, RIONEGRO, COLOMBIA

Akulov sat at the airport coffee shop, drank his espresso and chewed on an overpriced, artisan Tibitó chocolate bar. It had been agreed that he would greet Racine, as he was the only one out of the three men the French intelligence officer knew. Outside the airport terminal, Vince Casey waited in the front passenger seat of a white Toyota SW4 Fortuner, whilst Mike Parnell, the CIA paramilitary operative permanently attached to his division, sat behind the wheel. It had been Parnell who had met Casey and him at the airport some twenty minutes before, when their chartered chopper had deposited them. José María Córdova International Airport, like many international airports around the world, was not actually in the city it supposedly served. It was some twelve miles to the south-east of Medellín, just outside the smaller city of Rionegro.

Beard freshly trimmed, and dressed in jeans and a battered trucker jacket, both courtesy of Parnell, Akulov felt as though he resembled The Marlborough Man. But the jacket did enable him to wear a Glock 19 under his left arm in a pancake holster which, for the time being, he had left in the car so as not to get pinged by airport security. Akulov did not ask how and where the equipment and clothing had come from. The CIA had battled cartels around Colombia for so long that Akulov expected there to be designated CIA safe houses dotted here and there with everything a state sanctioned assassin could possibly need. The CIA had clearly thought ahead. But this was a "rush job", and Akulov hated rushed jobs, or "fastballs" as they were known in the trade. He allowed himself a thin smile as he remembered the British military mantra of the "Five P's" Tishina told the Werewolves about years before – "Proper Planning Prevents Piss-poor Performance". She'd then had to explain the meaning of the word "piss" to several of the others. He checked his G-Shock and then looked at the Arrivals board. Racine's flight had landed and, as it was a short domestic hop, he imagined its passengers would soon be streaming into the arrivals hall. Akulov finished both his chocolate and his espresso and slowly walked towards the crowd of waiting family members, lovers and hopeful taxi drivers.

Less than a quarter of an hour later, he saw Racine saunter out through the sliding doors. She was taller than most of the passengers around her, and she had also changed her clothes. She saw him and instantly a large smile appeared on her face. Akulov moved towards her and was taken aback when she threw her arms around him.

"My love!"

Akulov accepted the hug, realising that it made the pair of them look less conspicuous than if they had not embraced. "Hello."

"Hello? Is that all I get?" Racine pulled away just enough to look up at him and kissed him on the lips. "You taste of coffee and chocolate."

"I bought a three pack of the local brand; I have two in my jacket pocket if you fancied some."

"You know how to treat a girl!" She took his hand. "Let's go."

"This way."

"Through the doors, really? How unusual."

Akulov said, "I like the outfit."

"Ruslan, I don't. We look like a Roxette tribute act."

This time Akulov did laugh. "True."

"The iceman cracks!"

Outside the late afternoon sun was warm but, thankfully, not burning as Akulov led Racine towards the waiting SUV. He opened the rear door for her, she climbed in, and he scooted around the other side. The engine was running, and the interior was icy cold.

Casey turned in his seat. "Sophie Racine, so good to meet you."

"Just Racine," she said.

"My mistake. And the hippy here is Mike Parnell."

Parnell nodded his head, his dark blond ponytail undulating. "Enchanté."

Racine said, "Parnell, do you have the address?"

"No, I was going to stop and ask a sympathetic local," Parnell replied as he pulled the Toyota SUV out of its parking spot. "It's going to be fifty minutes or so, if we take the *Túnel de Oriente*, depending on the traffic, which can be nuts."

"I need to make this clear," Racine said, "Richard Halbert is not a desk officer or an analyst. He is a weapons trained DGSE field operative, which is the reason he was posted to Bogotá, and why I seconded him for my mission. He is my responsibility, and I have the authority to either take him in or take him out."

"If he draws a gun on me, he's going down," Parnell stated.

"Fair point."

"My objective," Casey said, "which I assume is also yours, is to locate the photocopies of the passports so we can take direct action against the men travelling on them."

Akulov had no intention of getting in the middle of a pissing contest between the CIA and the DGSE, so he said, "They have a two-day head start. Any attack they have planned could be happening as we speak."

"And that's what worries me, Ruslan." Casey sighed.

"What about logistics?" Parnell said. "Think about it. They arrive on several flights, so as not to arouse suspicion, or in case they've been found out. They're also tired. So, they sleep, they eat and then of course they need to get their arms and munitions. Then they need to get to the target. I'd say we have perhaps another day, max, until the *mierda* hits the fan."

"Racine, have you any idea as to what the targets could be?"

"I have a list," she stated, "but it is based on data from previous attacks which were carried out by other terror networks. You are right, we need those passport details."

As they negotiated the traffic out of the airport complex, Parnell said, "I managed to get some real time satellite feed. There are two vehicles parked at the property."

"A Q7 and a Toyota Hi-Lux?" Racine asked.

"Yes, but how did you know?"

"They're on the Google Earth images, which means these vehicles are probably used regularly by whoever is guarding and or maintaining the property."

"Which means," Parnell continued, "that we have possible multiple hostiles."

"And as you said," Racine added, "anyone with a gun is fair game."

"True, absolutely true."

"Once we have the passport details, I'll send them to Langley," Casey stated.

"And I will have them sent to Paris," Racine said.

"Madrid and Paris would seem the most likely places to target," Akulov mused, "however if Espinosa and Orosco really did want to emulate ETA, they'll probably attack Spain."

"What worries me is that twelve men is a whole lot of lunatics," Casey stated.

"Twelve angry men," Parnell added.

"Thinking tactically," Casey continued, "it could be one team of twelve – which is unlikely unless they want to carry out a single spectacular. Two teams of six? Well, that's two targets. Four teams of three? Now that's possible. Six teams of two? That's six targets, which takes a lot of planning. I doubt it's going to be twelve individual attacks, that's lone gunman or jihadi tactics."

"These men are different," Racine said, "they do not have a religious motive. They are not motivated by some belief that what they are doing is for the good of their god or for mankind. They are driven by money and opportunity. These are disadvantaged young Colombian men who grew up with poverty and violence, were possibly forced to become gang members, who have now been offered the freedom to travel to Europe – with an EU passport, and receive, I imagine, what is for them, a huge financial payout for attacking a specific target or targets. Apart from the cash, what's to stop them from simply taking their passport and running off?"

"Nothing," Casey said.

Akulov understood Racine's train of thought but added, "What intel have we got to say they are going to attack immediately? An insurgency, carried out over time would surely achieve more."

"Sleeper cells," Parnell added, "although the longer they stay, the less likely they will want to say goodbye to easy EU living."

Casey sighed. "Look, people, we can all debate this till the cows come home. The simple fact is we need to get those passport details and see where they are."

The SUV lapsed into silence, and then Akulov felt Racine's hand on his. He looked her in the eyes, not quite knowing what to do.

"You said you had chocolate?"

Akulov dug into his chest pocket. "Here. It's quite dark."

"Like me," Racine said as she took it.

Casey's hand appeared by his headrest. "You have chocolate? Give."

Akulov handed him the last of his bars.

"This is not Hershey's."

"Here comes the tunnel," Parnell stated.

They entered the *Túnel de Oriente*, a five-mile toll road, which together with a second, shorter tunnel and nine viaducts spanning two valleys, connected Medellín to the airport. In some ways the route through the hills reminded Akulov of the coast road from France to Monaco, however the verdant greens of the rainforest were much starker. Akulov wondered if someday he'd be allowed just to travel for travel's sake, neither hunting nor being hunted? Even his few days in Dubai had been interrupted by Tishina, and that had led him to this.

"OK. Can you please tell me your plan for gaining access to the villa?"

"Racine," Casey said, "we are simply going to ring the bell and walk straight in."

"Really?"

"It worked in Buenos Aires," Akulov said.

Racine gave him a sharp look.

"As I explained to Wolf Six earlier, we've been to the place. Espinosa kept on inviting me. The last time was a little over two years ago, and unless they've massively refitted the place since then, I know the layout and exactly where this darn clock is."

"We also know the staff," Parnell added. "The security guard who owns the Q7 is called Matías and the gardener-cum-handyman who drives the truck is called Carlos."

"Matías," Casey said, "is former military, but very out of shape, and Carlos, well he's good with a wheelbarrow."

"OK. So, we just walk in and say what?"

"We just walk in and say we've come from Botero to see the Frenchman."

"And if Matías says no?"

Parnell chuckled. "The guy will be wasted by the time we get there, and if I hand him a bottle of Jack Daniels, he'll say 'Sí' to anything."

"You whacking Espinosa created a void, and nature abhors a void. Botero was trying to fill this, before Wolf Six slotted him. We know Maximiliano Lopez, the guy who ran the clan business in Medellín for Espinosa is going to make his move. So, it is reasonable to presume if there are any other *banditos* at the house, they are Max's men watching the place, and of course the Frenchman."

"So, we go in armed," Racine stated.

"Of course we do, this is Medellín not Monaco."

"Twenty-five minutes," Parnell noted, "and then it's showtime."

"There's two tactical packs in the back, I suggest you take what you want," Casey added, "pretend it's Christmas."

* * *

Leaving the *Túnel de Oriente* at its junction with route fifty-six, they headed south skirting the city on an undulating route with dense foliage and glimpses of jagged peaks on their left, and high-rise tower blocks on their right. Eventually the tower blocks gave out to much lower, yet far grander, structures as they approached the suburb of El Poblado. In the dying light of day, the place took on a dreamlike quality as the trees gradually became dark, amorphous shadows, whilst the mountains resembled solemn, dark giants and both seemed to be watching the upmarket homes twinkling like stars in the twilight. Racine now had a thin, ballistic vest under her denim jacket and a Glock 19 in her pocket. Akulov had the same, whilst both Americans had opted for the larger Glock 17. The treeline roads became narrower, and the streetlights less abundant as they entered the exclusive San Lucas enclave.

"Parnell, you drive straight in. I'll get out, then the rest of you can follow. No disrespect Racine, but most four-man hit squads are four men, so hopefully your presence will make any potential hostiles we encounter less so."

"Perhaps I should have worn a dress."

"I had the same idea," Parnell said, dryly, "but nothing goes with these boots."

Akulov said, "So where is the clock?"

"It's in the living room, directly opposite the fireplace. Don't worry, I'll lead us there."

The SUV slowed, and Parnell said, "We have arrived at our destination."

Turning right they came to a stop at a set of eight-foot-tall electric gates. Beyond this the villa stood illuminated by a series of uplighters. Parnell powered down the window and pressed a button on the intercom panel. There was no answer. He pressed again and this time it crackled and a voice said, "Sí?"

Parnell spoke in Spanish. "Hey, Matías, it's Parnell and Casey! I've got a bottle of Jack for you."

There was a pause then Matías replied, in English, "Parnell and Casey? And a bottle of Jack?"

"Yeah."

There was a buzzing and then the gates started to slide apart.

"I told ya."

Parnell manoeuvred the Fortuner through the space and onto the large brick drive. A light switched on over the front door and it opened to reveal a short, squat form wearing a white vest and brown slacks. The man stepped forward and placed his hand on his forehead like a sunshade so he could peer through the overpowering exterior lights.

"Parnell? Casey?"

Casey stepped out of the SUV, bottle in hand. "Don't forget Jack."

Racine watched as the veteran CIA operator walked towards the old guard, shook his hand and handed him the bottle. The pair exchanged some words, then a moment later Casey waved them to join him. Racine was out of the car, just behind Parnell, and casually moving towards the pair. Akulov, she noticed in her peripheral vision, hung back as though protecting the rear of an advancing military column.

"Who is this?" Matías asked, gawping at Racine.

"Jack's sister, Jill." Parnell said.

"You are always too funny."

"I'm Sophie," Racine said.

"Hello Sophie," Matías held out his hand, Racine shook it. It was clammy.

"Hello."

"And you?" Matías's eyes fell on Akulov.

"That's Wolf Six," Casey said casually.

Matías looked at Casey as though he was speaking in tongues then his eyes abruptly widened. "The Wolf Six?"

"Oh yes, we go way back."

"This truly is an honour."

"Thank you," Akulov said, curtly.

"Please, all of you come in. Casey, you want to see the Frenchman?"

"Yes, if I can."

"Max gave me orders to take his phone and to lock him in the guesthouse, but at this precise moment I have locked him in the gym. He is one of those crazy people who likes to run."

"He can run but he can't hide," Parnell said.

Bottle of Jack in his right hand, Matías gestured with his left. "This way."

The group followed Matías into the hallway. The interior of the house was a mixture of cream-coloured walls, beige tiles, and wooden flooring and display units stained in the most unnatural copper hue.

"You say Botero asked you to speak to the Frenchman?" Matías asked.

"He did. The guy has some information he needs," Casey confided, "information the CIA needs too."

"I see."

"Can I meet him in the lounge? You could bring him in?"

"Like a butler?"

"Exactly like a butler."

"For a bottle of Jack, I'll even dress like one. OK, you know where it is. I'll bring him."

Casey turned left, and Matías went right. Parnell followed Casey, again Akulov hung back.

"What are you thinking?" Racine asked the Ukrainian.

"It's too easy."

"Sometimes it doesn't have to be hard."

"I'll stay here in case Halbert makes a break for it."

"Agreed," Racine said and followed the two men from the CIA along the corridor.

They entered the lounge area. Here the colour scheme continued, it was as though, in Racine's opinion, the owner, or interior designer, had something wrong with their vision. A cream leather settee and armchair, again with orangish stained wood accents, sat in the middle of the space. A large marble fireplace sat in one corner and opposite this, in the other, was the grandfather clock. It too had received the "Orangina" treatment.

"Close the curtains," Casey instructed Parnell.

"Oui oui, mon Capitan," Parnell quipped as he quickly pulled the drapes across the floor-to-ceiling French windows.

Casey knelt by the clock and started to run his finger along its underside. "Tell me about the Frenchman."

"He was tasked with keeping Greiner's family safe. He sold them out to Botero, who then kidnapped them and killed the two local staff we had on the security detail."

"So, are you going to punch his ticket?" Parnell asked.

"If he hasn't got any intel for us. I can't believe no one, apart from Espinosa and Orosco Senior, knew about the planned attacks."

There was a loud click from the clock. Racine watched on as the bottom slid forward. Inside was a space comparable to a standard sized suitcase.

Casey reached his hand inside, took out the contents and stood. "Now let's see what we've got here."

He crossed to the settee and sat, placing a thin envelope on the matching coffee table, then a second much thicker next to it. Racine took a seat next to him, whilst Parnell crossed the room and leant against the fireplace. Casey pulled out a bundle of letter-sized sheets from the envelope, which had been fastened together with a paperclip, removed the clip then fanned them out across the table. The top sheet was a printed list. Racine felt her pulse race as she was sure it was a list of passport numbers, and names. The next twelve sheets were individual black-and-white photocopies of the photograph page of Spanish passports.

"Bingo," Casey said. "I'll scan these and email them to Grillot and cc you."

"Agreed," Racine said.

Rather than a satphone, this time Casey retrieved an iPhone from his pocket, popped on a pair of thin, frameless reading glasses and started the scanning process.

"Get to it, Professor," Parnell said.

"You'll need a pair too, just give it a few years."

"OK, Boomer."

There was a noise from outside, sounds like very angry French. Sophie stood and exited the room. Akulov was walking towards her, pushing the rogue DGSE officer, whose right arm was twisted behind his back. He was wearing a pair of running shorts, T-shirt, and his trainers squeaked on the polished, wooden flooring. The man's eyes met hers and she saw a micro expression of terror flash across his face. Sometimes, she mused, a reputation was worth it.

"No..." Halbert said.

"Oui," Racine replied.

"Racine?"

"C'est moi."

Akulov nodded to a door to the left, Racine returned the nod, and the Ukrainian marched the Frenchman into the space. Racine followed them to find herself in a games room. To her direct right, taking up the corner space was a fully stocked bar, to the left sat a card table topped with green baize. Past that, a full-sized pool table took up the other end of the room and, directly in front of her, by the window, was another settee set, this one in a grey suede and thankfully wood free.

"Have a seat," Akulov said, pushing the Frenchman towards the settee.

"How very considerate," Halbert replied.

Akulov turned and addressed Racine, "I'll be outside, if you need me."

"Thank you, but I won't."

Akulov shut the door and left.

"Are you part of this?" Halbert asked. Racine remained silent, her eyes boring into his. "I was kidnapped in Bogotá. I've been held here against my will." Halbert raised the hem of his Puma T-shirt and used it to mop the sweat from his brow. Racine noted his well-defined stomach muscles.

"Who was holding you, that fat alcoholic?"

"There were others. Thugs with guns. They ordered me to not attempt to leave."

"Nonsense. They told you to stay if you wanted your money, isn't that the case?"

"W… what money?"

"Or were they going to pay you in gold? Was that it?"

"I don't know what you are talking about."

"You know the last time I encountered a traitor to France and the DGSE, it didn't end well for him."

"Look, I'm tired, and I'm thirsty. They've kept me here for three days."

"Two."

"Can we just go?"

"What, you don't want your money? I thought that was what it was all about for traitors who weren't doing it for ideological reasons?"

Halbert sighed, as though to show he was either disinterested or tired, or perhaps bored. Racine assumed it was a mixture of all three, or simply petulance. "Tell me what you want, Racine."

"What I want is your severed head on a platter, Halbert. What I need is for you to tell me everything you know about the operation."

Halbert sat back in the settee, and spread his arms along the back, as though he was utterly relaxed. Racine knew it was reverse psychology. "What operation would that be?"

"The one where your paymaster, Pablo Botero and his boss Espinosa, sent twelve terrorists to the EU."

"I don't know what you're talking about."

"Bullshit," Racine shook her head slowly. "OK, amuse me. Tell me what happened in Bogotá?"

"I was guarding the woman and her child—"

"Their names are Catherine and Nairo."

"I was guarding them, when suddenly Felipe opened the door and let Botero and his men in. He and Amira were working for him. I tried to stop them, but I couldn't. They took the woman and child and then killed Felipe and Amira."

"Where is your injury?"

"My what?"

"On the video Botero sent me, you were lying on the floor injured, there was a pool of blood around your torso. So where is the injury? You've just been dragged from the gym, how can an injured man run on a treadmill?"

"He knocked me out, hit me on the head."

"So you've been training with a concussion?"

"I feel better now."

"Why didn't he kill you?"

"Perhaps, Racine, because like you I am a French intelligence officer."

"And what were Felipe and Amira? Chopped liver?"

"They were local hires."

"Ah, so locals are what, not as important?"

"I wouldn't put it like that."

"OK. So what happened next?"

"I woke up here."

"You know, when I was growing up, I used to watch a lot of British television to improve my English. I learnt a lot of slang. One of my favourites came from a children's story-telling show. The British use it when they don't believe a tale they are being told. I'm going to use it now. Jackanory!"

"What?"

"Listen to me, you *fils de pute*, if you want to stay alive you are going to tell me exactly what I want to know."

"*Nique tes morts*, Racine!"

Halbert's left shoulder dropped and in a motion that was so quick, Racine almost missed it, the Frenchman swung a 9mm pistol up from behind the back of the settee. Hand still arching to acquire its target he squeezed the trigger, once, twice, three times. The first round went wide and slammed into the wall to his right, the second missed Racine's left thigh by the smallest of margins and, hand still rising, the third round slammed into her abdomen. Racine was jerked backwards, past the edge of the bar and into the closed door with a thud. Winded, she lay there for a second. Halbert rose to his feet, with what Racine could now see was a Beretta M9 held out in a two-handed grip. He advanced towards her. The door flew open and Akulov rushed into the space. He fired a single shot which slammed into Halbert's right forearm, jerking him sideways and biomechanically forcing his hold on the Beretta to break.

"Stop!" Racine commanded.

Akulov stood statue still, his Glock trained on the Frenchman's head. "OK. Why?"

"Because he's mine!" Racine pulled herself to her feet, her stomach was on fire, but she knew the vest, whilst still permitting a certain extent of blunt-force trauma, had prevented the 9mm round from penetrating her skin. Removing her Glock from her pocket she placed it on the top of the bar. To Akulov she said, "Wait outside."

"No."

"I said wait outside, dammit!"

Akulov backed away, a concerned expression on his face as he shut the door.

"*Enculé, tu vas me le payer!*" Racine looked down at Halbert who was holding his right arm with a shocked expression on his face.

"I… shot you…"

"And he shot you, *Trou du cul,* and now I'm going to kill you with my bare hands."

Halbert pushed himself to his feet, letting go of his right arm, letting the blood run and drip onto the floor. "Come on then, *poufiasse*!"

Halbert advanced, bouncing on the balls of his feet, hands up, unclenched but ready to either make fists, or to grab any incoming blow. Racine knew the fighting style; she had been trained in it too. He was attempting to back her into the corner, he threw out a tentative left foot, then immediately swung out his right fist. He was faster than she had anticipated, yet Racine managed to step inside it and shoot out her booted foot at his left knee. But Halbert jumped back, and the boot just grazed him. He then fired a pair of jabs directly into her stomach, which Racine did nothing to defend as the Kevlar would take the impact. In turn Racine swung her left elbow into the side of his head, connecting heavily, and he stumbled sideways. He kept his guard up to protect his head as he attempted to shake off the elbow strike. Racine went low, targeting the knee again. This time her boot made contact and there was an audible crack as the joint hyperextended, causing Halbert to howl and his leg to collapse. He twisted as he fell, landing heavily on his face.

Racine stood over the traitor and watched him for several seconds, before she drew her foot back to slam it into his side, but Halbert, nostrils flared, eyes wide and nose bloodied, grabbed her boot and rolled, causing her to crash to the floor, winded.

Halbert was now on top of her and immediately forced his good forearm across Racine's throat. Leaning forward, he put all his weight onto her larynx attempting to crush it, whilst his right fist now slammed into her face. "*Tu as merdé*, Racine! And now you are going to die."

Eyes starting to bulge, Racine noticed the edges of her vision start to grey out. She struggled to move her shoulders, but he moved with her. She bucked for all she was worth and then managed to clamp his damaged knee with her leg and squeeze it. Halbert grimaced in pain and recoiled just enough for Racine to twist her shoulders, making his forearm slide away from her throat.

Using all her strength, Racine managed to raise both shoulders and snap her head forward. Her forehead made heavy contact with the Frenchman's nose and there was an audible, and satisfying crack as the cartilage splintered. Halbert immediately pushed himself away and lay on his back with his hands over his face.

Racine rolled in the opposite direction and got up on her haunches. She pushed her long hair away from her face, and fixed her eyes on the man she was about to kill.

Halbert removed his hands from his face and roared with anger. He sat up and attempted to shuffle backwards towards the pool table. Racine watched, let him go, let him tire himself out. His eyes now reddened with rage and his face a bloody mess, fixed upon her. Racine held his gaze and slowly, and deliberately, got to her feet. Halbert reached the table and used the nearest of its heavy, carved wooden legs to hoist himself back up to his good leg. He stood, left leg bent, swollen, right forearm crimson and face almost unrecognisable. Racine collected her Glock from the bar.

"Alright. I give up. You let me live and I will tell you everything."

"The issue is, Halbert, that I don't think you know anything. In fact, I think you know nothing at all."

"I know about Durand. I will tell you all about him."

"By now Durand will have been collected by a security detail and taken on board an Air France flight in handcuffs."

"OK... OK... the men are going to hit Madrid."

Racine felt her neck with her left hand, there was going to be bruising, she'd have to wear a scarf. "Jackanory."

"It's true! I swear to you. There are two targets in Madrid."

"Which are?"

"No. I want a deal. I want a deal signed by the French President. I want immunity!"

"No." Racine raised the Glock and shot Halbert in his right shoulder. The Frenchman screamed and fell back against the pool table. "You tell me now, or the next round goes in your brain."

"You... you... are crazy!"

"Oui. The first target is?"

"The first target is the railway station..."

"Which one?"

"The main one... I... I need... help..."

"And the second target is?"

"The... the... sec... the second target..."

The glass in the window exploded inwards and instantaneously Halbert's head jerked sideways as a high calibre round tore through it. A second round zipped past Racine and tore into the wood behind the bar. Racine threw herself to the floor as more rounds peppered the room, tearing large holes through whatever they hit.

And then the lights went off.

She heard the door creak open. A voice she recognized as being Akulov shouted, "Racine! Racine!"

"I'm OK."

"Come to me."

Without replying, Racine commando crawled towards the open door. Outside in the inky darkness, she could vaguely make out Akulov's face. He said, "We need to get out."

"No shit."

"Six!" Parnell called out. "Get to the back of the house. Exfil via the garden."

"Copy that!" Akulov replied. "Let's go."

Racine rose to her feet, then keeping low, she followed the black form of Akulov down the slightly less dark hallway. Keeping close to the wall, they turned right into the kitchen and could now see the sky through the folding glass door which led to the terrace outside. Two thin, red shafts of light cut through the darkness behind them and then suppressed rounds tore into the wall by Racine's shoulder. She went prone and slithered towards the large island in the centre of the room. She saw red dots appear on the island in front of her and move to the right, and then there was footfall from behind. Whoever was attacking the villa seemed to be well equipped and well drilled. Racine turned onto her back and then abruptly sat up. She saw dancing shafts of red lights and opened fire, blindly, in the darkness towards them. The muzzle flash caused as each round left the barrel of her Glock ruined what little night vision her eyes had acquired, but it had the effect of making the gunmen back up and take cover around the corner.

"This way." Akulov's hand grabbed her shoulder and dragged her, feet scrabbling against the wooden flooring, around the side of the island, where they both crouched with their backs against the cold marble.

"How many?" Racine asked.

"No idea. One sniper, four-man assault team? OK? Move!"

In grey moonlight, Racine rose to her feet and, bent almost double, hurried out of the large, folding glass doors and into the outside terrace. Moments later, she heard the crash and smash of breaking glass as rounds impacted the doors and then the bark of unsuppressed rounds fired in return. Across the lawn and half-hidden behind a thick-trunked palm tree, Parnell beckoned to her. Rising to her full height she now sprinted over the damp grass. She reached the palm and took cover behind it. Moments later more unsuppressed rounds sounded within the villa and then Akulov rushed towards them.

"Casey's hit," Parnell said. "I chucked him over the back wall. We need to follow."

Without another word, the two intelligence operatives and the professional assassin, moved through the thick foliage of several other trees, towards the wall. It was no more than six foot in height and covered with a thick, knotted vine, which meant that even a child could climb it. Seconds later the trio landed on the other side.

"You… took your… damn time," Casey said.

"Where are you hit?" Racine asked.

"Left thigh. It's a through and through but it hurts like a bastard."

In the moonlight Racine now noticed the material tied tightly around Casey's thigh.

Parnell said, "Six, you take point – lead us out of here. Racine, you are tail end Charlie."

Racine nodded, although she was not ex-military, she understood the terms.

"C'mon, Boomer." Parnell hauled Casey to his feet, then bent forward and hoisted him into a fireman's carry.

* * *

Weapon up, Akulov proceeded down the dark garden. The house ahead was in darkness, as though its occupants were either hiding or out, it was too early for anyone to be asleep. The lawn was damp underfoot, the aftermath of the day's humidity, or perhaps just the villa's sprinkler system, and it wasn't flat. His right foot twisted as he missed a dip in the grass.

The elevation of the lawn abruptly changed, dropping down towards the pool, which did not have its lights on. Akulov paused and listened. He could hear nothing except for the clicking of the nocturnal insects, and a very distant police siren. Akulov looked back, Parnell was still carrying Casey, and behind them Racine was keeping an eye on the rear. Facing the house again, he continued to advance forward. Reaching the end of the lawn he waited again on the terrace. The house was still silent, and he could now make out blinds drawn at the kitchen windows. He moved to the left, following the wall of the house and arriving at the side of the building. Up ahead a single streetlight cast a dim light across the front garden and the road beyond. Ahead and to his left, and with a drive leading to it, was a small, single-storey construction. It had to be a garage.

Akulov advanced towards the garage and could now just

make out the edge of a fountain on a round patch of grass, in the middle of the turning circle. Overhead, the cloudless night sky sparkled and all around him the wealthy neighbourhood was silent. It seemed as though the attack had gone unnoticed or, if it had been, no one wanted to acknowledge it. Akulov peered into the garage through a small window and saw that there were two cars inside. One was under a cover, and by the look of it was a sports car and the other was an old looking, boxy saloon car. It looked early nineties, but it was too dark to see exactly what it was. Akulov moved to the door and noticed that it had what seemed to be a sophisticated alarm box and keypad attached to it. He wasn't going to risk it.

Akulov followed the drive in the direction of the streetlight and arrived at the front gates. They had no lock, so he pushed them open. Out on the street, he quickly moved into the shadows at the side of the gate. Looking both up and down the street, Akulov saw it was deserted. He darted back inside to see Parnell placing Casey on the grass, in the shadows by the front wall. Racine was slowly approaching from the back of the house, turning to look back every few paces.

Casey said, "How long until your guy arrives, Mike?"

"He said give him forty, but he'll be here sooner than that. So, I reckon we've got a good ten to wait."

"Who is your guy?" Akulov asked.

"Local talent, someone who will drive us outta here for a few grand."

"They are not following us," Racine said as she joined them. "It appears they wanted the house and not us."

"That'll be a takeover then," Casey said. "Looks like the Clan Del Oro is losing more than its management."

"Halbert told me the target is Madrid central railway station,"

Racine said, "he was about to tell me what the second target was when his head exploded."

"That's what keeping a secret will do to a man," Parnell stated.

"Whilst you were 'wrestling'," Casey noted, "I sent the scans of the passports to our people. If they've been used, we'll find out soon."

"I'm going out front to wait for my guy," Parnell started to walk away, "try not to get shot again while I'm gone."

Casey sighed. "What a mess, and I don't get a darn medal for being clipped."

"We need to get to Madrid," Akulov said.

"I'll lend you a jet," Casey replied, pulling his satphone from the pouch pocket of his jacket. "Take Parnell with you."

15

UNDISCLOSED LOCATION, NEAR MADRID, SPAIN

Ángel Martinez's fee had been guaranteed. It was being held by a Swiss bank, as had been José's demand. It would be released into a numbered account automatically in three days' time unless a specific cancellation code was delivered to the bank. That code was only known to three men: Franco Orosco and his two sons. José smirked, even in death he was punishing his father by taking his money, money he knew would otherwise go to his young stepmother to spend on her increasing number of high-end handbags. The team José had trained, under the guise of Martinez, had been in transit at the time of both sets of assassinations and had only learnt of the deaths a day later. The murders, however, had further inspired the team, who were committed to the cause, or so they had told him. All José cared about was that they continued with the planned operation.

José pushed his hair back from his face and studied his reflection in the mirror. He had let his stubble grow just enough that it now resembled a trendy, freshly trimmed, beard. He unscrewed the lid from his pot of hair wax, pasted a reasonably sized amount onto his palm, which he rubbed to warm it up before applying it to his hair. Once he had finished, he studied the result as he washed his hands in the sink. He nodded, he was happy, he looked different enough from the photograph in the passport he had used to enter the country to confuse any cursory check.

Leaving the bathroom on the first floor of the barn conversion, José took the stairs down. He had chosen the place specifically for both its rural location and its size. It was important that the entire team stay under one roof and not be observed when they did so. The twelve men were assembled and waited for him, eager nervousness in their faces. He understood what they were going through and remembered his first operation with his police unit. He moved to the centre of the large, open-plan space and stood with his hands on his hips. It was time for him to deliver the speech he had been rehearsing, the speech that would rouse the troops and make them ready to fight.

"Men, we have come a long way, geographically, physically and mentally. When I first met you all six months ago, you were a worthless bunch of dogs!" He noted a couple of smiles. "Now you remain dogs, but dogs of war! What we are going to do tomorrow, make no mistake about it, is the first strike in a war against those who oppose our existence. The government of Spain, they are the ones who have held you and our country down, yet we are the lucky ones. We can live freely, yet poorly in Colombia. But what of our brothers who have battled, using peaceful means only, for decades and decades to gain independence from Spain and their criminal partner France? They are prevented from speaking their own language! Like our forefathers in Colombia, they were forced to speak the language of the invaders, but at least our forebears remained Colombian. But our Basque brothers and sisters, they had to pledge allegiance to Spain or France. Well, that is not good enough any more! That must not continue to happen! You all know me, you know that I am like you, I came from the poorest of the poor, and I was like you before I joined the Spanish Legion. But let me tell you, and I have spoken of this before, my eyes were open, not to the opportunities that Spain gave me, but to the opportunities that Spain has taken, not just from me but from you, your parents, grandparents and their grandparents. Now we will take it back! We will take Basque back for the Basque!"

The assembled men cheered and hooted, as José knew they would. He had been like them once, that much was true, but unlike them he had moved on. He was no longer a pawn. The money they had been paid by the clan would have set them up for life in rural Colombia but wouldn't last them a year in Madrid. They were expendable, in fact as terrorists attacking the capital city of an EU member state, they were already dead. Now José let himself smile, not because he was proud of the twelve men he had trained, and brainwashed, but because he was anticipating what he was going to do with the five million euros which would drop into the bank account he had set up.

"Tonight there shall be no time for partying, today is not the time for that. Nor is tomorrow, or the day after that. But the night after that will be a different matter. In three days' time we shall celebrate! Once we bring the city of Madrid to its knees, we will party like never before, and this will be only the beginning of the war! This is our first step to being free!"

* * *

International Airspace, somewhere over the North Atlantic

Including the two pilots there were just five people on the CIA Gulfstream G550, kindly loaned to them by Casey, as it tore towards Spain. Akulov had no qualms about accepting the assistance of the Agency, even though Racine had been far less happy with the idea. This however was the fastest way, in the limited time given, to get to Europe and potentially halt the terror attack. Akulov didn't know who else Casey had alerted regarding the potential attacks, and frankly did not care, his sole concern was stopping those who were attempting to carry them out. After all these years of state sponsored and then freelance assassinations, he realised that he may finally be undertaking a contract for the greater good. The jet was eerily silent save for the gentle snores of Parnell, who had crashed out on the settee. Akulov shuddered as he remembered his own crash six months before, he wouldn't be using that or any other "in air" settee to sleep on for a while. Racine dropped into the seat opposite him, she had a can of Fanta in one hand, and a Pepsi in the other. She handed him the cola.

"Tell me about the train," Akulov said.

"The train?"

"Where we met."

"Ah, that train. Oui."

"So?" Akulov popped open his drink.

"The Spanish Environment Minister was in the next carriage. He was travelling to a meeting with his French counterpart. I had received intel two days before that an unknown group planned to assassinate him. My superiors and the Spanish authorities didn't believe it was credible, as they had received no other verified intelligence."

"Yet it was."

"I am rarely wrong."

"I know."

"I was not sanctioned to be there." She opened her Fanta, took a mouthful and grimaced. "Why were you on the train?"

"Travelling. Attempting to improve my Spanish."

"Did you?"

"I am never satisfied."

"Nor am I, which is probably why I am single."

"Is it too late to say I am sorry about your dog?"

Racine nearly spat out her Fanta. "There was no bloody dog!"

"Bloody dog? Are you trying to be British?"

"I spent two years doing A Levels at a boarding school in England. It left its mark."

"That's why your accent is so good, there is no trace of French."

"And you sound like you are from Washington D.C."

Akulov nodded. "Did you know who I was?"

"I thought you were British."

"Like James Bond."

"I knew you were definitely not James Bond; he would have assisted me with my case. You were not at all gallant."

"I am sorry."

"You've now said 'sorry' twice in the space of a minute, perhaps you really are British?"

"Perhaps."

"On the train, I was attempting to assess all possible threats. The hit squad was very obvious, almost amateur or reckless or overconfident. You seemed, well, you seemed a little odd."

"Odd?"

"Odd, out of the ordinary. I knew you were not a regular passenger."

"Yet I was."

"I shall rephrase that. You were not a regular person, yet you were a passenger. Now that I know you, I know that you are odd, full stop."

"Merci."

"This is an odd conversation, Ruslan. At any given time, you could become an enemy of the Republic of France. If you attack a French national."

Akulov remembered the last Frenchman he had killed, the man had been a menace to French society. "I understand."

"However, here we sit. Each trusting the other with our own lives."

"The enemy of my enemy is my friend."

"Am I your friend?"

"You are not my enemy."

Racine took another swig from her can. "This stuff is awful; I would much prefer Orangina. Tell me about Tishina."

"Tishina?"

"Your controller."

"She is not my controller."

"I apologise. Your broker."

"What would you like to know?"

"Everything."

"That I will not tell you."

"Very well, I will tell you what I know."

"Please do so."

"She is legendary. She was one of the GRU's top operators. She also was loaned to the KGB, and then she moved from covert field operations to strategic duties. This included aiding in the selection and formation of the Werewolves, before leaving and taking you for her Lone Wolf project."

Akulov frowned, "Lone Wolf" was an ultra-classified program that, as far as he was aware, only three people knew the existence of: him, Tishina and the man who, at the time, had been the head of the GRU.

Racine continued. "Then she used this as the basis for her

'freelance' work, which of course initially was sanctioned by the Kremlin."

Akulov said, attempting to suppress his annoyance, "I have not accepted orders from the Kremlin for over a decade."

"Yes. I know," Racine replied calmly. "Other operators took those jobs. The Kremlin is your enemy, as they are mine. So, we are friends."

Akulov picked up his can of Pepsi and drank. He felt uncomfortable and was not sure what he was supposed to say.

"You had a relationship with her, didn't you?"

"I have a relationship with her now, as you say, she is my broker." Akulov took a mouthful of cola.

"That is not what I meant, and you know it. You and her were, how shall I put it, 'an item'. You were shagging."

Akulov tried not to choke on his cola, "Shagging?"

"You don't know the word?"

"I do, but I've not heard it used for a while."

"So?"

"So, what?"

"Is that a yes?"

"Why do you want to know? Is it so important?"

"Due diligence."

"I see," Akulov said, but he didn't.

"I have always wanted to meet her." Racine asked, "Have you ever refused a contract from Tishina?"

"I have but not often."

"This is because of your moral kill code."

"It is."

"That is to be commended."

"There is nothing honourable in killing another human being."

"I know. Yet you and I are both killers."

Akulov said, "What are we doing chatting here, simply killing time?"

"Yes, and no," Racine leaned forward and lowered the level of her voice. "I know how lonely you are, Ruslan. I am the same. There is no one I can talk to. Even at the DGSE, if I open up to them, they are likely to send me for a psychological evaluation, but at least I do have the support of a team, and an organisation behind me."

And then Akulov understood. "Are you trying to recruit me?"

Racine fixed her eyes squarely on his. "Yes."

"No, thank you."

"You haven't heard my offer."

"I do not need to. It does not matter."

"My department needs another 'specialist'."

"I am sure there are many French specialists you could take on."

"Like Martin Basson?"

Akulov's eyes narrowed on hearing the name of the operator known as "The Bang Bang Man", who had also once worked for Tishina. "There must be others, former or current Legionnaires like him."

"I need someone I can trust. An operator with no current allegiance to flag or state. Someone whose only allegiance is justice."

"You sound like you need a superhero."

"So, what are you, Wolf Six?"

"What I am, Sophie Racine, is tired."

She nodded at the can of cola. "You should have slept, that caffeine is not going to help you."

"I know, but the last time I fell asleep on a Gulfstream jet, it crashed."

Racine's eyes widened, and Akulov realised he had shared

too much. She said, "I am good at what I do, you are too. I know we think the same way. This is why we should work together."

"What are we doing now?"

"I mean on a permanent basis, Ruslan. I am officially sanctioned to offer you a position in The Department."

"Which I am respectfully declining."

Racine sighed. "Where do you get this stubborn streak from? Your mother or your father."

"My grandmother."

"She was the woman who raised you, wasn't she?"

Akulov saw no reason to lie. "How did you know that?"

"Intuition. I'm guessing you lost your parents, and she took their place."

"Yes," Akulov replied as he started to feel the cold shadow of grief pass over him again. "She was all I had, and then she died."

"We all have to go sometime."

"It was not her time. She was murdered."

Racine seemed shocked. "How?"

"The Moscow apartment bombings. At the time it was blamed on the Chechens, so Tishina sent me to Chechnya."

The interior of the jet became quiet as both assassins drank, and Parnell continued to snore.

Racine said, "We have all lost someone. My aunt was a DGSE officer. She was murdered by her boyfriend – he was a Russian sleeper – in her own department. She is the reason I joined the DGSE. I wanted revenge."

"You and I are not normal people, are we?"

Racine said, "No Ruslan, we certainly are not."

A phone rang. It was Parnell's. He immediately sat and pulled it from his pocket. "Parnell?"

"Could be Casey," Racine said.

"Could be anyone," Akulov replied.

"How's the leg?" Parnell turned around. "It is Casey and I'm putting him on speaker." Parnell got up from his seat then sat down next to Racine, facing Akulov. "Go ahead Vince."

"We got hits on twelve of the names," Casey sounded out of breath, "they all entered Spain within twenty-four hours of each other. So, we found out each passport had a valid ESTA! They flew in small groups to the US via Bogotá, Medellín, and Cartagena. Landed at different destinations, stayed overnight then entered Spain via Madrid, Barcelona, Málaga, Valencia and Bilbao."

Racine asked, "Have you shared this with the French and the Spanish authorities?"

"Of course. They've fed their passport photos into their facial recognition system. Europol are now involved as is Spain's National Intelligence Centre."

Akulov said, "The Spanish will close the railway station, they'll have to, they can't risk even a single life being taken."

"Of course," Casey replied, "which is why we are going to have to find these banditos before they launch their attack."

Akulov said, "You got hits on twelve? Who is missing?"

"Their leader."

"What's the situation on him?" Parnell asked.

"We now have a face for Ángel Martinez, and some background. Would you believe he was trained by us?"

"Us?" Parnell repeated.

"He's former Spanish Legion and was part of their 19th Legion Special Operations Battalion – as it was known then. Being the 'Good Ole Uncle Sam', we trained them for the Spanish government at Fort Bragg."

"Shit, so we've got twelve irregulars led by one real deal?"

"Yep. The issue is that none of the pinged passports have photos which bear a close enough resemblance to him to be

Ángel Martinez. Neither do the as yet unused ones. So, either he didn't go with the rest of his team, or he's had some type of surgery, or we've got the wrong man."

Akulov started to process the puzzle, he knew he had the answer or at least part of it somewhere.

Casey continued. "Look he, whoever and wherever he is, is one man. We've got eyes looking for the twelve. That's all I've got now, all we can do is wait for any pings and, once you land, get you within visual of the railway station. Right, bye." Casey ended the call.

Racine sat forward and put her head in her hands. "They close the station, they stop this attack. But where the next attack will happen, we don't know."

"If they don't attack their primary, they'll move on straight to their secondary," Parnell noted, "and we don't have a damn clue where that is!" Parnell yawned. "I'm going to go back to resting my eyes, I suggest you get some too."

Racine moved seats to the other side of the plane, took a blanket and lay down. Akulov stayed resolutely staring out of the window at the clouds below them.

* * *

Madrid, Spain

The hotel room was booked using his second Spanish passport, like the one he had used to enter and then leave the US, this was also genuine, and also not from the same batch as those given to the men he had trained. This was the first time José Orosco had been to Madrid since he was a child, and he found it overwhelming. It wasn't the volume of tourists, or the number of shops, nor was it the sheer luxury of the Four Seasons Hotel he was staying at, it was the absence of the dirt, poverty and the fear that he felt when he ventured to cities in his home country.

He had been brought up to be a proud Argentinian, and his country was one of the safest in South America, yet, he had never wholly felt as though he belonged. Standing on the balcony of his suite, he surveyed the street below. The city looked like a giant model made by a gifted architect, not because the buildings were new or outlandish but because the symmetry was just too perfect. He watched people pass below, going about their daily business without a care in the world, they were the elderly, businesspeople, the young and of course the tourists. All moving, either enjoying or simply using the city.

José had not partaken of any narcotics now for twenty-four hours, neither the uppers nor the downers, and this was usually the time that he would feel the need to start snorting again. Although he felt decidedly shaky, he had to admit that those urges for more had not as yet manifested themselves. He took a sip from the large glass of expensive sherry the hotel had provided him with and enjoyed its sweet, full-bodied richness. It was not something he drank, in fact he could not actually remember the last time he had imbibed sherry, but he realised he liked it. In fact, he liked it a lot. He emptied his glass and wandered back inside his room. José decided it was time to pretend to be a tourist, he still had two days until the attacks he had rescheduled were to take place, so essentially he was a free man, and this free man wanted an experience.

His brother would enjoy this place, José thought and picked up his phone from the bed. He'd just send him a WhatsApp to see what he was doing... José suddenly felt cold. He sat on the edge of the bed, his hand shaking as the wave of grief struck him. His brother was dead. There would be no sending and receiving of messages. Not today, not ever. José dropped his phone and reached over to the credenza and grabbed the bottle of Gonzalez Byass. He looked out of the balcony window at the blue sky above and said, his eyes watering, "Here's to you, Hector!"

The sherry slipped down his throat so easily, it soothed his suffering and also made him come to a realisation. His brother would have wanted him to carry on with his life, to take over the entirety of the family business and become a success story.

The family business, José thought, as he sipped his sherry straight from the bottle. The transportation business was highly profitable, and he had a team who oversaw that, it was the other business which he would need to devote his time to, and that was the importation of gold from the Clan. But what about the overarching plan that his brother and father had devised, and the reason he was now half-drunk in a Madrid hotel room? What about the fight for the independence of their ancestral home, the Basque country? Had he forgotten all about that?

People died in wars, and generally the more people that died on one side, the quicker that side capitulated. From his reckoning, all they had to do was kill multiples of thirteen to make this first incursion into enemy territory worthwhile, meaningful and impactful and yet the people... the people who would die and suffer, were they the enemy? Were they in any way at all responsible for Spain not recognising the Basque's right for self-determination? José knew of his lineage, of course, he knew that his grandparents had been highly active members of the Basque Nationalist party, he knew they had fled Spain for Argentina after Franco took power in 1939. And he also knew his grandparents had wired funds to help ETA's formation two decades later. This was family history, this is why his father had started the whole program, and this was why his brother had too, with noble intentions, wanted to fight for the people to right the historical wrongs. But did any of it matter? Did any of it make a difference?

What would happen if the old territory of the Basque really became a country? José didn't have any answers to these questions, and all he had seen since he had arrived in Spain was the evidence of everyday, regular people living in a peaceful, democratic society, and who was he, who even had his father and his brother been, to deem it necessary to destroy this? He took another swig of sherry. Did the Scots have an insurgent force demanding freedom from the English? Not for several hundred years at least, but what they did have were politicians, who discussed matters like adults and they had internationally recognised referendums. But his brother, the politician in waiting who would have brought about this change, was now dead. And he had been killed by an instrument of one of the opposing imperialist invaders, Sophie Racine of the Republic of France's DGSE.

And that was when José felt as though he had been hit by a lightning bolt.

If he did not let the attacks proceed, that would dishonour his father, and his brother, but would they be dishonoured further if the world knew they had been the masterminds of a terrorist plot? Yet no one knew of their involvement. His father was dead, his brother was dead and Espinosa, the only man in Colombia who had known that he was not Ángel Martinez, was also unhappily rotting away somewhere. He took another swig of sherry, realising he had perhaps one move left, as he decided he knew what he had to do, it would be a way of killing two birds with one stone, and if it worked, he would be able to leave Madrid undamaged and have revenged his brother's murder. Picking his phone back up, he used the internet to search for the details he needed. He found a number, switched on his VPN, choosing Colombia, and called it. The ringtone sounded odd to him, but the phone did connect.

The voice was female, the tone was curt and the language

was French. "Direction Générale de la Sécurité Extérieure, bonjour."

José didn't speak French, so he replied in English. "Hello. I have some important information for Sophie Racine."

The woman switched to English. "This is the Direction Générale de la Sécurité Extérieure – the French foreign intelligence service. We do not have any Sophie Racine here."

"Yes, you do. She is currently in Colombia working with DGSE officers Paul Durand and Richard Halbert. I have information about an imminent terrorist attack in Madrid. There are two targets. I need to speak to her, immediately."

"I see," the woman replied. José could now hear a low hissing on the line and a click, and then the woman spoke again. "Putting you through."

There was another pause, more unusual noises, then a man's voice said, "This is Colonel Grillot, to whom am I speaking?"

José took a deep breath, and then started to talk. "I asked for Sophie Racine."

"I am her director. Who are you?"

"Listen to me. There are two targets. The first is the railway station – Madrid Puerta de Atocha, and the second is..." José's words started to slow as now he saw before him, like spectres, both his father and his brother. His brother was shaking his head, and his father was silently mouthing the word "traitor."

"And the second target? The second target is?" Grillot's voice sounded in his ear.

José felt his whole body start to jerk, as though an unseen force was shaking him. He screwed his eyes up tight, but he could hear the word in his head, "Traitor... traitor... TRAITOR!"

He opened his eyes. He was alone in his hotel room once more. Yet now he realised the monumental error he had been on the verge of making. He was standing on a precipice, he mentally took a firm step back, at the same time as physically pushing up from his bed. He strode to the window, head now held high. "You asked me who I am, Grillot? I will tell you exactly who I am. I am the man who is going to kill Sophie Racine! I am the man who is going to bring the Spanish authorities to their knees! The Basque demands independence!"

Before the French intelligence director could reply further, José ended the call. He had come so close to making a mistake, but he hadn't, and now he never would. He had two missions to carry out. The first was of course to attack Madrid, and the second was to murder the French puta. José took his jacket from the back of the chair, found the small, plastic ziplock bag, tore it open and hungrily plunged his tongue inside, coating it completely with powder.

16

MADRID, SPAIN

Akulov shut the door of his hotel room behind him and kicked off his boots. He was dog-tired after not sleeping on the transatlantic flight but knew there was no time for any now. In the Spetsnaz he had been issued with uppers to combat fatigue and had been loathe to take them as they had the side effect of making his trigger finger jitter, which was no good for a sniper. Now he would have gladly popped a pair of pills.

He padded across the thick piled carpet to the cabinet which concealed the minibar and opened it. Inside was the usual selection of sugary confectionery, and even more highly sugared soft drinks plus, of course, a selection of international beers and branded spirits in miniature bottles. He selected a Snickers bar, a can of regular Coke and sat on the end of the bed gazing out of his window at the sky and the cityscape beyond. Ripping open the chocolate bar he took a large bite, then he cracked the ring-pull of the Coke can and had a swig. As far as energy food went, it wasn't bad and at least he wasn't counting calories. He ate the rest of the chocolate and finished the Coke before he reached for his burner iPhone. Swiping it open he navigated to his internet-based Proton email, signed in, and clicked on the draft folder. This was where he left messages for Tishina. The text remained in the draft folder unsent and therefore untraceable. When Tishina opened the folder, she would then read the message, delete the text and add her own. It was a simple system, largely foolproof and of course secure. Until it wasn't. He typed his message:

Any news on W9 and family?

And then he added to this:

Any update on location of Spanish operator?

Akulov closed the web page and turned off his phone. He still felt tired, so took a second can of Coke as he crossed to the window. Sipping from it he peered out at the world below. The three of them – Parnell, Racine and him – had agreed to meet in the hotel lobby in thirty minutes and, checking his watch, Akulov noted that he had a little over fifteen left. He yawned, undressed and then walked into the bathroom as he finished his Coke. Using the hotel amenity kit, he lathered up his face and shaved off his beard, immediately blunting the cheap, plastic disposable razor, before he stepped into the shower. First, he ran it at a moderately hot temperature whilst he washed off the dirt and grime of travel before he switched the dial all the way to what felt like Arctic sub-zero on his skin. He did this to will his body to wake up and not give in to the consequences of international travel. Still shivering, he stepped out of the shower, grabbed a towel and proceeded to dry himself when his doorbell rang. Although he was expecting the concierge, a delivery he had arranged at the desk earlier, Akulov still checked the image of his visitor through the fish-eye spyhole in the door. The man was holding up a pair of shopping bags with the name of a menswear store on them, the same store which had a concession adjacent to the hotel lobby. Akulov tightened the towel around his waist and opened the door.

"Your clothes, sir," the man stated, with a practised smile.

"Thank you," Akulov replied, as he took his shopping.

The concierge nodded curtly and turned away as Akulov closed the door.

Crossing back to the bed, Akulov unpacked the clothes, inspected them and then dressed. In addition to plain black underwear, he'd chosen muted, practical colours – khaki-coloured jeans, a navy-blue cotton shirt and black denim jacket. He wasn't a fan of fashion and whilst he knew the brand, would not have sought it out at a mall. He collected his burner phone from the bedside table, turned it back on and navigated into his email account once more. There was a message. It was from Tishina.

> We need to talk. Send me the number of this phone. We'll use WhatsApp

Akulov deleted the message and replaced it with the number for his burner phone. He crossed to the minibar again and this time took out a bottle of water. Phone in left hand he once more took up a position by the window. His room was not overlooked, and as far as he could see there was no obvious perch for anyone to take a shot at him, which he reasoned was not very likely to happen, yet did always play on his mind.

The phone rang. It was Tishina.

"Ruslan. You arrived safely without crashing the jet?"

Akulov sighed. "Yes. This one did not fall out of the sky."

"That's progress, at least. I have no updates on Kizlyar as yet. If anything untoward had happened to him or his family I would have heard from my contacts in Canada. So, no news is good news – as the saying goes."

"Good."

"Now, about our Spaniard."

"Yes?"

"His was not a name I knew, which usually indicates that he is not a top-level operator, however I did have some luck with a Spanish contact of mine. A small-time arms dealer, based to the north of Madrid had a meeting with him two days ago. Please tell Casey I'm thinking of sending him an invoice for the ten thousand euros I had to pay for this information, that's at least a decent handbag."

"What was the information?"

"He sold Martinez thirteen nine-millimetre Glocks, with ammunition and ten HG85 grenades."

"No longs?"

"Correct. No assault rifles. So, this would suggest any attack would be concealable, until of course the first shot is fired, or the first pin is pulled."

"Up close and personal," Akulov said.

"Yes."

"I also have a still of Martinez, from the CCTV outside the dealer's address. Which I will send to both you and Casey now, but the only issue is that this man is not Ángel Martinez."

"Then who is he?"

"The man is José Orosco, the son of the man you were contracted to liquidate, and the brother of Hector Orosco."

"We have to find him."

"This is true, but first you need to find his men."

Akulov took a sip of water as he let his eyes follow the trail of a high-altitude passenger jet as it traced a line through the Spanish sky.

"How is your new friend?"

Akulov blinked. "Friend?"

"The client, Racine?"

"Fine."

"Fine?"

"She's professional and fearless."

"I've heard she's also beautiful. Goodbye for now."

The call ended and Akulov found himself looking at the handset and wondering what he was missing.

* * *

José Orosco had changed hotels. Not because there was anything wrong with the Four Seasons but, even though he had used a VPN, he did not believe it would fully hide him from the clutches of the all-seeing French intelligence agency. He didn't want them to find him before he found Racine. This meeting, however, he was taking in the café of yet another hotel, a four-star establishment on a corner directly across the street from the Four Seasons in one direction and his new hotel in another. He had a view of both five-star hotels from his table and felt somewhat reassured that he'd not seen a SWAT team storm either as yet.

José slurped his coffee, and reasoned that he was perhaps being a tad paranoid. He twiddled his room key in his fingers as he idly awaited the hacker he had paid a considerable sum to. He sipped from his grande Americano, as he watched the female barista at the bar of the hotel coffee shop. Her uniform was tight-fitting, which he approved of, and her lipstick and nails were painted a bright shade of red. He imagined she had been out the night before and had not yet bothered to change her nail colour as, he imagined, such a colour would be frowned upon in a service environment in a four-star hotel. But what did he know about fashion, or even morals for that matter? All he knew was he found her highly attractive. The woman looked in his direction. He returned her gaze. She smiled politely and continued to wipe the counter.

He checked his watch, a yellow gold, Rolex GMT-Master II with a flashy tiger iron dial, and noted he had an hour before he was due to rendezvous with the two teams when he would assign their targets and lead the attack. He smiled as he sipped his coffee, there was no way on earth that the Spanish authorities would know where they were heading and what they were about to attack. He knew his brother, and perhaps even his bastard of a father, would be proud.

José noted a man approach the café area from across the lobby. His hair was an unkempt jagged mess, or perhaps that was a style, José didn't know. He was not dressed in the correct attire for such an establishment, in his baggy jeans and logo T-shirt, and was too old to be a wayward child. He had a courier style bag across his chest and a pair of large headphones over his ears, the padded, noise-cancelling type that José had worn on first class flights, the type which music enthusiasts wore at home, the type which made anyone wearing them out in public look ridiculous. This character looked ridiculous, so he had to be the hacker he had ordered. The man looked around, trying to see who he had come to meet. José picked up his phone from the coffee table and sent him a WhatsApp:

> Over here. Dark blue shirt, maroon jeans, blue blazer.

The man flinched as his phone bleeped, then retrieved it from his pocket and swiped at the screen, perhaps the arrival of the message had sounded an alert which his headphones had magnified too much? Either way, José thought it looked comical. Eyes up now from his screen, the man saw José and started to hurry towards him. He sat himself down directly opposite José and pushed his headphones back from his ears.

"Hello. I am Daniel," he said, his prominent Adam's apple bobbing.

"Hello, Daniel, would you like a coffee?"

"Yes."

José raised his hand. The barista saw him and immediately started to approach.

"What can I get your friend?" she asked as she arrived.

Daniel said, "Do you have any vanilla sweet cream cold brew?"

The barista frowned. "No, I'm sorry we don't have that."

"How about a nitro cold brew?"

"I'm sorry we don't have that either."

"Hmm, OK, then I'll just take an iced white chocolate mocha."

"I can make you an iced Frappuccino with white chocolate shavings?"

"Hmm, no. I'll just have an iced latte then."

"Of course." She made eye contact with José. "And for you, sir, do you need a refill?"

"Why not." José smiled widely.

"I'll be back in a moment with your order."

José watched the barista walk away, then turned his attention to Daniel. "I paid you quite a considerable sum online to secure your services, as I was told by my sources that you are one of the best at what you do."

"The best."

"OK. So, what must I give you then?"

"Do you have a photograph?"

"No."

"Hmm, what about a name?"

"Yes. Sophie Racine."

Daniel opened his laptop and tapped at the screen. "Age?"

"Hmm, late twenties to early thirties, perhaps."

More tapping. "Nationality?"

"French."

"When did this person arrive in Spain?"

"Today."

"Hmm. OK, well, I've got nothing with those details on flight arrivals."

José sighed. "Yes. I know that."

"Hmm." Daniel continued to tap away at his keyboard.

"You said you were the best."

"I am, that is why I am now interrogating several closed systems."

José nodded, he didn't understand any of that reply.

"Your order, sir." The barista placed both drinks on the table.

"Just a moment." José reached into his wallet and gave her a fifty euro note.

"I'll be back over with your change."

"No need."

"Sir?"

José read her name tag, "Lucia, this is a personal tip for you."

"But this is too much."

"Your service is excellent, and I wish to pay for it."

She smiled, and this time it was genuine. "Thank you, sir."

"Not a problem at all, Lucia."

She smiled again and walked away. And he very much enjoyed watching her walk away.

"Hmm, I see," Daniel muttered. "It looks like this person's details are being protected... but... a-ha!"

"A-ha? What, *The Sun Always Shines on TV*?"

Daniel looked up. "Excuse me?"

"What have you found?"

"What I have found is an older photograph of Sophie Racine, which was taken at school. She's about sixteen here, look." Daniel turned the laptop around so José could see, and then turned it back. "So now if I take the image, run it through my facial recognition software, extrapolate the data and then... a-ha!"

"*Take On Me*?"

"Hmm?"

"Then what?"

"One moment... and done."

"What is?"

"I am. Here." Daniel turned the laptop around again. It now showed an image from a passport. It was Sophie Racine, but the name and the nationality were different. Here she was a UK citizen, and her name was Claire Kenmuir. "She arrived on a charted Gulfstream jet this morning."

"Where is she staying?"

Daniel cocked his head. "You want to know that too?"

"Yes."

"Well, that will cost you more."

"I do not care." José retrieved his wallet and pulled out a hundred euro note, Daniel shook his head, so he took a second one. He pushed the pair across the table.

"Why do you want to find her so much?"

José's eyes narrowed. "Perhaps you are not the best? Perhaps you cannot find her? Is that the issue?"

Daniel's mouth dropped open. "No. That is not true." He took the notes and slowly pushed them into his pocket. "Hmm. Right." He started to tap again, made a show of tilting his head, first left and the right, and then folded his arms. "Well, you are staying at the JW Marriott."

"How did you know that?"

Daniel looked up. "Your key."

José quickly pocketed it. "What about her? Have you found her?"

"Yes."

"So, tell me, where is she?"

"She is also staying at the JW Marriott, in a room along the hallway from you."

Now it was José's turn for his jaw to drop.

* * *

JW Marriott, Madrid

Now that they were back in a country with a steady mobile phone network, Racine had returned to using her encrypted iPhone. She sat in the lobby of the JW Marriott after a very quick shower, feeling out of place. Her hair was damp and tied back, and she was still wearing the Colombian denim outfit, which she desperately wanted to change. Perhaps she'd pop to a shop and grab a few items, there had to be somewhere halfway acceptable somewhere. They had three suites in the hotel, one each for her, Parnell and Akulov, and all paid courtesy of the Central Intelligence Agency. Perhaps, she thought, Casey was feeling guilty. His whole operation in Colombia with the Clan Del Oro and Espinosa seemed ill-conceived and without the necessary oversight, yet she knew Casey was an experienced deputy director.

Was that how the Americans did things, she wondered,

picking the least worse candidate and then supporting them with whatever they needed? It seemed to be their modus operandi with their two main domestic political parties, so why would their international operations be any different?

She yawned. She wanted to sleep. She wanted red wine. Nice red wine and not the supermarket crap. Perhaps when all this was over, she'd manage to find some Spanish red that would be suitable? Racine was under no illusions as to the scale of the undertaking that she, Parnell and Akulov were involved with. They had twelve gunmen to locate and liquidate, and all this without the loss of a single civilian life. Since arriving earlier that morning, she had already noticed a heightened police presence on the streets, and if she, as a "tourist", had noticed it she knew that the locals would have too, and of course also the very gunmen they had come to stop. So, the task then was that she and the two men would set up OPs near the railway station – Madrid Puerta de Atocha, and watch for the men from Colombia to arrive. She, Parnell and Akulov had studied the images from their passport photo pages and as much as they could do, had memorised the faces. But of course, their own eyes would be augmented by the feed from the myriad of CCTV units trained on the area, and central Madrid. Racine again looked up the station online and brought up a quick crib sheet written by a tourist blog which explained that the station complex was actually made up of three completely separate sections. The original Madrid Atocha train shed, which opened in eighteen eighty-two and was now a botanical garden and café complex. Madrid Puerta de Atocha, the modern terminus of fifteen platforms for high-speed intercity trains, and the Madrid Atocha Cercanias, with ten underground platforms to service cross-Madrid suburban trains.

The more she read and studied the plans, the more she

realised it was not just a simple task of closing the station, as it would have been say at Paris Gare du Nord. There was a question nagging at the back of her mind. Were the gunmen here to target the Spanish railway infrastructure or to target the travellers using it, or worse still, both?

Her iPhone rang. It was Grillot. "Hello?"

Colonel Grillot wasted no time with unnecessary pleasantries. "I have received intelligence on the planned attacks. There are two targets. The first is the Madrid Puerta de Atocha."

"Is this verified?"

"As much as it can be. The caller I spoke to was anonymous. He asked for you by name. He also mentioned Durand and Halbert."

"So, this could be misdirection?"

"We know from the intelligence you gathered that the railway station is one of the targets, so it would be reasonable to believe that, because the caller mentioned that exact target, it would be correct."

"That does follow, sir. What was the second?"

"That we still do not know. The caller refused to say and rang off."

"So, it could well be misdirection?"

"I don't think so. It was as though the man had changed his mind or was talking to himself. He started to rant about Basque independence, and also about you."

"Me?"

"Yes, Racine. He said he was going to kill you."

"He can join the queue."

"We are attempting to trace his call. It was routed via Colombia, but that could be just a digital location. I do however have more intel, which may tie in directly to our mystery caller."

"Sir?"

"An individual was caught on camera taking a delivery of arms north of Madrid from a known arms dealer. I shall send you the details. However, the man was not Ángel Martinez. He has been identified as José Orosco."

Racine's mind whirred. "So you are saying José Orosco is leading the attack, is in Madrid and called you to say what, he was going to kill me?"

"Yes, but the call could well be coincidence. It seemed as though the caller wanted to halt the attacks but then had a change of heart. Why would Orosco make such a call? It is not rational."

"Are terrorists ever rational, sir?"

"Good point."

"Will you now be informing the Spanish authorities, about the station and about Orosco?"

"Of course, Racine, why would I not? Were you expecting to single-handedly stop a thirteen-man terror cell?"

"Presumably it would only be six per target, sir, plus Orosco."

"Racine. Whilst I do not underestimate your abilities, I do believe that there is a time when you need to step back and accept that the Madrid anti-terror police units can handle this. However, I would still like you to observe, as this was your operation."

"I understand."

"The National Intelligence Centre has drawn up a list of possible targets. I shall email this to you to consider. Good luck." Grillot ended the call.

So, someone in Colombia, or Orosco, was after her? She shrugged it off – let them come at her, and let them die trying. Racine checked her watch, why were the two men taking so long? Perhaps Parnell was drying his hair? She smirked, and then the lift doors opened, and she saw Akulov. He had shaved; in fact, it was the first time she had seen him clean-shaven. He was also wearing a fresh set of clothes.

"You took your time."

"I emailed Tishina asking for an update on our Spanish mercenary. When I came out of the shower she had replied, and wanted to call me."

"And?"

"And Ángel Martinez is not Ángel Martinez."

"I know. He is José Orosco."

"How did you know?"

"Grillot told me."

Akulov nodded. "So Martinez, or Orosco operating as Martinez, was known to her network."

"So, is this a bit like 'Villains R Us'?"

Akulov sighed. "Two days ago, north of Madrid, Orosco took delivery of thirteen nine-millimetre Glocks, with ammunition and ten HG85 grenades."

"At least there were no assault rifles."

"That's what I said. This confirms the attack will be up close and personal."

Now it was time for Racine to share. "Grillot also had intel on the first target."

"Which is?"

"As our intel suggested, the Puerta de Atocha railway station. He received an anonymous call. The caller was about to give him the second target when he changed his mind."

Akulov frowned. "Misdirection?"

"That's what I thought, but we have little else to go on."

"So why give us the location? Do they want the Spanish authorities to be prepared or do they want, what, a confrontation?"

"Your guess is as good as mine." Her phone pinged. She

swiped it open. It was the list of potential targets from Grillot. "Look at this."

Akulov studied the list. "I'd choose the Royal Palace."

"That makes sense. One target is government controlled, and the other symbolic of royal power."

"Either way people die."

The lift opened again, and Parnell stepped out with a phone to his right ear, and a sports bag in his left hand.

Racine noted he too was wearing a new outfit. "Why am I the only one dressed like I'm homeless?"

"I thought it was fashion?" Akulov said.

"Seriously, where did you get your new clothes from?"

"I asked the concierge."

Racine sighed. "Yep, of course, of course you did."

"Listen up, people," Parnell said. "We got a ping twenty minutes ago at a petrol station forty minutes' drive south of here."

"Who was it?" Akulov asked.

"Two pings, two vehicles. The two drivers were filling up with petrol, and they are our guys. We have the plates too and they are being tracked. The Spanish don't want to stop them unless they're somewhere safe to do so."

Racine was exasperated. "And a motorway isn't safe?"

Akulov said, "How many passengers?"

"They were a pair of large SUVs – both VW Touaregs. I've seen the footage, they were not empty."

"So, we are supposed to assume that's the entire team?"

"To assume, Ruslan, well that just makes an 'ass' out of 'u' and 'me'. But we've got nothing else."

"So, we wait," Racine said.

Parnell sat on the long settee next to Racine, and placed his bag between them. "Here, there are three Glock 19s in there. Each in its own bag. Take one."

"In the lobby of a five-star hotel?" Racine asked.

"You'd rather it was a three-star?"

Racine reached into the bag. The Glock was in a padded, cloth bag. To the casual observer it could have been anything. "Thanks."

"Six."

"Thanks." Akulov now took his and sat at a right angle to them in the matching chair to the settee.

"We have a confirmed target," Racine said, matter-of-fact.

"Yeah, I know everything about the target and the ID of the bad guy. Tishina messaged Casey and Grillot, Grillot called Casey, and Casey told me, and then he told me that you knew. It's like the UN." Parnell stretched and started to raise his legs to place them on the coffee table.

"No." Racine tapped his leg. "Were you raised in a barn?"

"Almost," Parnell chuckled, "a ranch in Colorado."

"So, what, we just sit?" Racine was impatient.

"The Spanish have eyes on."

Parnell's phone rang.

"Yo, big dog. Talk to me?"

Akulov met her eyes, which she rolled dramatically.

"On my way." Parnell ended the call. "The Guardia Civil have just stopped a different vehicle. It was a car, on the way to the railway station. It contained two of our tangos. That leaves us with ten to find, plus their boss." Parnell made a call. "Eddie, it's 'go' time."

Racine frowned. "What's happening?"

"The Spanish police have the tangos in the car, so now we're cleared to intercept the two SUVs."

"The Spanish have agreed to this?" Akulov asked.

"Yes, and no." Parnell stood then hurried through the hotel exit and out onto the street. Akulov and Racine followed. An Audi Q7 came to a fast stop outside. The driver waved away the waiting hotel staff. Parnell pulled open the front passenger seat. "Get in then!"

Akulov and Racine followed.

"This is Fast Eddie, he's local talent."

"I'm a CIA desk officer, Mr. Parnell."

Parnell held up his phone. "Take us there, and fast, Eddie, fast!"

"OK." The Audi pulled away and into traffic, with a squeal of tyres.

Racine looked out at the city as it passed them. All those innocent people going about their daily lives in a European capital city, not knowing that any moment could be their last because a group of armed Colombian cartel soldiers had decided it would be so. It was not often that Racine felt the weight of her role on her shoulders, but as she sat there in the Audi with two CIA officers and the world's supposedly deadliest assassin by her side, she did. And it was crushing. She closed her mouth and started to breathe in, long and deep, then out slowly. She'd never had a panic attack, well not as an adult, not since she had been a teenager, but she knew the signs. Red wine usually helped, but of course she didn't have a bottle handy. No, she decided, she was bloody good at what she did, and so were those with her in the car now. They would prevail. They would prevent this attack. And then afterwards, she would get pissed on at least two bottles of the best red their hotel had to offer.

The Q7 left Madrid and took the motorway south, the location the Colombians had been spotted at was just ten clicks away.

"Huh, that's odd."

"What is?" Racine asked.

Parnell was studying his phone. "Those two SUVs have reversed course, according to the traffic cameras. They are now heading south. Wait. They've split up at Toledo. They are now heading south and east."

"They've been tasked with new targets," Akulov said.

"Which are?"

"That would be a guess, Mike."

"C'mon, Six, live a little. Have a bet, put your money all on black."

"They were originally going to hit the railway station, yes?"

"Yes," Parnell nodded, "stop drawing this out."

"Why?"

"Why?"

"Why the railway station? Because they wanted to cause disruption to the civilian infrastructure."

"If you say so, Six."

"So, what's south and east of here?"

"Sheesh, Wolf Six, just goddamn tell me."

"Wolf Six?" Eddie asked. "*The* Wolf Six?"

Racine realised what Akulov was getting at. "Railway lines?"

Akulov nodded. "Railway lines."

"There are two major ones that head straight to Madrid," Eddie confirmed, "both popular with commuters and tourists, always busy. It's the AVE high-speed lines."

"Small arms, grenades, up close and personal," Akulov added, flatly.

Racine looked at Akulov, remembering the last time they rode a train together. He looked back at her, she imagined he was also remembering.

"Right, let me think." Parnell started swiping on his phone.

"The two rail routes," Eddie spoke again, "well, the one to the east is the line up from the coast. It has two branches, one serves

Valencia and Alicante, the other comes direct from Cartagena. They then converge at Albacete. The route up from the south serves Cádiz, Seville, Córdoba, with one branch and the other Málaga. Both routes merge at Toledo."

"Impressive," Parnell said.

"Hey," Eddie shrugged, "I like trains, always have, and there are so many in Europe."

"The bad guys split at Toledo," Parnell noted, "so that means it's the trains."

Akulov saw the sign for a service station. "Pull in over there."

"Mr. Parnell?"

"Follow his request, Eddie. Six?"

"We need two cars."

* * *

The Q7 slowed, as Eddie indicated and swerved into the service station. Without a word, Akulov got out. He looked around. There were three cars being refuelled. One a small hatchback, by a woman in a burnt orange coat, the second an older looking sedan by a grey-haired man who was almost bent double, and the third an Alfa Romeo saloon being refuelled by a portly man in a business suit. Akulov slowly walked towards the man in the suit. As he did so, the motorist withdrew the pump from his car, replaced it in its holder then screwed the petrol cap back on. Akulov saw the man had his car keys in his right hand. He blipped the locks and turned his back to start to walk towards the kiosk. Akulov bounded the last few steps towards the man, snaked his arms around his neck and put him in a "Hadaka Jime" guillotine choke. He applied pressure to the carotid arteries and within seconds the man went limp. Akulov eased him to the ground, once he regained consciousness in a matter of a minute or two, he'd be fine. Akulov took his car keys and strode towards the waiting car. As he drew nearer, he was pleased to see it wasn't an average Giulia but the powerful Quadrifoglio edition. He blipped the locks and climbed in behind the wheel and started the engine. There was a knocking on the passenger door. Akulov expected an angry onlooker, what he saw was Racine. He opened the door, and she climbed in.

"You don't get away from me that quickly."

Akulov drove towards the Q7 and opened his window. Parnell powered down his own. "We'll take east, you take south."

"Copy that." Parnell shot Akulov a mock salute.

From behind, angry voices started to react to what had happened. Akulov closed the window, stabbed the accelerator and shot back out and onto the motorway.

17

The Alfa Romeo was powerful, and it handled as well as any sports saloon car Akulov had driven. With the onboard satnav and Racine reading the roads, they soon reached the fork and took the road east.

"What do you think we're looking for?" Racine asked.

"A large SUV," Akulov replied.

"Funny. That's not what I meant. I know they are going to hit the railway line but how?"

"Your guess is as good as mine. Do they derail a train, block the line and then take out the passengers or do they just leave the passengers alone? Or do they get to a station and board a train as passengers?"

"This is rushed, Ruslan. This had to be a decision taken on the fly. When they found out about the police presence at the station in Madrid."

"I agree. So that makes which option more probable?"

"They'll attack a train and derail it."

"OK, and how will they do that?"

"A bridge."

"Yes. We need to look for a bridge."

"On it." Racine searched the online map, whilst Akulov sped like a practised lunatic between the much slower motorway traffic. "Got it. There's a large bridge about thirteen kilometres ahead. It's where this motorway and a smaller, local route meets. Take the turning there."

"You're sure?"

"If they are not there, we carry on."

"OK."

Racine said, "I'm going to tell Parnell." She swiped on her screen and connected to the CIA operative. "We think they may be attempting to derail a train by attacking it from the bridge above. So look for a bridge. Yes, have that." She ended the call.

"What did he say?"

"He said thank you and that Fast Eddie agrees that's the probable plan."

Akulov now floored the accelerator pedal, making the Alfa's powerful engine roar. Streaking past the slower traffic like a missile, he just had to hope their assumption was correct, and he also had to hope that they didn't run into any Guardia Civil Tráfico vehicles otherwise they'd have an issue in the short term. The kilometres ticked by, with Racine giving him an update each minute. Akulov had a thought. "Are any trains actually scheduled to run today? Presumably if Madrid is closed where would they go to?"

Racine shrugged. "They'd probably stop elsewhere, perhaps a couple of stations short. I don't know. OK, I can see the bridge, you'd better start to slow."

Akulov now saw it too. There was an off-ramp with the name of a small town on it and the number of the road. He slowed the Alfa to the permitted motorway cruising speed and changed to the correct lane. As they started to take the road up and off the motorway, the large concrete bridge became visible and Akulov had a flash of déjà vu. It wasn't the same bridge from six years before, that would just be silly, a coincidence, but it was possible. And then they saw the SUV. It was a VW Touareg and it was parked, purposefully, on the dirt at the side of the bridge to minimise its profile.

"I am going to drive on past them. Get an eyeball on, tell me what you can see. We can't be the only car that's used this turning so they shouldn't suspect us."

"Agreed."

Akulov slowed the Alfa even further as they reached the top of the ramp and turned right. On the bridge Akulov kept his speed sensible, and his eyes pointed forward.

"That's one by the VW," Racine noted. "Two more are climbing down the gully towards the tracks and there's another two already on the tracks."

"Have that, so a five-man team. Call Parnell, tell him what we have. That means he's also got a team of five."

Whilst Racine made the call to Parnell, Akulov carried on driving until the ground dipped and they lost sight of the bridge. He pulled over onto the dirt. "You ready?"

"Always," Racine replied. She placed her hand on his arm and gave it a quick squeeze.

They both got out of the car, weapons up and ready to take on any targets. They were under no illusions that anyone they saw they had to engage. There would be no taking of prisoners, and no remorse. This was a terrorist act they were going to prevent and their actions were black and white. They jogged along the side of the road and then slowed and moved into the ditch when the bridge came back into view. Akulov squinted, trying to make out any movement on the bridge, but at this distance it was impossible. Then they heard the sound. It was like a distant whistling and rattling, which could mean only one thing: a train was on its way, and they were too late.

"We need to move!" Racine said, needlessly.

The pair of assassins now started to run towards the bridge. Akulov could now make out a single figure standing on it, and the man had a shape in his hands both assassins recognised.

And then he threw it over the edge of the bridge.

And then the first of the explosions happened.

From below there was a rumble and a crack and then smoke rose. A metallic screeching came from the rails and they saw the fast intercity train hove into view, sparks flying from its emergency braking systems. The man tossed another grenade and a second explosion tore through the gully.

Akulov came to a stop, took aim and fired a double tap into the grenade throwing Colombian on the bridge. A third grenade was still clutched in his hand, the terrorist was propelled forward and over the edge of the railing to the track below before his brain had comprehended that he was dead. There was a third explosion and now a shuddering, and an almighty metallic scraping and a thud, then clouds of dust rose from the tracks. Akulov and Racine reached the bridge less than half a minute later to see the train below had been derailed, and clambering into the driver's cab through the smashed windscreen was a further man. Another three were attempting to break into the train proper, one placed a hand grenade against the door before the trio darted down the side of the train for cover. Racine pulled her trigger twice and despatched the last in the line with a pair of rounds to the torso whilst the others made their escape, running down the side of the troubled train. Both Akulov and Racine ducked away as the grenade exploded in the gully below them several seconds later.

"There's one extra, tango!" Racine, now back to her full

height, she pointed and shouted over the noise of the metal continuing to buckle below. "It's Orosco!"

Akulov looked back down at the train and saw she was right. Two men were now exiting the front of the train through the cab's shattered windscreen where only one had entered. The first, handgun held by his side, started to briskly move back up the slope attempting to reach the road, whilst the other followed just behind with a phone to his left ear and a Glock in his right hand. Akulov noted the second man seemed older, heavier and more rugged than the other Colombians. Akulov realised Racine was right, he had to be the leader, Ángel Martinez aka José Orosco. They were bugging out, making their escape before the authorities were alerted of the attack. And then the man glared directly up at them. Orosco shouted to his man ahead, and both swung their handguns upwards, snapping off wild shots forcing Akulov and Racine to duck again.

"We can't let Orosco is get away!" Racine shouted.

"I've got him. You go after the two runners."

"No," Racine held eye contact with Akulov, and he noticed the start of an argument form on her face, but instead of wasting time they didn't have, she sighed and started to jog at a crouch towards the end of the bridge furthest from the approaching men, and the slope which led to the train below.

Akulov watched her for a moment before he turned and sprinted for the other side of the bridge and where José was angling to come back up as now the rounds from two handguns tore towards him. Sirens sounded, and a Guardia Civil car came to a screeching halt on the asphalt. Its occupants burst out at the same time as José and the other man appeared just in front of them. José immediately pushed his Glock into the back pocket of his jeans, waved his arms at the pair and started to speak quick-fire Spanish which, at this distance, Akulov could not discern.

The two police officers turned towards Akulov, drawing their service issue weapons. Akulov was caught, Glock in hand, he had no choice, he was not going to get into a firefight with a pair of law enforcement officers. He started to crouch, to place his handgun on the ground, when two shots rang out, not a double tap, but one after another. To his horror, Akulov watched as both the officers fell forward, having been shot in the backs of their heads. José and the second man quickly climbed into the Guardia Civil cruiser, and tyres chirping fled the scene. But Akulov was not giving up, he was Wolf Six, he was the Machine. Sprinting for all he was worth, Akulov headed back to the Alfa. It took him almost two minutes to reach it then a further twenty seconds to get back to the bridge. He skidded to a halt, looking at the two possible routes, one back on the motorway and the other via the older, winding local road which seemed to be heading into a series of low hills. He took the latter and driving the Italian sports saloon as quickly as he dared, given the nature of the winding, dusty road, he charged forward. The road climbed, and rounding a corner he came face to face with a truck coming down. With nowhere to go, he turned into the rocky wall of the hill and the Alfa bounced and screeched along for several seconds, leaving red paints streaks on the unforgiving rocks, while its flanks were scrubbed back to bare metal. He crested the hill and saw that the road plateaued. About a kilometre ahead he could see several cars, two were approaching in his direction and one was heading away. It was the Guardia Civil cruiser, and it was moving fast, but not as fast as he was. Akulov powered past both cars at speed, the first an older model BMW sedan, driven by a man with white hair, and the second a small SEAT hatchback, the driver of this sporting sunglasses and a baseball cap. It took him just five minutes to catch up with the cruiser. He slammed the nose of the Alfa into the rear end of the Cruiser with a satisfying crunch. The car in front bucked and jerked, and then Akulov noticed the small bridge they were about to cross a hundred yards ahead. The cruiser attempted to pull away, but as it did so the rear tyre burst and it started to fishtail, and then the driver lost control. Akulov slammed on his brakes and the Alfa came to a skidding, juddering stop. The Guardia Civil cruiser meanwhile caught the concrete edge of the bridge, rebounded from it and rolled off the road and down towards the river below.

Akulov leapt from the Alfa and scrabbled down the dirt verge, towards the stricken cruiser. The rear of the car was in the water, whilst its nose and front half were still on the bank. The driver's door opened, and a figure fell out. His face was a bloodied mess, yet even through this Akulov could see it was not Orosco.

The man threw up his hands, and started to plead in Spanish, "Pl... please... I am injured..."

Glock trained directly at the man's ruined face, Akulov said, "Where is Orosco?"

"Wh... what?"

"Where is your boss?"

The man started to raise his right hand, as if to point. "He... he took his car... he went..."

"Where was he going?"

"Ma... Madrid..."

"What type of car?"

"It... was... small... please... h... help... me."

"No." Akulov shot the Colombian terrorist in the face.

Wolf Six trudged back up the bank, turned his battle-damaged stolen car around and sped back towards Racine. Orosco was in the wind, because of him, and he had to be found, but for the moment at least Akulov had more pressing matters.

Ten minutes later he found her, amongst the passengers from

the train on the bridge. Two men were placing their jackets over the faces of the dead police officers. Akulov stepped out of the car, Racine advanced towards him, an angry expression on her face.

"Where's Orosco?"

"He got away."

"Parnell got his targets before they hit the train. Five passengers died on ours. We weren't fast enough."

Nothing Akulov could say would bring the dead back to life, so he remained silent.

18

Akulov didn't know the name of the bar, or even its exact location because "Fast Eddie" had taken the three of them there. And then they had found Vince Casey sitting, with his leg in a cast in a private room.

"Well," he said greeting the trio as they arrived, "forgive me if I don't stand up."

"You OK, boss?" Parnell asked.

"Never better. We did it, team. We stopped them."

"Five commuters died," Racine stated.

"Yes, which is a terrible thing, and yet it could have been so much worse, for us all."

Each of them took a seat.

"So, what happens now?" Akulov asked.

"We get drunk, is what happens now," Casey replied.

Racine said, "What about Orosco?"

"The National Intelligence Centre have taken over that hunt. The Spanish have insisted only they must apprehend him. He's one man, and now they know what he looks like, and have the details of the passports he used to enter both the US and the EU.

Unless he gets on a boat he won't get far. There are cameras everywhere, they'll get their man."

Akulov knew it wasn't as simple as that but made no reply.

The curtain to their side opened and a server stepped through. She held the curtain whilst two more servers brought in a pair of large silver trays. One contained a selection of tapas, and the other a selection of wines. They arranged the plates, bottles and glasses on the table and then left. Without being asked, Racine reached for the nearest wine bottle and read the label.

Casey took a second bottle and started to open it. "You know, as a kid, growing up—"

"In the Stone Age," Parnell added.

"Yes, Mike, in the Stone Age, I used to think the world was a huge place. Now it's shrinking year by year, month by month. I mean we keep on running into the same people – take you for instance, Ruslan. One minute you're bumping into me in Morocco, then I'm finding you in some damn awful town in Michigan and then the next, you appear in some goddamn awful drug dealer's mansion in the Colombian rainforest." He addressed Racine, "Wine?"

"Always."

Casey poured a large measure into her glass. "Ruslan?"

"No thanks," Akulov said.

Parnell pushed Akulov's glass forward. "No is not an option, Six."

"What I'm trying to say, to you all, is that well, I'm pretty darn pleased with what we've done, and I of course would be thankful to the pair of you – Wolf Six, Racine, if you kept our little operation in El Bagre a secret."

Akulov understood. He took his glass and said nothing.

Parnell said, "Less chat and more drinking."

"And rightly so." Casey filled Parnell's glass, and then his own, "I'm going to raise my glass, if you'll allow me? To all the bad guys, and the badder guys who stop them!"

Akulov offered the wine to his mouth. It was rich, full-bodied and surprisingly he liked it.

"Eat," Casey said.

The two men from the CIA, and the pair of assassins did just that and Akulov realised just how hungry he had been.

Parnell wiped his mouth with a napkin and said, "Well, if we're doing toasts how about I say one."

"You, Mike? I thought you were scared of public speaking?" Casey winked.

"No, I'd like to be serious for a moment. Here's to those of us who didn't make it, wherever they may be."

Casey nodded, and became solemn. "To the fallen."

Akulov drank again, his mind wandering back to his memories.

Parnell emptied his glass, and took the bottle and refilled his own, then topped up the others. The table started to eat again.

"Racine?" Casey said, after finishing a mouthful of food.

She wiped her lips with a napkin, "It's not my turn to toast. There's a tradition, isn't that true, Ruslan?"

Akulov blinked, he was back in the present. "Tradition?"

"The third toast?"

"Yes, there is."

"Tell us?" Casey said, a half-smile forming about his lips.

"In Ukrainian culture, the third toast is always to the women."

"So?" Racine said.

Akulov raised his glass. "To women."

"Thank you," Racine said, "and I thought you hadn't noticed."

Akulov drank.

* * *

Racine opened her eyes. Something had woken her. It was a sound outside her door. What was it, someone walking to their room, or perhaps a member of staff from room service collecting a tray of leftovers, or perhaps it was Ruslan Akulov attempting to raise enough courage to knock on the door and profess his love for her? She smiled, the wine was still working, and she was feeling fanciful, and farcical. She wiggled her shoulders, to get comfortable again, and closed her eyes. It was a shame it was not Ruslan...

The electronic note of key card opened her eyes again. It had to be the room next door, or the room opposite. Then the door creaked. It was her door and she sensed the slight change in pressure, as air from the hallway met the much colder air of her room. And then the door closed, extremely slowly, as though whoever had opened it did not want to make a sound, which of course they did not, whoever they were.

Racine reached under her pillow, was that where she had put her Glock? No. Without moving her head, she scanned the room seeking out her handgun. There was a sudden noise, the brush of a shoe on thick pile carpet and then something flashed in her peripheral vision, a blade.

Instinctively, Racine rolled to her right and out of the bed. She landed with a muted thud on the carpeted floor, and now she remembered she was naked. Ahead, under the credenza, a pile of clothes lay on the floor and in the dim moonlight which was poking in through a gap in the curtains, she could see the barrel end of the Glock.

"Puta!" a low voice cursed, in Spanish, and she heard the springs on the bed contract as the owner of the voice climbed onto it.

The knife flashed again. Racine had no time to move or cover, so she attempted to push herself into the carpet. In the semi-darkness the tip of the blade missed her cheek by a millimetre. It rose, and she knew this was the time to react. Throwing her legs up in the air blindly, she felt her left shin collide with the blade and the hand that held it. There was a flash and then a metallic clunk as the blade landed on the glass-topped coffee table in front of the balcony window. Racine rocked forward and using her momentum and core strength rapidly rose to her feet. Her attacker was still on the bed and backing away, attempting to get off, but his short legs not yet making contact with the floor. The man gazed up as he scurried backwards. He looked manic; he looked familiar. Swinging her right leg up and onto the bed Racine kicked him in the head. It was a stupid move she realised, and she over balanced and fell to the floor once again, but at least she had struck him.

"I am going to kill you!" the man said, his words Spanish but his accent from somewhere else.

Racine pushed herself back to her feet. She grabbed for the knife, as she saw the man reaching for something in his pocket... Racine launched herself forwards, and brought the knife down in a stabbing action, forcing it straight through his forearm and impaling it on the bed.

The scream was loud, and it was anguished, and there was no way the people in the rooms around her did not hear it. The man tugged his arm free. She now saw that he was holding what looked like a printed photograph in his hand.

"Who are you?"

"You do not even recognize me, Racine? Even though you murdered my brother?"

Racine stepped back. "José Orosco."

Orosco roared and pulled himself up from the bed. "You are going to die!"

Racine stepped forward and launched a straight kick at the rotund man, slamming into his chest and knocking him back against the wooden unit affixed to the wall. Before he could react, she slammed first a left hook then a right jab into his flabby frame. Taking a step back she watched, the fury racing through her veins at the man who had, in part, been responsible for all the deaths that had happened that day. She wanted to kill him, that much was certain, but she wanted to really hurt him first.

"José, do you know the funniest part of all of this? I was not the one who pulled the trigger on your brother, but I am going to be the one who ends your life," her words were fast. Anger and wine were not a good mix.

There was a banging on the door. It was Akulov. "Racine? Racine?"

José saw his chance. "Help me! This madwoman is trying to kill me!"

The door crashed open, and for a moment Racine saw a smile on José's face as the light from the hallway illuminated him.

"Do you need help?" Akulov asked.

"No, I can deal with this little shit on my own."

"W... what? Pl... please, she is a madwoman."

"Yeah, I'm livid."

Akulov said, "Racine you are naked."

Racine put her hands on her hips. "You'd have seen me naked sooner or later."

Akulov paused for a moment, his eyes on hers, then said, "I'll be outside."

As the door shut, José charged forward. Fists up, blade still in his right forearm, and the television controller held like a dagger in his left. If she hadn't been so angry she would have laughed. He swung at her. She sidestepped him, grabbed his head and drove it into the centre of the glass-topped coffee table. The glass smashed and José's head became stuck on the underside, the round steel edge of the table acting like a frame. She didn't know if he was dead or unconscious, so she kicked him hard in the stomach just because she could. She strode to the bathroom, grabbed two towelling bath robes, put one on and then used the belt from the other to bind José's hands behind his back. And then she stepped out of her room.

Akulov met her with a concerned expression on his face. "Are you OK?"

"I am fine. I just need a drink."

"The bar is closed."

"Merde."

He looked at her legs. "You are bleeding."

"I'm bleeding angry."

Akulov said, "Where is José?"

"He's having a coffee."

"What?"

"Never mind. Can I sleep in your room, please."

"That is fine, I'll take the settee."

"That is not what I meant."

"I understand, but it is what is right."

Akulov turned and headed for his room. As he reached it, Parnell's head poked out of his own. He was squinting and his hair was down, and to Racine's tipsy eyes he resembled a member of Bon Jovi.

"Hello," Parnell said, to Akulov, then on noticing her he said, "Oh, hellllo!"

"Goodnight, Parnell," Akulov said, ushering Racine into the room.

* * *

Akulov pointed to the bed. "Get in, and sleep."

Racine slipped off the robe, "You giving me orders now? Ooh, Wolf Six!"

In the semi-darkness Akulov rolled his eyes, "I'll be back."

Akulov left his room and shut the door. Across the hallway he entered Racine's room through the damaged door. He turned on the light. And then he blinked. Orosco had gone. He reversed back out of the room as his eyes now picked up a trail of blood on the grey hotel carpet. It was leading to the lift. Akulov turned right and took the stairs. They were on the sixth floor and taking the stairs down was just as fast as taking the lift. Pushing through the fire door, Akulov's feet pounded on the uncarpeted steps as he hurtled downstairs. It was a little after three a.m. and he met no one as he appeared in the hotel foyer, with the exception of the night porter who gave him a bemused look.

"Did you see a man—"

The porter pointed at the main entrance. "That way."

Without replying, Akulov ran across the lobby and pushed through the doors. Outside a Madrid Municipal Police vehicle pulled up and two officers clambered out. The driver, on seeing Akulov fleeing the hotel, held up his right hand in a stop motion. Akulov frantically looked right then left down the deserted street and saw a lumbering figure flagging down a taxi on the corner of the block. It was Orosco.

"Sorry," Akulov said and punched the driver in the stomach, grabbed the car keys which were still in his other hand and dived into the cruiser. Before the second officer was able to react, Akulov had the SEAT Ateca squealing away from the hotel towards the fleeing man in the taxi. Akulov found the button for the lights and sirens and pressed it. Ahead he saw the taxi slow and then veer to the left as though it was about to pull over. But it didn't. Instead the driver's door opened and a man fell out. Then within the space of two seconds, the taxi moved off again, the still open-door slamming shut by virtue of colliding with a large, cast-iron lamppost.

Zig-zagging now, the taxi accelerated away from Akulov, towards the Plaza de Canalejas, mounting the kerb and cutting the corner to join a narrow bollard-lined one-way street. Flooring the accelerator, Akulov followed, with the occasional light from the passing windows on either side flashing in the corners of his eyes. There was nowhere to go, and the taxi could not slow to take any of the right angle turns onto a different route. Akulov started to close the gap and then the street widened, giving out to a cobbled square, empty at this time of night. Yet the road itself was still lined by concrete bollards on either side so neither vehicle was able to turn. They were like trains on rails, and unlike several hours before, it was now going to be Akulov who derailed this train.

The road reached an intersection and the taxi's brake lights flashed as Orosco tried to slow to make his escape by the only turn possible. But Akulov was now too close, and he was too determined.

In an explosion of airbags, Akulov slammed the SEAT into the back of the taxi, propelling it up and over the high kerb. It skidded across the intersection, and its nose crashed through a glass-fronted storefront before it came to a shuddering halt half inside what looked like a furniture shop. A high decibel alarm started to clang from within the store.

Neck now numb, from what he imagined was whiplash, Akulov climbed out of the police SEAT and advanced towards the taxi, as he did so, he realised that his right ankle was in pain, and he began to hobble. On reaching the taxi, he grabbed the handle of the driver's door and pulled it open. The car was empty. And then something hard slammed into his shoulder. Akulov slumped forward against the taxi and the same weapon struck him again. Before it hit him a third time, he managed to duck away, sliding down the bonnet of the taxi and onto the broken glass which had once been a storefront window. Looking up he saw Orosco standing over him with what looked like a brass poker in his hands, and he was bringing it down to strike again. Akulov rolled from the front of the crumpled car and onto the glass covered tiles of the store, as what felt like a million needles injected him through his thin cotton shirt. The poker missed his torso but struck him on his left leg. Akulov was surprised by the force of the blow. He crawled to his right and using a thick armchair, pulled himself back up to his feet. With anger in his eyes, he now faced Orosco, one on one, man to man.

"You are the assassin?" Orosco spat.

"I killed your father," Akulov said.

"Good," Orosco replied, "as I had planned."

Akulov attempted to understand the words. "As you had planned?"

"I hated him." The poker now dropped to his side. "But my brother I loved. You and I have no quarrel. My enemy is that French puta!"

Akulov wet his lips. "I shot your brother too."

In the half-darkness, Akulov saw the Argentinian's face start to contort, and then the poker flashed. It slammed into Akulov's left side, but Wolf Six felt no pain. In his right hand was a shard of broken glass, shaped like a dagger and razor edged. In one swift movement, Wolf Six lunged forwards and slashed the makeshift blade across Orosco's throat. Wide-eyed, Orosco dropped the poker and grabbed at his neck, then fell to the floor. Akulov watched the man bleed to death, and then he limped away, back the route he had come as more police sirens joined the cacophony he had left behind.

* * *

The settee was more comfortable than it looked. Akulov realised he must have been more tired than he realised, as it was a knocking on the door which woke him. He checked his watch, it was a little after ten in the morning. Wearing a T-shirt and boxer shorts, he opened the door to find Mike Parnell, looking fresher than ever, standing on the other side.

"Good morning, how did you sleep?" Parnell winked.

"Deeply and on the couch," Akulov replied, "which was my decision."

Parnell held up his palms. "Hey, I'm not prying, but just think of what gifted kids the pair of you could make."

Akulov rubbed his face. "So?"

"Oh right, the 'cleaners' came during the night and sanitised Racine's room. Casey spoke to the director of the National Intelligence Centre, and well, let's just say that if you saw José Orosco last night it was an hallucination brought on by bad chorizo. They've also been persuaded that you did not steal a police vehicle, assault an officer, destroy a furniture shop and, oh yes, murder a man on the street."

"I see."

"You see? Sheesh, even for you, Six, that's one night of fun. You're damn lucky Vince likes you so much. And that he's so persuasive."

"Thanks."

"Thanks, he says. Listen, if you want to catch a ride back to the US, we're leaving here in an hour, wheels up in two."

"Thank you, but I think I will stay here for a while."

Parnell touched his forehead. "Understood."

"I guess I will see you around, Parnell?"

Parnell flashed him a smile. "See you around, you goddamn bad hombre."

Parnell walked away and Akulov shut the door. He stretched, padded to the bathroom, and stepped into the shower. His head was aching from what had been for him an excessive amount of alcohol the night before, and the rest of him ached from a culmination of what he called battle booboos. He felt himself drifting back to sleep as he stood in the shower, so suddenly turned the thermostat to full Arctic. Stepping out shivering, he dried himself before he grabbed a hotel robe and headed quietly for the bedroom, noting the dull ache in both his neck and his right ankle.

Racine was lying on her stomach with the thick duvet pulled up to the nape of her neck. Akulov had no idea why, but he sat in the chair at the side of the bed and watched her sleep. She looked to be at peace, and he had the unnerving feeling that he was too.

Racine opened her eyes. "My head hurts, and my leg does too, and why are you in my room?"

"You are in my room. Don't you remember?"

"I am. Oh, I am." She looked under the covers. "And I'm naked."

"That's how most people sleep."

"Last night, did I do anything stupid?"

"You fought a man whilst you were naked and drunk, and your finishing move was to put his head through a glass coffee table. Does that answer your question?"

"Merde!" Racine closed her eyes. "José Orosco tried to kill me."

"Which was a big mistake."

"Is he dead?"

"Yes, I killed him."

Racine turned and sat up, covering her chest with the duvet. "How?"

"That's not important, but it was a close shave."

"Ah, I don't care either way, but thank you." Racine paused, and she wet her lips with her tongue. "Ruslan, did we…"

"Did we what, Racine?"

"No. You can call me Sophie. Because we are friends and because Racine is not here now. Did we, 'do' anything?"

"No."

"No? Why ever not?"

"Because I'd rather be memorable."

"Ah."

"Parnell and Casey are flying to the States, they offered me a ride."

"Are you going to take it?"

"No. I am going the other way; I need to grab some down time."

"Where?"

"Why do you want to know?"

"Ruslan, will you ever be able to have a normal conversation?"

"This is as normal as I can get, whilst sitting in a chair chatting to a beautiful naked woman."

"Ah, so I am beautiful, am I?"

"You do not need me to tell you that, Sophie."

"So, what happens now?"

"Now? I expect the DGSE to pay Tishina, and then she'll pay me."

"That is not what I meant, Ruslan, and you know it."

"Dubai. I am going to Dubai."

"What? Why? Are you a fan of camels?"

"Yes, it's the long eyelashes, but I am going there because it is one of the safest places on earth, and no one can bother me without the authorities finding out."

"I suppose. I'd never thought of it like that. What happens if anyone does need bothering, whilst you are there?"

"I won't be bothered." Akulov stood. "I am going to dress, and then I am going to pack."

"What am I doing?"

"Sleeping more, I would imagine, and then probably heading back to Paris for a debrief with your Colonel Grillot."

"Ah! Why do I have to work!"

"Because you would get bored killing bad people for free." Akulov strode away and into the lounge.

EPILOGUE

ATLANTIS THE ROYAL, DUBAI, UNITED ARAB EMIRATES

Akulov looked out across the view of the Palm Jumeirah from his outside seat at the Kaleidoscope restaurant. It was still early enough to see the rising sun glinting off an ever-increasing number of windows as it rose, and also for him to feel a chill in the air. Akulov had chosen to stay at the other Atlantis hotel, "The Royal", this time, and had opted for a suite on one of its highest floors. He felt relaxed and the madness and danger, and of course the killing of the last week, seemed as though it had been experienced by another person. Just behind him, through the doors and inside the restaurant, the innumerable plates of cuisines from around the globe, and around the corner, sat awaiting ravenous guests. At this early hour, on a Saturday morning, however, he was only one of four guests partaking in the feast.

He sipped his reassuringly rich Royal coffee and found it to be as good as that he'd had in Atlantis The Palm. Most non-coffee drinkers believed coffee was just coffee, but that was nonsense. A great coffee was a wonderful work of art, and the caffeine boost helped as well. Akulov thought about the day he had planned. He would take his hired Jeep Grand Cherokee and drive out of Dubai, up through Sharjah, into Ras Al Khaimah and then up to the tallest peak in the UAE – the Jebal Jais. It was a drive he had not done before and he figured that, whilst he was a tourist, he should at least attempt a few touristy things. He heard a noise from behind and saw a family come out onto the terrace. They looked as though their flight had just landed in the UAE, they were bleary-eyed, and wearing outfits not appropriate for the desert heat. The mother and father moved with a slowness Akulov could only imagine came from a red-eye flight on which their son had not slept. The little boy was running around and pointing at the birds that had perched on the railings. He ran up and peered over the edge two tables ahead of Akulov before turning around and realising he was being watched. Akulov guessed he was probably the same age as Nairo, but then as he had no experience with children he had no frame of reference.

"Come on, Toby," his British mother called out, with a received pronunciation accent, "don't worry the man when he's having his breakfast."

"Can I worry the man when he's having his breakfast?" another English-accented voice asked.

Akulov turned his head to see Valentina Tishina strolling towards him. She was dressed in a long, flowing dress, with a high split on either side which flashed her shapely thighs. Akulov imagined it was both extremely expensive and extremely fashionable.

She pointed to the chair next to him. "May I?"

Akulov nodded.

"Oh hello, Valentina, so nice to see you. How have you been? Thank you for the large payment you have just made into my account."

"I am sorry, I was not attempting to be rude."

"The issue is, Ruslan, that you never are." She stared at the panorama of the city, as Akulov had done. "Tell me how Argentina was?"

"Unusual."

"Hmm. How was Wolf Nine?"

"Alive."

"And Racine?"

"Different."

"Ruslan, are you attempting to be particularly difficult today?"

"Yes."

"I see."

Akulov sighed. "Argentina was unusually difficult. Did you have any idea Racine would be there when you gave me the contract to take out Franco Orosco?"

"No. Not at all. However it all worked out well, you now have the intelligence agencies of two countries on your side. If you keep this up you'll have no enemies anywhere."

"But do I want to keep it up?"

"What? Really, Ruslan? Please don't you start on with that 'retirement' talk again. For starters, how would I eat? You don't want to see me out on the streets begging for scraps because you retired, do you?"

"Valentina, I doubt that would ever happen."

"True. How was Kizlyar?"

"He was attempting to make something of his life."

"So that was why he went AWOL?"

"Yes. It is difficult for me to explain, but he seemed to have found himself, at least until his wife and child were taken."

"And then you got them back, so everything became hunky-dory again?"

"Yes. It was good to see him. In fact, it was nice to find out he was alive."

"Nice?"

"You know, there are only four of us left."

"True, the four best ones. Tell me, what did you think of Racine? I have never met the woman but, of course, she is a woman who has a reputation."

What did he think of Racine? That was a difficult question to answer, as he didn't know how to. She was as skilled an operative an anyone he had met, she was courageous, caring and most of all... what was she most of all? "I liked her."

Tishina seemed shocked. "You liked her, Ruslan? What does that mean?"

"It means what it means, Valentina."

"Oh, you men. You are all either emotionally unavailable, emotionally stunted or emotionally stilted."

"I have emotions, yet I rather prefer to keep them to myself."

Akulov heard voices from behind, more guests arriving he imagined, but then he didn't have to imagine any more.

"Ah, I see you've got company, Ruslan."

Akulov turned his head to see Sophie Racine standing behind him with a plate of food in one hand and a glass of champagne in the other. He suddenly felt a little short of breath. "Isn't it a little early for that?"

"Nonsense, Ruslan," Tishina said. "It is never too early for champagne."

Racine said, "Hello, Valentina, I'm Sophie."

Tishina stood. "Yes, I know who you are."

"May I?" Racine asked.

"Go ahead, if you wait for Ruslan to invite you to sit, you'll still be standing at supper time."

Racine took the seat on Akulov's other side. Akulov noticed that she moved it away from him a little.

"How are you?" Akulov asked.

"I'm fine, I think. I'm dressed now. And you?"

"I think I may be happy."

Tishina stood. "I am going to get a glass of champagne."

Racine finished her glass in two gulps. "I'll come with you. There seems to be a problem with my flute."

The two women in his life started to walk away. Tishina called back to him, "We're going to compare notes, Ruslan."

"There's so much I want to ask you," Racine said.

"About him?" Tishina asked.

"Him? No, about you."

Akulov sipped his coffee and attempted to understand what was happening.

* * *

Jenner, California

Tomas Torres sipped his whisky and settled into his thickly padded leather armchair. It was almost nine o'clock and he had helped his daughter put the children to bed. Tonight he had read them a bedtime story. The living room was lit by the flickering flames from the log fire, which Christian had insisted upon starting up and, for once, Torres approved of his son-in-law's decision. Both men sat in their own armchairs, both nursing their large measure of whisky.

"I have never told anyone the full story before, and the full truth," Torres said.

"Does that include the courts?" Christian asked.

"Oh they had most of it, enough for a conviction, but now I

imagine those files have been burnt – tossed on a fire like yours, or shredded to save embarrassment. But this time what happened will be known and remembered by all. As an American, it is difficult for you to understand, Christian, but what happened in Argentina all those years ago, what was done to her young men in the name of nationalism, has caused a collective scar on our subconscious. Some say you should never pick at a scar, I say you should wear it with pride, as an act of remembrance."

"We all have things we regret, Tomas."

"I know, Christian, I know, and they sound like an echo in our dreams."

"Has it started yet, Papa?"

Torres turned his head and smiled at his daughter as she entered the room, with a glass of wine in her hand. "No, you are just in time."

"Good." She sat on the settee which was placed between the two armchairs. On the large television screen in front of them the commercials finished, and the opening credits started to play for the Argentinian investigative reporting series.

Torres savoured his whisky as the presenter introduced the programme, mentioned him by name and then the feed cut briefly to historical footage of the Malvinas crisis before his prerecorded interview started. Now, Tomas Torres, with a tear in his eye, truly had justice, and so did the relatives of all the other men the Orosco family had murdered.

* * *

Halifax Stanfield International Airport, Nova Scotia, Canada

The rental car was a Ford Escape, which Akulov thought was ironic. Akulov ignored the on board GPS and tapped the address he had found into the Waze app on his burner iPhone. Modern technology informed him it was a one hour and four minute drive, which after the almost twenty-hour flight from Dubai via Boston, was more than enough. He was tired but apprehensive, and he wasn't alone.

"People will talk," Racine said, "if they see us together."

"The only people who know us here are the ones we are going to visit, and if they do not talk, it will be quite embarrassing."

"You know, Ruslan, sometimes I understand why the other Werewolves called you 'Machine', you need to lighten up a little."

"I thought I was the embodiment of sweetness and light?" Akulov replied.

"Ha," Racine unwrapped a chocolate and popped it into her mouth, "I hope they've got some decent wine."

Akulov was relaxed, and for once he thought he may actually be happy as well. Which he realised was an almost alien concept. They left the airport taking the Veterans Memorial Highway, which again he found ironic, and headed south. The route was scenic and skirted three different lakes before they turned east onto the Harvest Highway. Forests now lined each side of the road and although he knew there were the occasional housing developments and small towns just beyond these, the route felt remote. It reminded him of driving through rural Ukraine and his mind started to drift back to what he remembered of his parents. Family, to Akulov, had always been an intangible concept. It was something he knew he once had but he had no real recollection of it. His grandmother, of course, had stepped in and taken over after his parents' deaths, and that had been all the family he had known until he had made new brothers in the army. Then there was his sole remaining blood relative – Devyat, a man who had followed the same path he had but several decades before.

Akulov said, "You are an only child?"

"As far as I know."

Akulov glanced sideways. "Meaning?"

"My mother ran off when I was a teenager. I may have brothers and sisters, even nephews and nieces."

"You've not seen her since?"

"That's what 'run off' usually means, Ruslan. My dad was a much better parent. No, that's unfair. My mother had issues, and they took over."

"I am sorry."

"Like you were for my dog?"

"This is different, your mother was real."

"I hope she still is."

"I am not used to this, Sophie."

"What? Talking like a human being?"

"Yes."

"Well, I would never have guessed."

"Thank you."

"I was being sarcastic."

"I know. So was I."

"Ha."

As they reached the outskirts of Windsor, the road narrowed, the trees receded, and houses stated to dot the sides of the roads.

"Civilisation," Racine said, with a smirk.

Their route took them around the edge of town, whitewashed wooden houses and grassy driveways now greeting them on either side until they passed the River Avon and the landscape changed. For several miles the horizon seemed to widen and all other evidence of human habitation, save for the black strip of tarmac they were using, vanished. They continued on the Harvest Highway until Akulov saw the first sign printed with the name of the place they were heading for. A thin smile formed at the corners of his lip. He glanced over at Racine, wanting to see if she had noticed it too.

"Is this some sort of a joke?"

"No."

"So, are you telling me out of all the places in the vast country, he decided to settle here?"

"I think it's ironic."

"That's one way of putting it."

The houses once more started to appear and this time there were commercial buildings too, which were also wooden clad but here they were brightly coloured like a seaside town. To their right, the trees fell away to give a view out across the Bay of Fundy to the distant, towering dark form of Cape Blomidon.

"Welcome to Wolfsville," Akulov said.

Racine started to laugh. "Stop!"

"Why?"

"That shop sells wine. Stay in the car."

Racine exited, leaving Akulov manoeuvring the mid-sized SUV into a parking space, and imagining that he'd soon receive a ticket. Less than two minutes later, Racine reappeared with a heavy looking carrier bag, which clinked as she climbed into the car.

"It's not French, but apparently it's very good, and it's very local."

"Can we carry on?"

"Oui."

Akulov pulled away and once more followed the turn-by-turn directions until they reached Fowler Street. The house was a large family home, wooden clad, as per the norm and painted a pastel green. It was on a slight rise, and its front lawn was bordered on both its boundary sides by tall, mature trees. It was at the very end of the street by a turning circle. Akulov slowly crunched up the grey gravel drive and parked the Ford Escape Together Racine and Akulov opened their doors and stepped out. Akulov saw the, not too subtle, twitch of a curtain at a downstairs window and before the pair of them had managed to reach the steps up to the front door, it opened and a little boy came out.

"Uncle Machine!" he yelled and ran towards Akulov.

Akulov crouched down, not knowing quite what to do, and let the boy jump at him. He caught him in his arms and stood up.

Nairo looked into his eyes with a now serious expression on his face. "Who is she?"

Before Akulov could reply a voice from the door shouted, "She's a friend!"

Akulov smiled at Kizlyar, who trotted down the steps towards them. Akulov put Nairo down. He stood and looked at Racine.

Racine said, "I spoke to you on the telephone. Do you remember?"

Nairo inclined his head as though attempting to remember. "Are you thirty-two?"

"Yes. Are you six?"

Nairo shook his head. "No. I'm now six and a half."

Akulov walked towards his brother Werewolf. The pair embraced awkwardly.

"You found us," Kizlyar said.

"We did."

"How?"

"I sent them our address," Catherine said, appearing from the side of the house.

Racine held up the bag to Catherine. "I've brought wine. Shall we go inside?"

"That's a good idea."

"Oh, just wine!" Nairo folded his arms.

Racine crouched down. "And chocolate, for you!"

Akulov watched the two women and Nairo walk back inside before he asked, "How are you?"

"Now? I am happy."

"That is good."

"So, er, you and Racine?"

"We are friends." Akulov said.

"That's how it starts."

Akulov stated, "And that has to be how it ends."

"Nonsense."

Akulov felt his burner phone vibrate in his pocket. Frowning, he retrieved it. It was an incoming call from a withheld number. He looked around before he raised it to his ear. "Hello?"

"Ruslan, I do not have much time." The voice was dry, and sounded weak but there was no mistaking as to who it was. "I am going to send you a location. Please. You must come!"

"Devyat?"

"Yes, nephew. It is me, I need..." the line dropped.

"Business?"

"Personal. That was my uncle."

"You have an uncle?"

"Only recently."

"Where is he?"

"I don't know." The iPhone still in Akulov's hand bleeped and displayed an incoming WhatsApp message. And that message was just three words long.

"What's that?"

"It looks like a What3Words location code."

"Where is it?"

"I don't have the app."

"Wait, I do." Kizlyar pulled his iPhone from his back pocket, swiped, looked at the words on Akulov's screen, then typed them in.

"Where is it?"

"Hotel Khreshchatyk, Kyiv."

* * *

MORE FROM ALEX SHAW

ABOUT THE AUTHOR

Alex Shaw is a member of the International Thriller Writers organisation and the Crime Writers Association. He is the author of three bestselling thriller series featuring Aidan Snow, Jack Tate and Sophie Racine. *Total Blackout*, the first in his Jack Tate series, was shortlisted for the 2021 Wilbur Smith Adventure Writing Prize.

Download your exclusive bonus content from Alex Shaw here:

Visit Alex Shaw's website: www.alexwshaw.co.uk

Follow Alex Shaw on social media here:

facebook.com/alex.shaw.982292
x.com/alexshawhetman
instagram.com/alexshawthrillerwriter

ALSO BY ALEX SHAW

Wolf Six Thrillers

Wolf Six

Kill Code

Target Echo

Printed in Dunstable, United Kingdom

77891021R00161